Grandmère

Grandmère

by *VIÑA DELMAR*

HARCOURT, BRACE & WORLD, INC.

New York

Grandmère

A worldly, fashionable divorcée flies from New York to Paris to take temporary custody of her two grandchildren when she fears that they are about to become a part of their father's French family.

$\mathcal{S}$*tanding in* the unexpectedly chill wind of noon, she shivered, then tensed herself against such weakness. Other people might run before the wind, clutching coat collars closely to their throats and rubbing dust-filled eyes, but she would not run and she would not shiver. She would stand quietly on the pavement in front of this rather seedy-looking building until she chose to move. She did not look at the building, though she had a long acquaintance with it. In the early part of the century it had been a private residence, but in her day it had already become a distinguished speakeasy where dress clothes had been obligatory. Law-breaking had had more style then, she thought. In retrospect a speakeasy could radiate a nostalgic charm so poignant as to make it seem an irreverence that now its basement housed a restaurant of uncertain quality while abovestairs the rooms were there for anyone to rent.

Taxis, irritably enmeshed in luncheon traffic, inched past her slowly. Occasionally a driver who had dropped his passengers at the glitter spot a half block west glanced at her, then looked away, surprised that she had not rushed toward him.

Rebecca understood the surprise. If not in need of a taxi, then for what reason did a lady with a chic gray hairdo stand motionless on the curb? Well, perhaps to murmur a greeting to the restaurant's cat that came, shining black, up the basement steps, narrowing its eyes against the dust and deciding, after only a moment, to withdraw completely from October.

Rebecca turned her head at a sudden shout from the corner. The newspaper vendor, a rough-skinned woman wearing a navy peajacket, was fighting the wind as it tried to rob her of a stack of dailies. There was a small commotion as the newspapers doubled in width, exposing their inner pages to loss and destruction. Passers-by helped a little, their expressions bored and bitter, as though every day some old woman in a peajacket called out to them for assistance. A tabloid came to rest in the street and was run over by a taxi. Rebecca saw the woman pick it up, study it for signs of bruises, then pat it gently before returning it to the stand.

And now suddenly there was nothing more to look at except that which she had come to see. The brownstone house across the street. Never before had she stood observing it in quite this way. But then never before had she agreed to fly across the dark Atlantic in the middle of a windy night. There is some danger, she thought. I may not see the house again. But couldn't that be truly said at any time? She was as old as the woman in the peajacket.

She looked at the door of the brownstone house. When she had held its key the brasswork had gleamed against dark, satiny wood and the door had set the tone for all the beauty and grace to be found behind it. Had the house been a portion of her divorce settlement she would have guarded it as a treasure. But Torrey had kept the house, remarking mildly that since it had belonged to his father she had no sentimental involvement with it. The lawyers, he had added, were instructed to deal fairly with her in this matter as in all others. And she had been dealt with fairly. Only the house had suffered.

How could he bear the grimy windowpanes, the unswept steps and the broken doorbell with its rotting wires hanging dead and unburied? Wasn't he shamed by the torn, soiled shades cocked at crazy angles, betraying the sickness of even such simple mechanisms as theirs? How could—

She remembered suddenly that Torrey lived in London and saw the house infrequently. There were others to blame for its appearance, and they were not strangers, not casually accepted tenants from God knows where. They were her children. Hers and Torrey's.

Three steps down from street level, in what had once been the kitchen and the servants' dining room, was Juanita's shop. There was a sign that said so. Juanita's Shop. Above it, in the space quaintly known, in her day, as the parlor floor, Barrett conducted his business. Happily, he needed no sign. She peered upward to the former family bedrooms. They had been remodeled so that Torrey had a *pied-à-terre* when in New York. She looked long and hard at the rain-spotted windows and the splintered frames, then her gaze traveled to the rooftop. Directly beneath it had been the servants' quarters, converted now into an apartment in which Barrett and Flower lived. No shades at all. Just limp, faded draperies and a cracked windowpane. She felt disgust and anger. She had known the house was neglected, but viewing it from the opposite side of the street, seeing it squarely from basement to roof, was a shock. It was dirty and dismal like the houses of lazy, irresponsible people who watched deterioration without interest. Money was not the question. Torrey would respond generously to an appeal for repairs and replacements. Only no one noticed. No one cared.

I can forgive Flower. Flower does not really belong to this house, so I can forgive her. What does that mean? Does it mean that I cannot forgive Juanita or Barrett? Do I expect the house to look as it did in the old days? Everything changes. The street has changed. Customs have changed. I have changed. Even Torrey has changed. When I came here he was rehearsing Romeo. Now he is playing Lear.

She stood quietly in the wind and gazed at the house to which Torrey had brought her when they were very young. It had been such a beautiful house. But everything was measured by time and desire. Time was no longer forever, and desire was a hushed, river-view apartment with a profusion of the latest conveniences.

I have all that an old lady could want. All. Then she strolled to the corner, smiled at the woman in the peajacket, and bought a magazine. And after a while she crossed the street, walked down the three steps, and entered Juanita's shop.

Juanita was busy with a customer, but she tossed a quick smile in the proper direction. Rebecca sat down on a gilded chair and waited. The shop was dimly lighted and had an odor that she associated with mice, living and dead. This basement had once been bright and warm. A gleaming monster of a stove, delicious fragrances, an enormous refrigerator, and beyond the stretch of orange baize that now curtained the archway, there had been the large, round table where she and Torrey had taken every Christmas dinner with their servants. What a nice idea that had been. Had the servants enjoyed it?

The customer who was consuming Juanita's time had apparently wandered into the wrong shop. She was a plain, little white-faced thing who wanted to buy a dress. A tangible, solid object of purchase that could be placed in a box and carried home.

"Our clothes are all custom-made," Juanita was saying. "We design for the individual. I see you in garden shades. Strong reds, audacious blues, sharp yellows."

The customer was wearing cautious beige and wondering how to leave.

6

Rebecca focused her attention on the shop. What a lot of material Juanita had stocked. Bolts and bolts of it, and remnants and dress lengths in every possible color and texture. There were baskets boiling over with buttons of all sizes and shapes. There were tape measures, pincushions, unwashed mirrors and unemptied ash trays. There were dress forms and drawings of Juanita's designs and, from behind the baize curtain, sounds of a sewing machine, a coffee percolator and the Chinese fitter yelling excitedly into the telephone.

"Do tell me how you think of yourself," Juanita pleaded. "Gamin? Sophisticate? Intellectual? Through clothes we can look any way we choose."

Rebecca eyed her daughter standing there in the corduroy pants and tailored shirt. Was this the way Juanita had chosen to look? Now if she were wearing smart Capris and the shirt were silk and Juanita had put on make-up and hadn't cut her hair so short, then one could understand somewhat. The girl had never been a beauty and, since she wasn't really very young any more, matters had reached near-disaster stage. Fortunate that she still had her slenderness and the wonderful smile.

"Perhaps another time," Juanita said, letting the customer go. She lighted a cigarette and untroubled by dust, pins or the inelegance of the position, she sat down on the floor in front of Rebecca. "So tomorrow you'll be seeing Vicki?"

"Yes. For a few hours. She'll introduce me to the house and the servants. Even to the children. They were too young to know me the times that she and Edouard brought them here."

Juanita waved her cigarette toward an ash tray and missed. Her untidiness was annoying and embarrassing. It seemed as elaborate as a teen-ager's plot to invite a scolding which could then be resented and rebelled against. How odd if Juanita thought that she could draw a rebuke. Rebukes had never been family policy. Rebecca had even resisted the temptation to present the shop with one of those clever magnetic gadgets that could rescue all the abandoned pins that were strewn from doorway to curtain and certainly beyond. The gift might be considered a criticism. Well, no matter. She smiled down at Juanita and said, "You'll be seeing Vicki almost as soon as I will. Are you glad about that?"

"Yes, but I wish she'd had a different reason for swapping cities with you."

"Vicki is Vicki. Should we expect her to be someone else?"

"I guess not. It would only lead to disappointment. Do you know what I think is strange? Not in one letter to me has she mentioned that s.o.b from Belfast."

"Now, why is he an s.o.b.?"

"Because though everyone knows about him and Vicki he gave out an interview in which he said that he's yet to meet the woman he would marry."

"Oh, what do press releases matter?"

"Of course," Juanita went on, "there's the possibility that Vicki doesn't want another marriage. Actually she doesn't deserve another."

"Isn't that an unfeeling thing to say, dear?"

Juanita shot her a quick gray glance of curiosity. "You don't find three divorces excessive?"

Rebecca shrugged. "I didn't always understand Vicki's thinking when she was twelve. Now that she's thirty-five I—"

"She's thirty-seven," Juanita said.

Rebecca did not reply to that. Instead, "I went to one of

8

those little art houses last night and saw Fallon McKee in an English movie."

"What's he like?"

"Black of hair, smoldering of eye. All gentle-rough and toneless mumble. You know the type. Once upon a time he couldn't have bribed his way into a tent-show company. I wouldn't have sat through his performance if I hadn't known that Vicki was involved with him."

Juanita, knees clasped in gracefully narrow hands, rocked forward on her corduroy bottom. "My question is, Why does she have to involve you?"

"She needs me. If she lets McKee come here alone to do the show, she'll lose him to some other woman. If she leaves the children in Paris with just Mademoiselle and servants, she's running the chance of forfeiting custody. Edouard could say she's not a responsible person and that he wants a new deal."

"And he bloody well deserves a new deal," Juanita said.

"Oh, no, honey. All children are better off with their mothers."

"But Vicki's won't be with their mother. She'll be here with McKee."

"So *I'll* be with the children. God knows Edouard can find no fault with that. Vicki is permitted to leave Paris. She isn't a prisoner."

"Does Father know this McKee fellow?"

"I shouldn't think so, though Vicki has gone to London several times. She might have introduced them. If you mean does your father know about the affair, I would say yes. It's had some rather high-candle attention in columns on both sides of the ocean."

Juanita put out her cigarette and lighted another, dropping the pack back into her shirt pocket where its shiny red brand-mark loomed clownishly through the thin material. "I was curious to know what Father thought of the pub-keeper's son. That's what McKee is, you know."

"I couldn't care less about that," Rebecca said. "It's his so-called acting that revolts me, though, in a way, I pity the new players. They have to conquer the public with their stunning ignorance. A star in today's world is in such demand that he hasn't any time to learn how to act."

The smile now. Something of Torrey but more of Juanita herself in that bright, unstudied smile. "I wonder if he'll be a sensation on Broadway."

"Of course he will. Everybody is a sensation on Broadway nowadays. Every week brings us an actor of a greatness not to be believed. I'll tell you the truth—I think a secret agreement on new criteria has been reached. What else could have produced such a grand harvest of artistry?"

"Talking of artists, real artists, I read that Father's Lear is a terrific smash in London."

"Did you see the review that said Jill Columbus was intense, magnificent and overwhelming?"

"Someone sent it to me. Someone who thought it very funny that his mistress is playing his daughter."

Rebecca had the impression that Juanita did not think it at all funny. She waited and let Juanita choose the next topic of conversation.

"Vicki will be living in your apartment?"

"Yes."

"And the pubkeeper's son?"

Rebecca said, "I'm sure he will be in a hotel or have an apartment of his own. I didn't ask. I rely on Vicki's judgment."

"Good grief! You do?"

"Well, let me say it this way: The man's a new, big

British name, and the newspapers will be very interested in him. She'll have to be discreet."

Juanita's eyes glinted. "You mean that for the sake of McKee's play and McKee's American movie contracts and McKee's precious career she'll refrain from humiliating her children and Edouard?"

Rebecca tilted her head and regarded Juanita thoughtfully. "Would you say that somewhere in the world today there is possibly an affair going on in which the people concerned sincerely, deeply love each other? And if so, would you concede that that affair might lead to marriage and the greatest happiness these people have ever known?"

"Of course. It's possible."

"Then why couldn't that couple be Fallon McKee and Vicki? If you're giving a break to any woman, then why can't you give it to your sister?"

Juanita grinned. "You're so right that I may never say another nasty thing about Vicki. Do you want a cup of coffee?"

"No. I'm going to lunch at the Plaza with Jennie Frost. We'll sit over three cups of coffee there and—"

The phone behind the curtain rang, and Juanita ran toward it. Rebecca picked up the magazine she had bought at the newsstand. There was a spread on Paris for the tourist. Someone had recommended it to her attention. "For a woman who's never been there, it will be very informative." Rebecca had not bothered to say that she had been to Paris. Once before and very long ago.

The door to the shop opened, and Midge Kent came in. She was the girl who shared Juanita's apartment somewhere downtown. She was a red-haired little thing with soft, dark eyes. Quite pretty. Midge was wearing one of the undisciplined designs that were pictured in the drawings around the shop and she was carrying a brown paper bag. Inside the bag would be homemade sandwiches and a custard, or a salad and a dish of gelatine. Midge, for some unexplained reason, always brought Juanita's lunch to the shop.

"Oh, hello, Mrs. Winton." Midge set the bag down, then looked about as though she were lost and slightly alarmed. "Where's Johnny?"

"Who?"

The baize curtain trembled, then hung secretive and still. Had the wind that followed Midge into the shop only reached the curtain now?

"Juanita," Midge said. "Juanita. We sometimes call her Johnny. It's a nickname, you know. We call her that sometimes. It's cold out today, isn't it? Don't you think it's cold?"

"Yes."

"It's hard to believe it's autumn already. Where did summer go?"

Rebecca was insulted by the banality of the question. She made no plans to reply.

Juanita came through the archway smiling at Midge. "Hi. What's new?"

"Nothing."

"No mail? No calls?"

"Not of any interest. Only a bill from the furniture-finishing man."

"How much?"

"I'd better tell you after you eat."

Rebecca rose from the gilded chair slapping in the general direction of her derriere. There was sure to be dust. "I really have to go."

Juanita gave her a hug. "Thanks for coming in to say

12

good-bye. And have yourself a ball in Paris, girl. A real ball."

Rebecca climbed the steps to the front door of the brownstone. The inside stairs had long ago been walled off along with the dumbwaiter and the laundry chute. She walked into the foyer. It was unfurnished except for a few cane-bottomed chairs. The sliding doors to what had been the front parlor were open. Flower sat in there, dark, glowering, her chin resting in her hand as she listened to a young man reading the Bill of Rights.

Flower's eyes wandered to Rebecca, then slid away from her. Rebecca understood and kept walking. She heard Flower's voice behind her.

"Dick, try to remember that the dramatic value of the scene rests on the character being a foreigner. You sound real American to me."

The back parlor housed Torrey's book collection and was closed off and locked. The dining room still clung to a shred of its old identity because the antique brass chandelier with its original candle sockets had never been removed. Torrey's father had loved that chandelier. How often he had told of finding it on a junk pile in Boston. Rebecca sighed and did not look at it. There would be cobwebs. And there would be the painful suspicion that her children would one day fling the chandelier upon another junk pile.

A young girl perched on a stool was staring sulkily at Barrett. He was pacing the floor, his brows drawn together in a scowl. There was a canvas chair. Rebecca sat on it. It sagged perilously, uncomfortably. Barrett and the girl, quite correctly, took no notice of her.

"Tell me," Barrett demanded, "the things you were thinking just now when you ran through the parking-lot bit."

The girl laughed and looked at him with icy-bright eyes. "You Method boys," she said, and reached into her purse for a cigarette. "What was I thinking! Really!"

Rebecca recognized the girl. Katie Cornwall, the twenty-year-old who had wrapped Broadway up into a neat package and taken it home with her the season before.

Barrett said, "I didn't send for you, you know. Your director asked me to take you. He doesn't think you're getting anything at all out of the scene. And neither do I."

Katie got down from the stool. "You make me tired. All of you. I'm going home."

She walked out of the room, and Barrett watched her go. "Sarah Cornwall Bernhardt," he said. "And to hell with her. How are you?"

"I'm fine, dear."

"Good," he said. "Good." But he spoke absently, his eyes on the doorway through which Katie Cornwall had walked.

Rebecca was silent, giving him time to accept that the girl was not coming back.

"They're opening a week from Friday in Philadelphia, and she's giving the scene nothing." He sat down dejectedly on the stool that Katie had abandoned. "God, I get fed up with this. Have you any idea how maddening it is to spend one's time offering help to people who think they're already perfect?"

Rebecca studied her gloved hands. "Maddening or not, you must often succeed in persuading them to accept your help. Producers and directors keep sending their problems to you."

"They sure do, and sometimes I think I'd be better off running a neighborhood dramatic school for eager amateurs. I'd see a lot of lousy acting, but at least I'd know the students were doing their best. Consider Katie Cornwall. One big hit and she's loafing. She thinks she can't fail."

"A natural mistake."

"Is it? I wouldn't know. I never had a big hit. Maybe that's why I can't stand Katie."

Rebecca felt suddenly weary. He had been reading those old reviews again. He had taken them from the bottom drawer of his desk last night and had read each lacerating word over and over. And then he had drunk too much, and Flower had held him close and let him cry. Perhaps it was an exaggeration to say that he had drunk too much. Surely he never did that. Or not very often. When he did, it was because the tempo of the times was so disturbing. Lots of people drank too much too often. And what a pity that Katie Cornwall had been nasty to him when, in all probability, his poor head was aching fiendishly.

She reached for his hand. "Darling, if you had cared enough to keep on with it, you'd have been a fine actor."

"That's what I like," he said pulling away from her, "the good objective criticism of a mother. But you're right about one thing. I didn't care enough. Maybe I always had a love-hate affair with the theater. God knows I hate every damned thing about it now. I wish I could get away from even hearing about it."

"What would you like to do?"

"What can I do? What else do I know besides theater?" His voice was sharp and, she thought, accusing.

She said, "What does any man know besides the subject he has studied for years and then practiced for many years more? The theater is your profession."

"You've heard of people who gave up their professions, haven't you?"

"Which brings us back to my question. What would you like to do?"

15

"Anything but what I'm doing."

"That's an empty answer, dear. It doesn't give the people who love you anything to go on. If you hate what you're doing, you must have some idea of what you'd rather do. You must have dreamed of something you'd prefer."

"Yes, I've dreamed of being a cowboy. Didn't you guess that?"

She glanced at him uncertainly.

"I'm telling you that I've never grown up. If I were a person of any maturity I'd have cleared out of here years ago. I'd have sold used cars or dug ditches or learned how to read gas meters or—"

"And then you would have been happy?"

"No, of course not. I'd have been whining just as I'm whining now." He began to pace again. She watched him, observing his thickening waistline, the jowliness and the pouches beneath his eyes. He had been handsome with a sort of golden freshness, she remembered. "My mistake was in not choosing a road of my own. Other Wintons had the guts to look for new destinations. The last English Winton was a soldier. Did his son become a soldier? No. He came to America and made a hell of a success in the banking business. Did his son become a banker? No. He made a hell of a success as a doctor. Did his son become a doctor? No. He made a hell of a success as an actor. Did his son become an actor? Yes. The poor jerk tried and was a hell of a flop and wound up complaining to his mother about it when he should have been making happy bon voyage prattle."

Rebecca said, "Your father didn't consciously search for a new destination. He was going to follow his father into the medical profession but the First World War came along and he enlisted at eighteen. He told me that when he returned he was still of a mind to study medicine but—"

"I know the story, Mother. It's retold and reprinted constantly. Old Phil Shiler was Grandfather's patient and needed a handsome young man for a small part et cetera, et cetera."

"Yes, et cetera, et cetera, except that the stories never mention your grandfather. When he saw that your father was growing serious about the theater he swallowed his disappointment and said, 'Acting isn't going to get you out of studying. Let's start preparing you properly.' He was a wonderful man. And a medical genius. Let me tell you that your father would never have walked in his footsteps successfully."

Barrett paused in his pacing and scooped up the clipboard he had left on the window sill. He snapped the spring noisily a few times, then spoke without looking at Rebecca. "How are you getting to Kennedy tonight?"

"The Bensons are taking me. It's easy for them with the chauffeur and the big car. But thank you for offering." She ignored the glance of surprise he cast at her. Where was the harm in their both believing that he had offered?

Flower came into the room. She was a large girl without style or charm. She had been born in eastern Europe and had traveled extensively enough to pick up a dozen languages. Nevertheless Rebecca had always felt that her daughter-in-law had no real rapport with words. Only utter insensibility to a delicate sound could account for this big, round-shouldered young woman adopting the literal translation of her name. Flower's smiling welcome was sincere, but her teeth were tiny. They seemed no more than a decorative edging for her fine, healthy gums.

"Barrett, did you invite your mother to have coffee?"

Rebecca said, "Oh, I don't have time. I only dropped in to say a quick good-bye."

"I am sorry I was busy when you came," Flower apolo-

17

gized. "Being familiar with different accents is very useful and has become an important part of our work together." She looked pleadingly toward Barrett. He was frowning down at the clipboard and making some notes. "Darling, your mother is here. What is so urgent that it must be written now?"

"Something I don't want to forget."

Flower asked no further questions. She smiled again at Rebecca. "Perhaps while you are in Paris my mother will be there. I would so love you to meet each other. She is in Athens now and has written that she expects to go to Paris very soon."

"Really?" None of this was believable. Had Flower made it up? Surely this girl's mother, while gathering firewood in the forest, had been devoured by wolves.

"You have already seen Juanita?" Flower asked.

"Yes. I've said good-bye to her and now I must say good-bye to you."

"Barrett," Flower said.

He looked up from the clipboard. "I just had to get that down while it was fresh in my mind," he said. "Well, Ma, what can I say? Have fun."

"I'll try." She embraced him, then turned to Flower.

Flower, who had little respect for clothes, make-up or coiffure, enfolded her affectionately. Rebecca died a little but preserved the major part of her careful grooming.

"You are to have a wonderful Parisian holiday. Let nothing worry you. Be lighthearted. You know that I will take good care of everything. Come, Barrett, let us walk to the door with your mother."

Rebecca hurried west toward the Plaza. The wind was less fierce now and the sky was a brighter, lovelier blue. That was the sort of thing to watch for. The bluer sky, the little boy roller-skating with his father, the woman trying to leash-break a Siamese cat. One found such things as a result of constant alertness and determination to find them.

I am on my way to the beautiful Plaza. I shall have a fine luncheon with a dear friend. And then this evening I will do what every woman would like to do. I will go to Paris. I am on my way to the beautiful Plaza. I shall have a fine luncheon with a dear friend. And then this evening—

She stopped walking to read with amiable interest the message posted in front of an unfashionable little church.

IS YOUR HARVEST SEASON BOUNTIFUL?
COME IN AND GIVE THANKS

Rebecca peered into the dimness beyond. Such a sweet old church and no doubt in need of the extra dollar one would drop in the collection box. She hesitated not another moment. She entered the chilly quiet and sank to her knees.

She thought about God. He had given her an apartment from which the sparkling windows looked out upon sun, sky and spunky little helicopters. And the apartment had six wonderful closets and a kitchen with a pink refrigerator, and in her apartment there was calm and— But it was frivolous to thank God for an apartment.

She thought about time. She had no quarrel with it. To destroy people was time's business, and that had always been known. One had to make a game of the thing, and the object was in seeing how long one could play, how long one could stand straight and tall. God had given her a face that had not defied time but had refused to grow slack and ugly. He had given her a body that she could still recognize as hers. He had given her— But this, too, was frivolous. One did not thank God because one's legs were prettier than those of one's daughters.

In speaking to God one cast aside the trivial, the unworthy. One did not speak to Him of legs or refrigerators or closet space or the friendly, efficient staff at the apartment house. No. One thanked God for the meaningful things in life, the blessings with which He brightened those declining years.

Silently she spoke to God. She said, "Thank You, dear God. Thank You for my wonderful children."

Barrett and Vicki were listening to a quiz show. Miss Emmett disapproved of radio. She thought it rather vulgar. "Why don't you fetch the parcheesi set?" she suggested to Juanita. "It's on the shelf with the jigsaw puzzles in Barrett's room."

It troubled Juanita that Miss Emmett was still trying to organize games in the interval between dinner and bedtime. She ought to know that people grew up and chose their own amusements. But how lonely and terrible her life must be now that even Vicki had no real need of her.

Juanita laid aside an exciting magazine serial and went to get the parcheesi set. Things have come full circle, she thought. Now *I* entertain Miss Emmett till *she* becomes sleepy.

Mother's door was open. She was sitting at her vanity table, dressing to go out to dinner with the Bensons. "Come in," she called. "Keep me company while I'm putting myself together."

Juanita stopped short on the threshold of Barrett's room and turned slowly. This was new. But then, when one was fifteen, there was something new every day. "Keep you company?" she asked.

"Yes. Come on in. I have an important letter from your father."

Juanita went in to Mother's bedroom and sat down. She sat very still and let waves of joy wash over her. Funny, how you could never guess what was going to happen next. She had been on her way to play parcheesi, and now here she was surrounded by fragrances of perfume and cosmetics and Mother was about to reveal that Father had asked for a reconciliation. She breathed deeply. Imagine having Father living with them as he used to do. . . . Perhaps in the brownstone house . . . At night there would be the sound of Father's voice in the hallway and his footsteps on the stairs and—

Mother was staring at her over the silver frame of her hand mirror. "Aren't you interested that I had an important letter from your father?"

"Yes."

"I couldn't tell. You never said a word." Mother opened a drawer in the vanity table. "In any case, here it is."

Juanita did not take the letter immediately. How ghastly if Father were rejected after she had read his impassioned plea to be reunited with the family. "Are you sure I should read it?"

"Of course you should read it. Stop making such high drama of everything. Honestly, you're the most emotional little somebody I ever knew."

Juanita threw a quick glance at herself in the full-length mirror on the closet door. All she saw was a long sliver of a girl with a narrow face and ropy hair. She had almost expected to see what Mother had called an "emotional little somebody." That had sounded appealing. Hesitantly, she drew the letter from its envelope.

Rebecca, my dear,

When I came to say good-bye to the children before embarking upon this adventure I told you quite a lot about it, so I will not go into it any further here. But it is really more marvelous than I had dreamed it would be. I have been given a magnificent toy to play with, and I am very pleased that Mr. Hector thought he needed me to get his theater world-wide attention. So much for that.

Now to the real reason for the letter. Among the things Mr. Hector provided along with the token salary is a beautiful home which is mine for the summer. (It belongs to his sister, who is in South America.) It is splendidly furnished and equipped with three servants. My life here is a blend of the artistic and the social. Mr. and Mrs. Hector are rather proud of having fetched me, and consequently I am meeting all the people we used to sneer at as Midwestern barbarians.

Becky, this house and the historical (theatrically speaking) first season of Mr. Hector's theater I want to share with one of my children. That would be Juanita, since she is the eldest. I think she would enjoy it. Many of my new acquaintances have teen-age sons and daughters, and it would be good for Juanita to know them. She could form friendships that would last all her life. Please let her come. I think that . . .

Juanita's eyes ran searchingly over the two remaining paragraphs. Where had he mentioned his hopes for a reconciliation? She placed the letter back in its envelope. "I'm going to play parcheesi now," she said.

Mother took a gray chiffon dress from its hanger. "Fine. But try to make up your mind soon about this thing. There will have to be shopping if you're going to spend an entire summer with your father."

An entire summer. Juanita felt a sudden shiver of excitement. She hadn't thought of it that way. An entire summer. Why, that was weeks and weeks that she would have with him. They would be inseparable. She would watch all of his performances, and perhaps even when he was rehearsing she would be allowed to sit in the back row of the theater. They would have every meal together, and they would talk about books and plays, and she would amuse him by making sketches of people and places.

She said, "Do you suppose he will meet me at the train?"

As it turned out, he didn't. Instead, there was a very correct chauffeur awaiting her on the station platform.

"Miss Winton? I'm Gus."

She smiled and said hello. She loved family chauffeurs. In the old days of the brownstone, chauffeurs had been

23

friends and confidants outranking Miss Emmett on all counts except in times of illness.

"Your trunk arrived this morning, Miss Winton. Now, which of these valises are yours?"

She pointed them out, and Gus led the way to a black limousine. He settled her in its luxurious depths, and the car glided smoothly away from the railroad station. She peered out the window at the hot, dirty city. It was crowded and busy, but there was an oddly raw look about the place. She caught a glimpse of two large department stores and several enormous office buildings, yet she had the feeling that the streets were not really paved and that here, in any tavern, one could meet a man who carried a keepsake from Jesse James. The past lingered on in dark, wooden houses that stood stubbornly right in the middle of the business district. The car passed a theater, and she caught a quick impression of a fancy, over-decorated lobby with large globes and ornate woodwork, and it was all seen through a veil of dust, as though a band of horsemen had just ridden by.

It was thirty minutes later that she became aware of a sudden cool breeze. The dusty city and its flat, dismal suburbs were behind them now. Freshness and the fragrance of sweet, green things suddenly filled the air. The car followed a tree-lined road, and at the end of it, shimmering softly in the sunlight, there was a very blue lake.

"The lake is artificial," Gus said. "And it's the center of a wheel. Everything spreads outward from the lake. Mr. Hector developed all this from nothing, and see how beautiful it is."

Juanita nodded. "Where is the theater?"

They drove around the lake, Juanita gazing excitedly up each spoke of the wheel.

"That is where Mr. Hector lives," Gus said.

It was a huge white brick house surrounded by lawns so satiny green that Juanita thought they, too, must be artificial.

"Look at the planting as we pass, Miss Winton. Famous throughout the whole state. They employ six full-time gardeners."

The thought of six full-time gardeners was mildly interesting, but she had not been conditioned to appreciate horticulture.

"Where is the theater?" she asked.

Gus left the lake drive and guided the car through a street of haughty little shops. On another day they might be fascinating. Now she had no time for them, for straight ahead, at the end of the street, was the theater. Superb in its simplicity, it stood white in the sunlight, its Greek columns delicate yet strong, its marble pavilion starkly unadorned save for a life-size painting of Father as Hamlet. And somewhere within those exquisite walls was Father himself.

"Can we stay here for just a minute, Gus?"

He rolled into a space marked "No Parking At Any Time." "Would you like me to take a look in the theater? Maybe they are resting for a minute and—"

"Oh, no. I wouldn't disturb my father for all the world. I just want to look."

"You didn't see pictures in the magazines of Mr. Hector's theater?"

"No." She had a sudden disquieting thought. "Do enough people live around the lake to make the theater successful?"

He shook his head. "But theater-lovers will come from all over. The admission price is very low and parking free. Also, buses will run from the city. Still, even that will not pay expenses. Never. Mr. Hector will give from his own pocket what is needed to make up the difference every year. It is his gift to everybody."

Juanita was pleased to classify Mr. Hector with the benevolent noblemen of ages past who had sponsored writers and actors. Very romantic. She must remember to tell Father how she regarded Mr. Hector.

They drove then to the house where she would live. Gus opened the front door and set her luggage in the foyer. "I will bring it upstairs in a few minutes. Sit, if you please; I will get Margaret or Clara."

The room to which Clara took her was all really too chartreuse, but it was spacious and furnished in elegant contemporary. It had its own chartreuse-tiled bathroom and an astonishing amount of closets. Juanita handed her luggage keys over to Clara.

"What time does my father usually return from the theater?"

"I would say seven, Miss."

It was earlier than that when she heard him in the corridor. He was calling, "Where is my daughter?" She flew to him, and he hugged her and spun her around, and they walked downstairs holding hands and talking nonsense. It wasn't till they reached the bottom step that Juanita knew he had not come home alone. He had brought a lady with him, and she was no one from the cast, for she did not look tired and used up. She was red-haired and smartly slim. Terror tore at Juanita. He has Someone. Now he'll never ask for a reconciliation.

It was a relief to discover that this was Mrs. Hector. Well, then the Hectors were young. Amazing. She had pictured Mr. Hector as a fat little man in his late sixties.

"How lovely to see you," Mrs. Hector said, and her throat was obviously lined with deep blue velvet. She

26

took Juanita's hand and led her into a room in which there was a white piano and, unbelievably, a harp. The room was all white and gold, and there were no draperies or carpet, only a gleaming golden floor and white cushioned chairs. On the wall, two violins in shadow-box frames. "We'll talk while your father arranges for cold drinks." But Mrs. Hector didn't talk. She fixed large blue eyes on Juanita and simply stared.

Father reappeared. "Gus is bringing Martinis. Iced tomato juice for you, Pumpkin. I hope that's all right. How was the trip?"

"Perfect. How are your rehearsals going?"

He closed his eyes and grimaced. "Awful. Polonius is still working with the script in his hand and Ophelia has a cold."

"It's probably not a cold at all," Juanita said. "More likely an allergy to those 'fantastic garlands of crow-flowers, nettles, daisies and long purples.'" She was very pleased with herself and even more pleased when she won a roar of laughter from Father. "I didn't tell you. I saw the theater. Only from outside, of course. I can't wait to see the inside. When may I?"

"We'll arrange it."

Gus arrived with the drinks. He murmured a greeting to Mrs. Hector, and she gave him a bright smile. Thriftily, while the smile was still intact, she turned it upon Juanita.

"We've forgotten to tell you what I've planned. Tomorrow evening at my house there will be a dinner party at which you'll meet all the very nicest people in your age group."

Juanita tried to think of something charming to say.

"Formal," Mrs. Hector went on. "There will be dancing. We'll have a real romp for you. When I added up

27

everybody's daughters and sons and nephews and nieces and a few odd grandchildren, I think the list came to about a hundred."

Juanita was stunned. A hundred. And they all knew each other. She looked shyly at Father. "Will you be there?"

"Sorry." He emptied his glass and poured again from the pleasantly frosted pitcher. "Who's calling for Juanita?"

"I have Keith Portwood standing by as her date," Mrs. Hector said. "But recently he's become so breathless over Marigold Reese that I'm not entirely certain."

"What do you mean?" The coldness in Father's voice suggested that Mrs. Hector was just anybody. It seemed to Juanita that Mrs. Hector was by way of being the boss's wife, but perhaps Father recognized no one as his boss. "You have Keith Portwood standing by as Juanita's date, but you're not entirely certain. That doesn't make sense. Especially since his mother is your best friend."

Mrs. Hector laughed lightly. "I'll test her influence, and we'll see what happens. Keith and Marigold may have promised to date only each other. It's a typical hostess problem and not very serious. There's always Sandy Houghton. He's a darling."

"If there's *always* Sandy Houghton, he can't be such a darling," Father said.

Juanita thought it a silly discussion. "Since I don't know any of these boys, it makes no difference at all who calls for me."

Mrs. Hector puckered her lovely brow musingly. "Actually, Torrey, you know, Juanita's right about that."

"Yes, and because it makes no difference at all who calls for her, let's just make sure that it's Keith Portwood."

And Mrs. Hector made sure that it was Keith Portwood.

Juanita, walking out the front door with Keith, understood why Father had been so insistent. Father loved her

28

tremendously and was anxious for her to have the special excitement of driving in an outrageously showy automobile and having for escort this broad-shouldered, narrow-waisted Adonis who was certainly seventeen, at the least. Father had made such an effort in her behalf that she must never let him know that she was amused by the self-consciousness with which Keith carried his handsome self. Amused, too, by the slim, crouching monster in the driveway. "What kind of car did he drive?" Barrett would ask. And she would say, "A foreign car. A sixteen-cylinder Nouveau Riche."

In the more pleasant sense of the word there was nothing amusing about Keith. He was sullen-eyed and, she thought, slightly stupid.

"I'm looking forward to seeing the Hector house," she said as they drove the short distance. "It's so lovely from outside."

He shrugged.

She had been taught that it was her responsibility to make conversation. "This is a beautiful place to live."

"What? Oh, yeh."

"Your car is beautiful, too."

He nodded.

She lost a minute in searching for another topic. "Have you seen the theater?"

He scowled as though she had posed an annoyingly difficult question. "What theater?"

"Mr. Hector's theater."

"Oh, that theater."

They were through the Hectors' gates and Keith had surrendered his car for parking before she thought of anything else to say. Or at least of anything that could have been said to this dull young man. There were people to whom she could have made the observation that even

Mother Nature paid dividends to the wealthy. If one could afford to build a white brick castle, then the moonlight would obligingly wash it in silver glow. Plant a garden that would perish without the attention of six employees, and the air will be filled with a fragrance unmatched by any bottled perfume. Not only that. As a special whimsical gift of love your trees will be inhabited by fireflies and your guests will stand spellbound in the summer night, unwilling to exchange rapture for a plate of hors d'oeuvres.

"Well, are we going in?" Keith asked.

"I was just looking," she said.

She walked beside him to the open door where Mrs. Hector was welcoming the arrivals. There were other ladies with her, and they all greeted Juanita expansively.

"I'm so glad you could come," Mrs. Hector was saying to everyone in her soft velvety voice. "Juanita, my dear, I want you to meet . . ."

Juanita said the proper thing a great many times. Keith had immediately found the girl who was obviously Marigold. She was pink and white and very pretty. At her side was a slim boy. Sandy Houghton, of course. He looked awkward in his dinner jacket. His black tie had somehow come undone.

Guests were streaming in through the open door, and Mrs. Hector was seeing that Juanita met everyone, but people had a habit of gathering in intimate groupings that grew more intimate as gossip and private opinions were exchanged. Juanita debated whether or not she should stand staring interestedly at nothing or join Keith, who, socially speaking, was responsible for her. He was laughing and talking animatedly to Marigold. Juanita had just decided against intruding upon them when a small thing happened. Marigold suddenly noticed the state of Sandy's tie. She turned from Keith and skillfully made a neat bow knot for Sandy. She smiled at him and as she resumed her conversation with Keith she drew the awkward boy into bright orbit by slipping her arm through his. Juanita was encouraged to move from her isolated position against the wall.

"Hello. I'm Juanita. Are you Marigold?"

"Oh, I've been dying to meet you, Juanita, but I saw you getting swamped with introductions so I held off. This is Sandy Houghton, and now that we're all together let's walk around and talk to people and let's sort of capture a table so we'll be seated together at dinner."

Long before dinner was announced Mrs. Hector had disappeared, leaving the ladies of her welcoming committee as chaperones and general advisers. They made certain that everyone was in line for the buffet dinner and suggested seating arrangements at the candlelit tables for four. Afterward, they gently herded their charges down the stairs and into the ballroom. The music had already begun. Keith turned hopefully toward Marigold, but she floated away with Sandy.

Keith looked then at Juanita. "Do you want to dance?"

She danced with him. He spoke to friends of his as they passed. He laughed with them and finally stopped dancing to join two couples who had paused at the edge of the floor, deep in discussion. Keith was admitted to their circle, and Juanita stood watching the antics of the drummer. She wished desperately that she had brought her sketch pad.

When she got home Father was sitting in the small parlor of the master suite. He looked up from a script as she walked in. "Tell me about the party. How was it?"

"It was marvelous. How did the rehearsal go?"

"Satisfactorily." He lowered his eyes to the script and made a few idle markings with his blue pencil. "A lot of the youngsters you met tonight are coming to my opening. It's quite an occasion." He glanced up at her. "Was anything said to you about it?"

"No." She was tempted to say quite bluntly that there was little chance of her having an escort to the opening, that tonight Marigold had generously sought out dancing partners for her. But he would suffer. He would refuse to believe that she was not sick with hurt and humiliation.

Because he loves me he wants me to be happy and he doesn't know that a plain girl can enjoy life just as much as someone who looks like Marigold. I must give him reasons to be sure that his ugly duckling is very happy. Tomorrow when he takes me to rehearsal I will prove to him that an intelligent girl is pleased by the important things in life and has no need for beauty.

It was wonderful to be shown around Mr. Hector's theater by Father, to be introduced to the cast and to see how impressed Father was with her comments and questions. At rehearsal break, when luncheon was brought in, she sat with him in his dressing room and they talked of Shakespeare and laughed because Father had never played Romeo in a company where Juliet wasn't older than her nurse.

"I have to get back to work now." He gave his notes a moment of cold, silent concentration. " 'Get thee to a nunnery' is coming up. Every time I've done *Hamlet* I've wondered how Shakespeare meant me to read that line. What do you think? With angry impatience? With contempt? Or is it a compassionate warning?"

"A compassionate warning," she said, and later in the back row of the theater she caught her breath in happy wonderment, for he read the line as she had suggested.

They drove back to the house in the fading afternoon with a lazy breeze beginning to stir in the treetops and the sky turning a delicate lavender beyond the church spire. There was the beautiful hush of approaching evening and the memory of the bright golden day.

"I have never been so happy," Juanita said.

Father smiled at her, and she was glad he had not spoken. His silence meant that he understood and that he was happy, too.

A pity the ride home was so short. She knew that a mood had a brief life and never flourished when taken from the place of its birth. It could be remembered but never recaptured. It could be mentioned but never described. She would walk with Father into the house, but the mood would not go with her. She could go back to the car and drive all night searching for it, but it would not be found again. Happiness would remain, of course, but the soft-sharp unearthliness that had touched her would be gone.

Father opened the door and called Gus. "Bring a Martini to my room, like a good fellow. I may be in the shower. Just set it down somewhere. Did I get any calls?"

"Yes, sir. There's a list on your upstairs table."

"Did Miss Juanita get any calls?"

She was startled by the question. Who would call her?

"Yes, sir."

Father turned to her and winked, then looked at Gus expectantly.

"Miss Marigold Reese called," Gus said.

"And who else?"

"That was all today, sir."

Father said, "Well, I'll be in the shower." And he walked upstairs.

Juanita went to the phone. It was rude not to return a call, Miss Emmett had always said. They're exactly the same as letters, you know, dear.

"Could you have lunch with me at the club tomorrow?" Marigold asked. "It's sort of fun there sometimes."

At dinner, when she told Father of the invitation, he was pleased.

"Good. You'll see people you met at the party, only this time they won't be strangers. Perhaps you'll ask a few of them here. I won't be home tomorrow evening."

Well, of course there would be times when he would dine out. Odd that she hadn't realized that.

"Would you enjoy having several boys and girls in for dinner?"

She stared at the silver flower bowl in the center of the table. This was the moment in which to be very honest. This was the moment in which to say, "No. I don't need anybody but you. I don't need anything except the theater, some books and my sketch pad."

Clara came into the dining room and served Father a small vegetable salad. It was one of his Spartan dinners which he had disciplined himself to accept three evenings a week. He selected a particularly crisp piece of toast and did not speak again till Clara had returned to the kitchen.

"I think tomorrow you had better murmur discreetly to Marigold and find out which lads have not yet arranged dates for opening night. Need I add that the unattached ones should be those you invite to dinner?"

"Why must I have a boy to go to the opening with me?"

"Because you young ones are not invited to the big party at the Hectors' house afterward, but there is going to be dancing at the club. I don't want you left out."

He looked at her so anxiously that she felt she must give him some reassurance. She remembered a pleasant, stout boy who was Marigold's brother. He had seemed quite unattached at the party. She smiled at Father. "Don't worry. I won't be left out."

Marigold was very considerate and understanding. She said, "Don't think I haven't gone through the stranger-in-town deal. It's terrible. When I visited my aunt in Texas last year I thought I'd never get to know anyone."

Juanita, gazing at Marigold in her little ruffled sunsuit, found it difficult not to laugh. Marigold probably had had a dozen aspiring escorts for every party that had been given. Just the same, it was awfully nice of Marigold to pretend.

"I'd get my brother to take you, but my mother promised Nancy Templeton's mother that he'd take Nancy. It's ridiculous. Nancy's only thirteen. She shouldn't even see *Hamlet*, but her mother thinks it's an event she shouldn't miss. You know what I mean. Your father being so famous and everything. Did you like Sandy Houghton? He might be free that evening."

A boy in bathing trunks threw himself on the chair beside Marigold. He had tousled dark hair and a sleek tan. "Why don't you take a swim? Water's wonderful today."

"I was in before lunch. Warren, you know Juanita. You met her at—"

"Oh, sure. Hi. What are you doing tonight, Marigold? There's going to be a horse auction at a farm out Glancette way and lots of the kids are going over and—"

Marigold nodded. "I know. I'm going with Keith. First we're going to eat at Nobie's, where they fix those wonderful Chinese dishes, then—"

"Okay. Just so long as you're going. I'll see you there." The boy jumped from the chair and back into the pool.

"He's such a nut," Marigold said. "How about a Coke?"

"No, thanks. It was a lovely day, but I have to go now."

Father came home earlier than usual from rehearsal. "How was your afternoon? Are you having dinner guests?"

"No. Everyone was busy this evening."

"Oh, too bad." He ran up the stairs, then paused to call from the landing. "Give me a minute to get into a dressing gown, and we'll have a visit while I'm resting."

That was so like him. It was evident that he had planned a brief nap. Now that she was to be alone all evening the nap must be sacrificed. She waited till after Gus had delivered the customary drink to him, then she went upstairs. Father was lying on the bed in a black linen robe. He looked tired, she thought, but very distinguished.

"Tell me what happened today, Pumpkin. Did you inquire about young gentlemen who have not yet sworn themselves to other ladies for the opening?" The question, though playfully put, did not disguise his concern.

She sat down on the edge of the bed and grinned at him. "It seems I'll have no problems," she said, airily. "There are a couple of possibilities, but I think I will choose Sandy Houghton."

"Who are the other possibilities?" Father asked.

She hadn't expected that. "Well, there's a boy whose name I think is Jim. I'm not sure, and I didn't get his last name. Then there's another boy who kept jumping out of the pool to talk to me. But right now I think I'll decide on Sandy."

"Don't decide on Sandy," Father said. "My daughter can do better than that."

"Do you know Sandy? He's a very nice boy."

"He isn't popular, Pumpkin. I hear he has no dash." Father raised himself on one elbow to take a swallow of his drink. "Why was it that you and Keith Portwood didn't get on better together?"

"We got on fine. It's just that he and Marigold are practically going steady."

"A pity. For the parties and dances and very definitely

for the opening you ought to have an escort who's pretty special."

She turned her face from him to conceal the trembling of her lips. Suppose it developed that there was no one at all to take her to the opening? Marigold hadn't been certain that even the scorned Sandy would be available. Father cared so terribly for her happiness that his wonderful night for which he had worked so hard would be completely ruined. He would be receiving congratulations from everyone, but it would be meaningless because his little girl had been left out of the party at the club. It mustn't be that way. She had to do something. Could she summon the courage it would take to call Marigold's brother and say, "I understand about Nancy Templeton, but she's too young to go dancing after the play, isn't she? Couldn't you take her home and meet me at the club?"

She felt herself reddening at the idea of such brazenness. What would he think of her? Why, he would think that a girl as nervy as that would be fair game for petting and all sorts of liberties. And, Juanita thought wryly, he would probably throw little Nancy down a well and come running because, as she understood it, boys were crazy about kissing and touching and that kind of thing.

She cast a sidelong glance at Father. He was scowling. It hurt to see him so troubled. Would it cheer him to know that she didn't even like Keith? Could they laugh together over his misapprehension that attention from Keith could have made her deliriously happy? "You know," she began, "there are lots of boys who are more entertaining companions than Keith."

"I'm quite sure of that, but he happens to be the beau ideal of the little world in which we find ourselves at this time. That's what matters, isn't it?" He pulled himself wearily off the bed. "Scoot. I must get dressed."

After she left him she sat stiffly on a chartreuse chair for a long while. When he walked past her door and called good night she was still sitting there. But she had not wasted her time. She had thought. She had thought about boys and about Father's disappointment and how happy she and he could be for the whole summer if only this business of her escort were settled. And it could be settled. Unless all the giggled, whispered information she had gathered was completely false, it could be settled. When the car drove away she went to Father's bedroom, where there was a private line without an extension. Even if they were going to eat Chinese food and go to a horse auction, perhaps she was early enough.

Someone who sounded very much like Gus answered the phone.

She said, "I would like to speak to Mr. Keith, please." Her heart fluttered, then seemed to lie cold and motionless. There was still time to hang up, still time to—

"Hello."

And now there was time for nothing but the sudden sharp stab of pain in her stomach and the determination to give a good performance.

"Keith? This is Juanita Winton."

He didn't quite say, "Who?" But his silence was eloquent.

"There, you see? You hardly remember me, and that's what I want to talk to you about. I didn't get through to you at all the other night, did I?"

"Who did you say this was?"

She had forgotten his blasted stupidity. She would have to begin again. "Keith, I'm Juanita, your date at Mrs. Hector's dinner party. I've been in a fog ever since, wondering why I struck out with you."

"What do you mean?"

"Well, I'm not used to being ignored. I come from a pretty big town, you know, and back there the boys really notice me. That is, when I'm given half a chance."

"This is *Juanita?*" he questioned.

"Yes, this is the girl you didn't want to dance with, the girl you didn't want to talk to, and the girl you dropped at the door as though she was poison."

She heard him laugh a little nervously.

"Keith, you're the best-looking thing I've ever seen, and I thought I'd at least get a good-night kiss."

There was a sudden resentful silence. Then, "Who are you trying to kid? Who is this? You're not Juanita Winton."

"I can prove I am."

"How?"

"Come on over."

"I have a date."

"Oh, that disappoints me terribly. I thought that perhaps you'd be curious to know what a big-town girl is like when there isn't a crowd around."

It took her fifteen minutes of repetition, of flattery and of derision before he agreed to break his date. She came away from the phone shaking. She washed her face in cold water and took an aspirin tablet. Then she put on some lipstick and went downstairs to tell Gus that there would be two for dinner.

She watched for Keith from the living-room window and when she saw his car in the driveway she stood staring in awe at this testimonial to the power of evil. One could behave oneself for a thousand years and be paid off in the coin of indifference. What lie had he told Marigold? And why did it matter? She was never going to think of Marigold again.

Conversation was sprightly at dinner. Keith talked

pleasantly of the ski lodge where he and his family spent the winter holidays. And she took note of his new attitude and she smiled at him and thought of him as a swine. After dinner she led him to the room with the harp and invited him to help find some dance records. They danced to a tango rhythm and held each other very close.

"So you're a big-town girl, are you? How are they different from any other kind?"

She moved even more closely to him, and they kissed. His hands went immediately to her breasts, and she wondered what delight that could bring, for she hadn't the soft, round things that lots of girls had. However, he seemed entertained and slid his hand inside her dress and kissed her again. They stopped pretending to dance.

"Take off your clothes," Keith said.

"No. Look for me inside of them."

He reacted excitedly to that, and it interested her to observe that words, too, had incendiary powers in such moments. Why, this was an easy game to learn. Only an idiot would fail to play it well. She brought her mouth close to his ear and she said, "Oo, that's wonderful." And she said it breathlessly many times till he was wild and aching for her. Then she scrambled away from him and laughed in the darkness.

He called her a very nasty name. She had never heard it before, but the meaning was clear.

"Wait," she said. "Tell the truth. Did you ever before know a girl you didn't have to behave properly with? I mean outside of cheap pickups and—"

"Thanks for nothing. You chickened out."

"I didn't chicken out. I never intended to go the entire distance tonight. I brought you here only to give you a sample. You get the full treatment next time, Keith. That is, if we reach an agreement."

"What do you mean, 'an agreement'?"

"Well, there's something you're going to have to do for me first. I'm mad about you, but I'd have to know that you like me a little bit, too, before I'd be willing to start a real fire. I'm not going to ask so much."

When Father came home it was very late, but her door was open and she was reading.

"Hi, Pumpkin. You must have quite a book there."

"Yes, it's wonderful. Was the dinner party nice?"

"Too nice, considering that there's an early rehearsal."

"Oh, that reminds me—I'm going to your opening and the party at the club with Keith Portwood. When he called to ask me I hadn't had dinner yet, so I told him to come over and he did."

Father stared at her incredulously, and she could see that he was delighted.

During the entire last week of rehearsals she went with Father every day. He even invited her to dress rehearsal, which was more than she had dared to pray for. Nobody but Father would have understood how much the dress rehearsal meant to her. Nobody but Father would have planned to surprise her so gloriously.

"Your father tells me that Keith is taking you to the opening," Mrs. Hector said. The chill blue eyes were wide with astonishment, and Juanita knew that the chaperones had reported that Keith had not been able to endure the sight of Juanita Winton. She also knew that Mrs. Hector, at first meeting, had marked her down as too plain to foist on the most popular boy in town.

At dress rehearsal Juanita was presented to Mr. Hector and was properly reverent. He was a fat little man in his late sixties.

He asked, "Are you enjoying yourself out here?"

"Yes, sir. Very much. Thank you."

"Everyone likes sham," he said. "I shall be remembered for an artificial lake and a cathedral built in honor of make-believe."

Though she had a reply she did not voice it. Mr. Hector had quite consciously spoken for quotation and an answer would have been in shocking poor taste.

It was two in the morning when Father and Juanita drove home. They had cake and hot chocolate in the kitchen. He was too stimulated for sleep and his mood was joyous.

"I won't see you at all tomorrow night," he said. "Owing to my commitments and yours, Pumpkin, we'll be off in different directions." He grinned mischievously. "I know your theater manners are impeccable and that you wouldn't dream of walking in late. But, on the other hand, don't come too early either. Let everyone see whose daughter it is Keith Portwood chose to squire."

What an absolute love he was, how anxious for her to draw every bit of delight possible from her summer visit. During this last week of rehearsals she could have been ecstatically happy had it not been for the bargain made with Keith. There were moments when she feared that Father's *Hamlet* would be spoiled for her. But even sitting beside Keith Portwood in the theater she was able to forget him. Her attention riveted on Father, she was lost to all but Elsinore.

"He's good," Keith said as they left the theater.

"Yes," she said. "Real good."

They went to the club, and she danced with Keith. Then she let him take her home, and on the gleaming golden floor of the room with the harp she lay down with Keith. The darkness was filled with pain and indignities, and when the room was light again she was sickened by the glow of contentment that enveloped Keith. He was talking on and on, and though she did not listen, she was conscious of a note of triumph in his voice. He had forgotten that this had been a bargain. He was thinking in terms of conquest.

"Come on. Let's go back to the club."

"You go if you want to, Keith. I don't feel like going." A sudden terrifying thought struck her. "Keith, you wouldn't—you wouldn't tell anybody, would you?"

"Don't be dopey."

She saw him out, then ran upstairs, filled the chartreuse tub and stepped gratefully into the hot water. So that's that, she thought. That's that. She welcomed the triteness of the words because it suggested that something disagreeable though not serious had been concluded. When one could say "That's that" then there was nothing saddening enough to cry over, nothing hateful enough to make one wonder if it was really good to be alive. That's that. That's that. That's that.

Only there was more. When she came down to breakfast Father was having his second cup of coffee. "Well, good morning," he said. He eyed with interest a slip of paper beside her plate. "That must have been a very successful party at the club."

She looked at the note in Gus's handwriting. Jack Howden called. Warren Fay called. Phillip Talcott called.

"Sit down and drink your orange juice, my pet. It will make your hair curl, though apparently you don't need curly hair."

She raised her head and looked at him. His eyes were shining and his smile was warmly affectionate.

"I don't know what these calls are all about," she said.

He laughed. "You must have been a great deal more vivacious at the club party than you were at Mrs. Hector's."

"Oh, yes. I danced on tables and tossed my pink garters to the cheering mob." She slid Gus's note out of sight beneath her plate. "Father, your performance last night. You were so wonderful, so—"

"Yes, I was good," he acknowledged. "I never felt more power and certainty. Mr. Hector was profoundly moved that I have given his theater as much respectful effort as I give New York or London. The magazine and newspaper people who were here from the big cities all promised rave notices for the theater and the production as well as for me personally. I feel very humble. That is to say, I feel only slightly superior to any other actor alive."

She wanted to laugh with him, but suddenly she was sobbing.

"Why, Pumpkin, such behavior on this, our happy day. We're both successes, and you've gone all hysterical over it. I understand. It's very exciting, but you must calm down."

"I'm all right," she said. "Really I am." She dried her tears and drank some orange juice.

"I know you are. We're just awfully emotional today because we're so proud of each other. Pumpkin dear, are you going to spend the morning returning the calls of those boys? Or would you like to go shopping with me? I want to buy you a memento of the *Hamlet* opening."

"Oh, I'll treasure it forever."

"Of course you will, darling. It will be something rather nice. You can call the boys later."

She said, "Wouldn't it be fun not to call them at all? I made a marvelous splash last night. I think now I'll retire into a very exclusive shell and spend my time reading and sketching."

"You can read and sketch all winter long. Now is the time for happy nonsense. I shall be very disappointed if you don't make the most of your visit here. Why, I expect you to have a date every night."

44

He bought her a lovely golden necklace, and she had a date every night. The loud-mouthed Keith had defeated himself with his boasting. He had created curiosity and competition. Father was very proud of her. He brought her all sorts of amusing gifts and he bragged outrageously about her army of admirers. And when they met, Juanita felt the cold, questioning gaze of Lois Hector upon her.

"You're having the wonderful summer I wanted for you," Father said.

She put her arms around him and buried her face against his shoulder. She hated the town and the people and the lake and herself and everything in the world except Father and his pride in her.

"Who's going to take you to the opening of the new play?"

She shrugged. "Do you have a preference?"

They laughed together over that, but it wasn't the same as when they had laughed over Juliet being older than her nurse. It wasn't the same at all for Juanita.

"I love you, Father."

"I love you, too, Pumpkin. Of course, I scarcely get to see you any more, but I remember your sweet little ways."

"Do you?" she asked earnestly. "Do you really?"

The opening of the second play was less important than *Hamlet* for many reasons, but it had its own quality of excitement. Juanita attended with the boy named Warren Fay. Warren Fay who had had no date for the horse auction but who had not cared to invite her.

She cried during the play because it was very sad and because Father's performance was exquisitely heartbreaking. When they left the theater there was a melancholy summer rain falling. They drove around in the night, and Juanita felt the fragrant mist upon her face, and there was the pain of loneliness and longing. The raindrops glittered

45

in the black trees, and the tires on the wet road sang a mournful song, and she wanted to talk to someone who understood the aching beauty of a summer rain, but there was no one.

"Let's drive to that sandwich place," she said. "I'm hungry."

They ate hamburgers with melted cheese and drank root beer, and after that she let Warren take her home and into the room with the harp. She had become very skillful at ending the ordeal rapidly. It was no longer agony, but neither was it enjoyable. She had discovered that meek surrender did nothing to speed up matters, whereas if she feigned feverish impatience it was not only accepted as a mighty compliment but was vastly effective in bringing swift conclusion. The art of love. What nonsense.

"When do I see you again?" Warren asked.

"I don't know. Call me."

She walked him to the front door and closed it sharply behind him. She turned then and ran up the stairs as she always did when once again she had guaranteed her popularity. But tonight Father was standing on the landing.

"You're home," she said, inanely.

"Yes. I came directly here from the theater. Mr. Hector is ill, so the little supper was called off." He was not looking at her, but she felt that he had looked. She was conscious of her disheveled hair and of the lipstick that must be smeared.

"Warren just left. Did I wake you when I closed the door?"

"No. I was on my way to the kitchen to get some ice."

"I'll get it for you."

He walked past her and disappeared in the shadows of the downstairs hall. She fled to her room and to the mirror. Her dress was wrinkled, but there was no conclusive evidence of wrongdoing. Her hair was less disordered than she had imagined. Only the blurred lipstick was beyond easy explanation.

She had thought herself clever. Now she must prove that she was. This was the time to think of something brilliant, something . . . Suddenly she knew what to do. She would call to him as he came along the corridor and when he had entered her room she would look at him shyly and she would say, "Father, I guess it's not serious, but perhaps I ought to tell you—I let Warren kiss me good night."

How relieved he would be. He would smile at her and when alone he would perhaps laugh over the foolish suspicion he had harbored. She heard his step upon the stairs and she readied her eyes for a look of candor and her manner for a certain winsome sheepishness.

"Father."

"Yes." But he did not stop walking.

"I want to tell you something."

"I'm very tired." He continued to walk till he had reached his room and he went inside and closed the door.

And for the first time she remembered that tonight he had played a new and difficult role. Of course he was tired. He was exhausted. And she had not said a word to him of his beautiful performance. Would it seem absurdly nonchalant to write a note extolling his genius when he was a victim of maddening worry concerning her? She decided that it would. The words of praise must be postponed until tomorrow and spoken only after she had played her own artful little scene. But how ghastly long the night would be. If only he had not closed the door.

She went to bed and slept fitfully, and all at once Clara came into the room carrying a tray.

"Miss, I thought you might like to have your breakfast here."

Juanita sat up and looked at the girl. "Why? Why here?" She became aware of the color of early morning and she was struck by a sudden nameless terror. "What time is it?"

"Seven o'clock. But I have all the packing to do and the train leaves at eleven thirty."

"What train?"

"The train for New York, Miss."

Juanita leaped from the bed and ran to Father's room. The door was open.

"Mr. Winton had to go somewhere very early, Miss, but he arranged for everything. He has telephoned your mother to meet you. Gus has the money to buy your ticket at the station and I'm to have your suitcases ready to go with you. The trunk will go tomorrow."

Afterward Juanita remembered standing in the corridor and screaming. She remembered Clara's bewilderment when the screaming didn't stop. She remembered Gus and Margaret rushing upstairs and she remembered the iced towels on her neck and forehead, the aspirin and the silence of the servants.

She never remembered getting on the train or getting off in New York. Vaguely she remembered the few hours or the few days spent in the apartment before she was driven to a sunny private hospital out on Long Island. After that, things began to take on shape and clarity again. The nurses were cheerful, the resident physician very kind. The doctor who came to sit and talk with her every morning was extremely sympathetic.

Even more sympathetic was the obstetrician who had delivered Mother's three children. He made a very gentle examination. Then a week later he had her wheeled toward the quiet little hospital's surgery, telling her that one more examination was necessary. This one, being more thorough, might be slightly painful and so, he had added, he would pamper her with an anesthetic.

In the hallway she heard him whisper, "Rebecca, go home and relax. This is a very simple deal. She's in no danger and, law or no law, with all my heart I believe it's the right thing to do."

Mother came every day to visit her. It was difficult to make conversation. During many weeks it was difficult. Then gradually Juanita turned again to books and to her sketch pad and there were things to talk about. By the first week in December she was home and completely normal.

All the doctors said so.

Orly was enormously chic. One had immediate and certain knowledge that this was Paris. Even a Venusian landing here would admit, after a glance, that he was off course and that this was not Kennedy Airport. Soft bells chimed. The gift bars shimmered with inimitable elegance. The cashmere sweaters, the glittering bottles of perfume, the ingeniously constructed toys, the sparkle of jewelry, the assortment of fine gloves and scarves, all caused one to ponder the necessity for driving into the city. But of course one would do so if only to please the officials who performed their duties with such dignified cordiality.

Rebecca, in the line of arriving passengers, searched the faces of those anxiously awaiting clearance of friends or relatives. She saw a young woman in stout shoes and a durable coat. So this was Mademoiselle. No possibility of a mistake. The children standing at her side were undeniably Vicki's. The little girl held a tiny poodle dog in her arms. The boy wore a dove-blue cape lined in scarlet.

Rebecca had not known till now the disappointment she would feel if Vicki failed to meet her. But one could rationalize the situation. Vicki was busy with her packing. Vicki had so many things to do today. Silly for Vicki to meet the plane when they would be together shortly.

Mademoiselle was directing the attention of the children toward her. They raised their dark eyes, and Rebecca waved. The little boy called, "Grandmère, Grandmère," and Rebecca dropped her hand. Grandmère? She experienced a sudden stab of loneliness. What am I doing here in a strange country? Look at all those people, and I don't know a single one of them. She fastened her gaze on a fabulous beaded sweater and thought about the shops on Faubourg-Saint-Honoré. What heaven for a woman with a purse full of traveler's checks. And suddenly the formalities were concluded, and she was free to join Mademoiselle and the children.

"Madame, I knew you instantly from the photographs I have seen. We are so happy that you are here."

"Thank you, Mademoiselle." Rebecca embraced the children. "Hello, my darlings. Ursule. Etienne."

The children glanced uncertainly at Mademoiselle. She spoke swiftly to them, and the children lifted their faces to be kissed.

"Ah, yes, that is nice," Mademoiselle approved. "How do they look to you?"

"French," Rebecca said.

Mademoiselle was not amused. "Yes, well . . . Shall we go now to the car?"

The children walked beside Rebecca with Mademoiselle leading the way, a porter bringing up the rear. Rebecca patted the small poodle. Ursule was pleased. "Fifi," she said.

"Naturally," Rebecca replied, although she knew she was talking to herself.

The car was a miniature station wagon. Surprising how it swallowed all the luggage without bulging. Mademoiselle attended to the gratuity for the porter, and it was Rebecca's guess that the man was dealt with too thriftily.

"You would care to sit up front with me, Madame?"

"Thank you."

Mademoiselle opened the door for Rebecca, and the children protested. It seemed they wished to ride in the front seat themselves, but if this privilege were denied then

Grandmère must ride with them. The protest was short-lived and restrained. Mademoiselle simply repeated an order, looked coldly at the children, and they climbed into the back seat.

"They could have ridden up here," Rebecca said, "if that's what they wanted. I wouldn't have minded."

Mademoiselle gave no sign that she had heard. She was the type of driver who must prepare herself and her clothing for the great undertaking. She unbuttoned her coat, smoothed her gloves, settled her hat, and narrowed her eyes on a distant point as though it were a target. She moved her shoulders to make certain that no sudden catastrophic attack of paralysis had beset her. She found just the right position for back and buttocks, arranged a crafty watchfulness upon her face, then started the car with a terrific jolt to all occupants and was off like a bat out of a burning barn.

Rebecca turned to smile at the children and to study them a little as they placed Fifi between themselves on the leather seat. How considerate they were in handling the small dog. What sweet little creatures with their cameolike faces and pale, silky skin. Rebecca thought it unfortunate that their hair was too cleverly cut and dressed, giving them the same high-fashion artificiality proper to the well-groomed poodle. Ursule's antelope trench coat and Etienne's dashing, though unidentifiable, uniform brought a memory to Rebecca.

"Does she really want children or does she want dolls?" Juanita had asked upon reading the letter from Paris.

"I am pregnant," Vicki had written. "Here I am, thirty years old and married for the third time and at last divinely happy. After mistakes and follies I have arrived at a place where I am so serene and joyous that now I want children."

Rebecca remembered, too, the letter that had come just a year after Ursule's birth.

"You'll never believe it, but I'm wildly, ecstatically happy to be pregnant again. Edouard is such a wonderful husband and father that I can think of nothing more desirable than to stay forever in my quiet house raising a family. Thank God, I never wanted children till I married Edouard. How unthinkable that I should have babies that did not belong to him."

Mademoiselle said, "There is a letter awaiting you from Madame, your daughter, with full explanations, I assume. Still, there is no harm in mentioning to you now that her plans were changed and she has already departed for the United States."

Rebecca caught her breath and stared unbelievingly at the young woman. "What! You mean she's gone? She's left? Why, I can't imagine . . . Are you sure?"

"Oh, yes, quite sure. I regret your disappointment, Madame, but it seemed sensible to tell you."

Rebecca said nothing. The sickening sensation of shock made conversation impossible at the moment. How could Vicki have done this to her? It was incredibly unkind and beyond any reasonable explanation. The French governess and the soft, incomprehensible chatter of the children seemed intolerable now that there was to be no end to the strangeness and loneliness. Had Vicki given her only a few hours, it would have made a difference.

Oh, God, this is going to be unbearable. Or am I just terribly tired? She looked about her. She supposed this was the outskirts of Paris. Swiftly moving traffic on a superb highway, a showcase for prosperity in itself, even if one failed to notice the impressive new housing developments. She wished she were driving from Kennedy Airport into New

York. Wouldn't the sight of Shea Stadium bring joyful tears? Oh, Vicki, Vicki, my girl, what a beast you are.

"How far is the house from the Plaza-Athénée Hotel?" she asked.

"It is very close, Madame. To walk the distance is not difficult."

Sue and Barker Kane were at the Plaza-Athénée. What fun that they were in Paris. How lucky she was to have both friends and family here. Most tourists had no one at all. She turned and smiled again at the children. Then to Mademoiselle, "The children speak no English?"

"No. The pursuit of flawless French is considered sufficient for now."

Rebecca felt a slight resentment. Disgraceful, she thought, to leave English till it becomes such a terrible chore that they'll hate it. They could have been picking it up all this time without any trouble at all. Outrageous, when one considers that Vicki is tenth-generation American— on my side.

"Quite a pity, I think. Their grandfather is one of the greatest actors alive. He may retire before they can appreciate him."

"Would that not be the case even if they understood English perfectly, Madame? One must be mature and an experienced playgoer to recognize Mr. Winton's superiority. Fortunately, his accomplishments in the cinema provide an enduring testimony to his greatness." Mademoiselle paused to frown at an automobile that had managed to pass her. "They have had the extreme pleasure of meeting their grandfather. He was in Paris and called upon them. He invited them to visit London, but I suppose that was merely a pleasantry."

Rebecca supposed so, too.

They were in the city now. She had come to it quite differently that other time. She had come by way of Le Havre after a voyage on the luxurious *Ile de France*. Such a magnificent ship. Dead for many years.

"We have not much farther to go," Mademoiselle said.

There it was. The biggest gimcrack in the world. The Eiffel Tower. Gimcrack? Was it really? That was how she had thought of it for years. "Trashy, pretentious," Torrey had said, averting his eyes from the Eiffel Tower. And it had been natural for her to accept Torrey Winton's conclusions when she was very young. A sign of atrophy to accept them now without re-examination. She looked long and hard at the tower as it stood piercing the gray mists of the autumn day. And because one could not go on record without words, she said to Mademoiselle, "It definitely has style."

"Oh, the tower. Yes, you are quite right. It has not beauty or majesty but, yes, style. There, Madame, is the Plaza-Athénée Hotel."

The street had a peculiar quality of existing under glass. Obviously, it was protected in some very special manner from the tread or even the view of ordinary citizens. Mademoiselle whisked the car around the block, then seemed to double back for the sake of utter confusion. "And so we are here," she said.

The children scrambled to the pavement and promptly disappeared. Mademoiselle hurried to inform someone of the arrival, and Rebecca stood regarding Vicki's house. It was on a curved corner opposite a grassy square, a narrow house four stories tall. Made of brick and stone and trimmed with ironwork, it was clearly a nineteenth-century structure and in its youth would have been designated a mansion. Its stately charm had been conscientiously preserved, and trees surrounding it had had as much loving care as the house itself.

A blond man in a striped apron came to carry the luggage. Mademoiselle led Rebecca into the house. The foyer with Regency paneling and a chandelier of gilt carved wood were unexpected. Vicki had never described her house in detail, and Rebecca had not guessed it to be so formal. In passing she noted a Queen Anne table and two frail chairs encrusted with mother-of-pearl. Amusing to recall that there had been a time when Vicki had regarded with contempt any piece of furniture that had not been designed the day before yesterday. The upper corridor was colored by light from a stained-glass window. Rebecca peered at the garden through a segment of deep amethyst, and it was a gloomy experience.

"Do you ever have bright, sunny days in the autumn?" she asked.

"Rarely. The smoke from the Seine obscures the sun."

The smoke from the Seine. If the words had meaning, it was lost on Rebecca. "Where did the children go?"

"To the kitchen, Madame. It is their responsibility to offer the little dog fresh drinking water on his return to the house."

Rebecca smiled. "And if they failed to remember, would the little dog go thirsty? Surely a servant would—"

"Yes, Madame, a servant would. And if that should be necessary, then the little dog must be given away to punish the children for neglecting him. It is a way of teaching them to be trustworthy. Turn to your left, Madame. Your room is there."

It was a very large room with high windows draped in pale gray velvet. Vicki had wittily balanced the ceremonious display of a massive canopied bedstead and a heavily carved armoire by installing a voluptuous chaise longue and a scarlet satin slipper chair. The fireplace and mantel were in marble of varied colors, and on a Boulle chest there was a vase of roses and a sealed letter.

Mademoiselle said, "I shall return presently."

Rebecca opened the letter.

Mother dear,

It seems I am always asking you to understand something. I had fully intended to be in Paris to receive you. I had even intended to meet you at Orly, but instead—he consulted the astrologer and was advised as to the luckiest hours for him to move toward a new phase in his career. He had to choose a plane which would enable him to leave here and arrive in New York within the same well-omened period of time. I said, "Go. By all means, go. I will take the plane we originally booked on." He was very upset, fearing that our relationship, being an important part of his life, would also be in danger if the signs were ignored. Please don't laugh at all this. I am the veriest beginner in astrology, but I know it is the only thing that humans have that will guide them truly. I beg you to forgive me for leaving before your arrival. Try to accept that I had to do the sensible thing.

I hope you will be happy in my house. I think you will find that I have excellent servants. I know you will adore the children. I will telephone or write soon. I love you dearly.

V.

Rebecca tore the letter to pieces and walked into the bathroom to burn it. Long ago, in its original form, the bathroom had evidently been another bedroom, perhaps the sleeping quarters for a personal maid. Now it had a jade-colored tub, toilet and washbasin with gilded dolphins for plumbing fixtures. There was a glass make-up counter with a fine mirror above it, and the comfortable, tufted chair swiveled sportively on the head of a larger dolphin. The room was carpeted in white, and there was a crystal chandelier with small green silk shades. There were no matches in the bathroom. There were no matches in the bedroom. Rebecca placed the pieces of the letter in her purse. She did not trust French plumbing with Vicki's pathetic secrets.

Mademoiselle appeared in the doorway. "Is there something I may do for you?"

"Yes. If you would be so kind, I'd like to look around a little. Just this floor for now. My daughter's room. The nursery. I'd like to see where there's an available telephone. Things like that."

Vicki's room turned out to be an apartment. Bedroom, bath, sitting room and a deep alcove secluded by a Coromandel screen. Black bookcases against a stark white wall. A black desk with a handsome brass lock. On the wall, two Picasso drawings. An armchair upholstered in black velvet had beside it a Louis Sixteenth pedestal table which served as a very special bookshelf. It took only a glance to verify the suspicion that here one would find a half dozen volumes on astrology.

The bedroom and sitting room were brilliant examples of Vicki's taste and imagination. The furniture was exquisite, and she had created a harmony that spanned the centuries from an ebony door done in a marquetry of ivory and silver to the stunning Vlaminck so cleverly hung that it was forced to blend rather than dominate. Rebecca was impressed by the precious objects Vicki had gathered and placed so expertly on brackets and tables throughout the apartment. Roman medallions, Egyptian cats, terra-cotta figures, African sculpture, Chinese porcelains, bronzes, goblets, hourglasses, silver candle lamps. Her bed table was a carved wedding chest with copper hasps, and her dressing-room walls were covered in velvet with a light tracery of embroidery in gold and silver thread. One could spend hours examining these rooms that Vicki had furnished when she had loved her husband and her house.

The nursery was also an apartment. Two small sleeping rooms for the children, a bathroom and a large playroom. Everything in vibrant shades of red and blue. Curtains of white *glacé* chintz. Gay, fanciful.

In the hallway there was a telephone. "I will help you if you encounter difficulties. Of course, you will be using the instrument in the room of Madame, your daughter, for most calls, but this one may prove more convenient."

Rebecca waited till Mademoiselle had left her, then began immediately to unpack. She opened the carved armoire and found it lined in fragrant quilted satin. A closet with sliding doors had been created by sacrificing five feet of the room's width. It had countless shelves, drawers and small inner cupboards and a compartment for fur coats. Rebecca thought of her New York apartment. She was fond of it. The apartment was convenient and attractive. But it was disturbing to think of Vicki rushing to live inside that pretty pink vacuum. How could a woman who belonged to this house breathe in the barren brightness of built-ins all shinily enameled with nice fresh paint?

She went to the window and gazed out at the small piece of Paris below. Very elegant. She could tell because there was a nursemaid just leaving the grassy square across the narrow street. She wore a vast, braid-trimmed mantle and the traditional white head veil. She was pushing a high, large-wheeled perambulator inside of which was a mass of yowling lace. The sky was the color of tarnished silver, and Rebecca became aware that the chill had invaded the room. She placed her hand upon the radiator and found there was no danger of having her fingers blistered. She remembered what Jennie Frost had said, "You'll freeze to death and go blind trying to read at night. I have a better light in my icebox than Parisians use on their bed tables."

Rebecca investigated. Jennie was right. The bulb in the lamp glowed feebly. Could one buy a finer, brighter bulb?

Probably not. It might lead to blown fuses for miles around. She snapped the wall switch. High up in the gilt-decorated ceiling the black iron chandelier leaped into action. Three little buttons of light beamed with the strength and splendor of the candle on baby's first birthday cake. She wondered if the artists in their garrets knew that the rich people were also freezing and had no lights by which to read.

There was a radiator in the corridor. Rebecca touched it, then went back to her room and put on the jacket of her suit. She walked toward the nursery. Perhaps the children were there with Mademoiselle. If not, she might just get into her mink coat and sit in Vicki's black velvet chair reading a book on astrology.

What had suddenly become the entire population of the world was in the nursery. A young Frenchwoman, a dog and two children with whom Rebecca could not communicate. She stood in the doorway, fascinated by the sight of living creatures who were conducting themselves quite normally. The children were coloring picture books. Mademoiselle was sewing, and the small dog dozed comfortably on a blue corduroy cushion. Then it could not be true that everything was different and disjointed and out of tune. The scene in the nursery offered promise that one might catch the rhythm of French life and learn to move with assurance and purpose.

Mademoiselle looked up from her sewing. "Ah, Madame, come in. Please seat yourself."

Rebecca sat down on a bright red chair. The children ran to her and displayed their work. A Martian colored in yellow. Superman in several shades of green. Their eagerness for her approval was gratifying.

"Why, I think these pictures are just wonderful," she said. She rather overdid the smile and the warmth of her tones so the children would be convinced of her enthusiasm. She was not pleased with Mademoiselle's translation which quite clearly was, "Grandmother is amused." But the children seemed satisfied and returned to their crayons.

Mademoiselle's needle flashed industriously. "Your room is pleasing to you, I hope, Madame."

"It's rather cold."

"You mean that you find the decor unfriendly?"

"No, the temperature. It's really quite chilly. Even in here it's not what I'd call warm."

Mademoiselle put her sewing aside and walked to the radiator. She touched her index finger to it experimentally, then brought Rebecca the good news. "The heat is functioning perfectly, Madame."

"I see," Rebecca said.

Mademoiselle took up her sewing again. "Would you care for a cup of tea or perhaps coffee?"

"No, thank you."

"Dinner is not till seven thirty. I am speaking, of course, of your dinner. The children and I eat earlier."

"Yes, I would suppose so. What time do they go to bed?"

"Eight thirty. Is it different for children in the United States?"

"About the same, I think."

Rebecca sat on the red chair shivering slightly. By next week, she thought, I shall be a very old woman. With a shawl over my shoulders I will sit here crocheting lace. Mademoiselle will be my only friend, and we will have long, stimulating conversations about children and weather.

A girl in black uniform appeared in the doorway. Her collar and cuffs were crisp and snowy white. Her hair was tidily covered by a net. She nodded politely to Rebecca, then addressed Mademoiselle. The children dropped their crayons and became wildly excited. Mademoiselle looked at them severely, demanded silence, and turned to Rebecca.

"Their father is downstairs," she explained. "He has come to pay a call on you, Madame."

Very surprising. Edouard. Rebecca rose from her chair, then noticed that Ursule's face was splashed with tears. Etienne was angrily destroying his yellow Martian.

"What's the matter with them?"

"The visits of Monsieur are great events. They love him very much. Naturally, they want to run downstairs immediately."

"And why can't they? They can come right along with me. They can—"

"Their father has not asked for their presence, Madame."

Rebecca forced herself to take a deep breath before replying. "He will," she said.

"And when he does I shall be very happy to tell the children so. For now, they must await their father's pleasure."

Rebecca walked downstairs remembering how her children used to rush at Torrey when he entered the house. They would surround him and cling to him and scream in his ears and propel him to a chair where they would sit all over him. Why, Miss Emmett would have been discharged had she ever suggested to Winton children that their father might not care to see them.

The servant in the black uniform was waiting at the foot of the staircase. Rebecca followed her to an octagonal room where the ceiling had apparently been lowered to create an atmosphere of intimacy. There were wide settees and a coffee table inlaid with copper and tortoise shell. Marquetry also in the uncarpeted walnut floor.

"Edouard, how kind of you to come."

He bent and kissed her on the cheek. "Madame, I am kind to myself."

They stood in silence for a moment, looking at each

other. The three years that had passed since their last meeting had made some changes. He was leaner, and the boyishness that had once promised to accompany him into a blithesome old age was gone from his eyes.

They sat down on one of the settees, Edouard holding her hand. "You had a good flight, Madame?"

"Very."

"I know you did not see Vicki. My secretary had occasion to call here today and she reported to me that Vicki had already departed."

"And you guessed that I would be ill at ease in this unfamiliar place. I do appreciate your coming over."

"It is my pleasure." He took his hand from her to accept a drink that was being offered him. "Would you like this? I can send for another."

"Oh, I need it, Edouard. This house is freezing cold."

He laughed. "No. It is just right. Americans keep their houses too warm. When I first entered your apartment in New York I thought you were attempting to grow orchids, so stifling was your living room."

"How I should love to stifle a little right now."

"Overheated houses are damaging to the health. However, so that you will not say you were treated abominably in Paris, I will arrange for the fireplace in your room to be in action at all times."

"Heavenly. Is there any chance of getting more light on my bed table?"

"Very unreasonable of you to ask. Paris is not as extravagantly wired as New York. Here one must sacrifice reading in bed for the joy of seeing fountains and monuments in a happy blaze of illumination. One must make some concessions for having Notre-Dame floodlighted so one may admire it while eating duck at Tour d'Argent."

"You mean that now Tour d'Argent actually permits a

view of Notre-Dame? Don't passers-by stare at the diners?
Don't—"

"The restaurant moved upstairs, Madame, very long
ago."

With the arrival of his drink she thought that perhaps it
was time to become more serious. "How are you really,
Edouard?"

"Well enough. Better than I guessed I would ever be
again. I have suffered shock and heartbreak since last I saw
you."

"I know that, and I'm very sorry."

He was silent for a moment and when he spoke it was
clear that he voiced thoughts which had crossed his mind a
thousand times. "If I had abused her, I could have asked
forgiveness and mended my ways. But when a woman simply tires of a man there is nothing he can do but accept with
grace and good manners." Abruptly he got to his feet.
"Come. I will show you the house. This is the room in
which we entertained when we had less than a dozen to
dinner. The room was affectionately known as 'Little
Louis.'" He pointed to the chair which he had occupied
while awaiting her. "Louis Thirteenth." To a black lacquer
table. "Louis Fifteenth." To a marble console. "Louis Sixteenth. And so forth, Madame. Let us continue elsewhere.
I am somewhat tired of Little Louis."

He led the way to the dining room. The walls were in
deep red flocking, and a fine crystal chandelier suspended
by a rope of red velvet glittered above an oval table. The
room had a marble fireplace flanked by silver urns. Rebecca
realized as she walked with Edouard that, though her attention might be caught by the huge twin Venetian mirrors
of the drawing room, his eyes doubtless sought out some
small article that had a meaning or a memory. She only
glanced at the paintings and sculpture and remarkable work-

manship that surrounded her. She would see it all another day unaccompanied by Edouard and his regrets.

"My library," he said, gesturing toward a suède-covered door which was now closed. "It was done in delightful modern. I have moved the furniture to my apartment. Let me show you the morning room."

Yellow and white sang cheerfully in the carpet, curtains and informal furnishings.

"And here is the children's dining room."

Rebecca lingered a moment there, smiling to herself. Only Vicki would have dreamed of reconstructing for her small French children an American dining room of the McKinley period. Golden oak furniture, stiff lace curtains and fruit in a cut-glass bowl. Above the table hung a large amber-colored lighting fixture ornamented with a bright edging of red and green squares.

"She had great difficulty collecting some of the items," Edouard said. "Observe the wall platter which commemorates Dewey's victory at Manila."

"A very odd whim," Rebecca remarked, "when one considers that the children have been taught no English."

"Do not suppose, Madame, that it was ever easy to understand Vicki. Are you interested in kitchens?"

"Only somewhat."

Vicki's kitchen was varnished pine panels and stainless steel. It was beams in the ceiling and all modern appliances. Herbs growing in curious little pots on the window sill and a chromium food scale from Hammacher Schlemmer's.

"Would you like to meet the cook?"

"I have taken too much of your time already, Edouard. I know you want to see the children."

"You can believe that I shan't leave without seeing them.

66

What is your guess? Would they prefer that I visit the nursery or have them join us downstairs?"

"Oh, by all means, downstairs."

The children were brought to the octagonal room, and Rebecca watched as Edouard talked to them and encouraged them to talk to him. He held Ursule on his lap. Etienne sat beside him, and Edouard kept an arm around the boy. Rebecca saw worship in the children's eyes, and she wondered what Edouard thought at such moments. Did he feel that he owed an apology to his son and daughter? Forgive me for choosing as your mother a woman who could not be faithful to you or to me. Forgive me for finding her so appealing that I could not resist her.

Rebecca excused herself and gave the children fifteen minutes alone with their father. When she returned there was a lively three-cornered conversation in progress. The eyes of the children glowed and there was a pink excitement in their cheeks.

"I am going to spend the weekend with my mother," Edouard explained. "She lives outside the city. I would take great pleasure in having you two ladies meet. Ursule and Etienne have accorded me the honor of agreeing to spend Sunday at my mother's house. May I hope that you will do the same?"

Rebecca said, "Oh, Edouard, please don't think you must invite me."

He looked at her intently. "You will discover that in France we do not embarrass ourselves or others with careless invitations. If to have you visit on Sunday would be, in any manner, inconvenient I would see no reason to pretend that you are welcome."

Rebecca laughed. "French courtesy might defeat honesty."

"Our courtesy is the result of our honesty. It is the Americans who say, 'We'd be delighted to have you,' when there is no room in the car and no wish for your company." He lifted Ursule from his lap and set her on a delicate chair that Rebecca knew was anomalous to Little Louis. Napoleon Third. He turned then and spoke to Etienne, who hurried away, returning with the man who had served the drinks. "Now," Edouard said, "we shall attend to the matter of a good warm fire for your bedroom, Madame."

The servant was amazed at the order he received. He looked at Rebecca wonderingly, then walked over to consult the radiator. She knew he was telling Edouard that the heat was working magnificently. Edouard, she saw with relief, was very firm. She would have her fire.

"I am afraid I must leave now. Mademoiselle will drive you to my mother's on Sunday. About noon, I should think."

From the threshold she looked back at him. He was kneeling and embracing his children, his voice gently bantering as he parted from them. She went to her room and watched from the window as he drove away. She hoped he was taking to dinner somebody rather sensational who was completely mad about him.

In the corridor the children were speaking to Mademoiselle. Rebecca heard the word "Grandmère" uttered several times. Of course. They would be explaining that on Sunday this Grandmère would be going with them to see that Grandmère. She walked out of her room to join them.

Mademoiselle said, "So we are all going visiting?"

"Yes."

"Oh, you will enjoy it, Madame. Mrs. Dover is a most wonderful person."

Rebecca rapidly paged through a stack of mental notes. Why am I "Madame" and Edouard's mother "Mrs.

68

Dover"? She's French. Not I. And, for that matter, why is their name so un-French? I used to know. What is it that Vicki told me about the family? I wish I could remember. There was something else that had never seemed important but now, considering Sunday, loomed fearfully on the direct horizon.

"Does Madame Dover speak English?"

"Oh, yes, extremely well. As a girl, Mrs. Dover was educated by Irish nuns in the convent at Bordeaux."

Rebecca observed that Mademoiselle very deliberately had not used the pronoun but had made a point of repeating "Mrs. Dover." She was delivering the message that this was the way, and the only way, to address Edouard's mother.

The story will come back to me, Rebecca thought. Not that it really matters, as long as I train myself to remember that *I'm* Madame.

"Mrs. Dover's house is very lovely," Mademoiselle went on. "Years ago she lived in this section, but during the war she moved far away from Paris. Afterward when she returned she was never content in the city and finally bought the place which you will see on Sunday."

Rebecca said nothing. She wished to avoid casual talk concerning Edouard's mother. Mademoiselle was well-bred and tactful, but Rebecca knew that conversation with an adult was an intoxicating experience in the lonely life of a governess. Unsolicited information must be discouraged.

She looked at the children. They were standing there in the corridor, their small faces raised to her. The soft colors from the window touched them with an ethereal glow, and she thought what a picture they would be for a Christmas card. Chic little angels, in their clothes from Avenue Victor-Hugo, and the light coming through stained glass to fall upon their shining black hair. They stood silently gazing at her, and she saw that their eyes were questioning and a little sad. Speak to us. Make us understand you, the eyes said. It's no good, you know, if you don't even try.

And Rebecca prayed for a word to offer her grandchildren. An international word, a wonderful word, but it was not exactly a word that came to her. Suddenly, in the uneasy stillness of the house, she was inspired. She bent toward them and shouted, "Boo!" The children sprang backward and for the slimmest split second were terrified; then they began to laugh, and their laughter filled the corridor and rolled down the staircase. Rebecca laughed with them, and it was a beginning.

Mademoiselle said, "Madame, you are a lady of much humor and merriment. It is charming, perfectly charming." And then she spoke to the children. Her smile was indulgent, but it was plain that there had been sufficient humor and merriment for now.

The laughter gradually subsided to only an occasional snicker. Rebecca knew it could be reanimated when she wished. The merest whispered "boo" would serve. She could afford to let Mademoiselle restore order.

"What will they do now?" Rebecca asked. "What is their daily routine? Do they go to school?"

"I will answer your questions in reverse, if you do not mind. They have lessons with me. I am a qualified, licensed teacher. Their routine was interrupted today by their mother's departure and your arrival. Usually we are very well organized and have lessons, walks and playtime on a regular schedule. Now we are going to take the little dog for his exercise. We will go no great distance at this time."

The telephone on the hall table rang. Mademoiselle ignored it and it was answered in another part of the house. "The children also attend a dancing class where they meet their friends and spend many pleasant afternoons. Occasionally there is a concert or a cinema for young people—"

The maid in the black uniform was coming up the stairs, her progress sedate and unhurried. Everyone knew that she brought a message, but it was unthinkable that she could speak till she stood in the upper corridor. When at last she did, she bobbed her head and smiled and made a statement which included the name "Madame Winton."

Rebecca went to the telephone.

"Ah, Madame Winton," said the male voice at the other end. "My information is that you are from the United States. A sincere salutation and welcome to you. Is it, by any chance, my great good fortune that you would like to buy some dirty post cards?"

Rebecca gazed nervously toward Mademoiselle. She need not have worried. Mademoiselle was on her way to the nursery with the children.

"Exactly what kind have you for sale? I'm pretty tired of the junk you can get at any *cinq*- and *dix*-cent store. I want something real artistic."

"Oh, Madame, I have just the thing. Sixty-eight—no, sixty-nine—very sentimental poses of my wife in affectionate communication with my best friend. You will love them."

"Bring them over."

"What time?"

"Now. I can't wait."

"Marvelous. How are you, Becky darling?"

"Fine. How are you and Sue?"

"Pretty good. What about dinner with us?"

"Sounds real friendly."

"Oh, great. Hey, Sue, she'll have dinner with us."

"You come here first for a drink."

"We'll be over in a few minutes."

So everyone knew that Vicki had not waited. Who had

told the Kanes? Perhaps Vicki herself. Why, of course. Wasn't it the most natural thing in the world that Vicki would call Sue and say, "Don't let my mother be alone for dinner this first night in a strange place. It would be so ghastly for her." Without doubt, that's what had happened. Oh, without any doubt at all.

In the nursery Mademoiselle was helping the children into their coats.

"I don't suppose it will disturb the kitchen greatly if I don't dine at home this evening, will it?" Rebecca asked.

"Madame, you must please yourself."

"Will you explain to the cook that I have been invited out?"

"Yes, of course."

"And will you also say that I am expecting my friends within the next half hour? I should like them to have a drink here and perhaps a simple appetizer. I don't expect fancy hors d'oeuvres on short notice. Sorry to trouble you with this, Mademoiselle, but I assume none of the servants speak English."

"They do not. I will attend to it for you with pleasure."

Ursule and Etienne had been listening attentively, watching, hoping to grasp some notion of what was involved here. How good they were. Though obviously consumed with curiosity, they asked not a single question.

"Mademoiselle, would I be inconveniencing you if I asked that, when you return from your walk, you send the children to me? I would like Mr. and Mrs. Kane to see them."

Mademoiselle's eyebrows twitched eloquently. She said, "We find ourselves in confusing circumstances, do we not, Madame? I think you were left as uninformed as I regarding the matter of authority. Let us try to arrive at a working agreement. I am an employee. You are the mother of

72

Madame Dover. I perhaps shall make a suggestion or an explanation to you at times, but certainly I can never disregard your wishes. For instance, you ask me to send the children so they may be presented to your friends. I shall say to you, 'Yes, Madame.' But I shall also say that this has not been the custom of the house."

"You mean my daughter never introduces the children to her friends?"

"Madame, here parents do not compel their guests to listen to the prattle of children, nor do parents take it for granted that their guests wish to give up their own conversation for the joy of entertaining the little ones. But that is not the entire reason for drawing a sharp line between the world of adults and the world of children. We feel we do a great service to the young by preparing them for the drawing room instead of merely setting them loose in it."

Rebecca smiled amiably. "Mademoiselle, we'll have no serious disagreements. But do answer my question. Doesn't my daughter show these delightful children to her friends?"

"Of course, she does, Madame. There are special times for that. A luncheon in the garden or an informal afternoon gathering indoors. Also there are the holidays when parties are given for children and are attended by adults as well who come to observe the jollity."

"Sounds very nice."

"Oh, it is, Madame. It is the only civilized way. In France we have a very tender regard for the years of childhood, but French people are horrified at the idea of youngsters intruding upon the cocktail hour."

"Well," Rebecca said, "the Kanes are Americans. They won't be horrified. If I acquire any French friends, I'll remember what you've told me. After the children have exercised the little dog and given him his bowl of water, send them to me. I will be in the octagonal room."

"Yes, Madame." Mademoiselle handed Fifi's scarlet lizard lead to Etienne, who snapped it on the small collar. "I will give you my key, Madame. You may keep it. I shan't be taking any evenings away from the house. And I will bring the children for you to present to Mr. and Mrs. Kane."

The Kanes were wonderfully comfortable companions, and Rebecca had known them a very long while. It had been rather a curious relationship inasmuch as there had never been a close intimacy which demanded constant meetings or even phone calls. Sometimes a year passed without communication between Rebecca and the Kanes. Yet, Rebecca realized, something like kinship existed here. One might not include a cousin at a dinner party, but he would not be forgotten at a wedding, and somehow the Wintons and the Kanes always had been involved in each other's important moments.

Barker, gray-haired and angular, was of utterly undistinguished appearance. One might look at him and listen for the tick of the middle-price watch he had received for slaving fifty years at the draftiest desk in the office. Sue still had the hair and complexion that had inspired a columnist to describe Barker Kane's wife as Aphrodite sculptured of honey and snow. No longer Aphrodite, Sue was chubby as a pincushion and her hair was processed honey, but she had kept the dazzling white skin, and the sea-blue eyes had paled only a little.

The hastily assembled appetizers suggested that Vicki's cook was not only obliging but something of a magician. She had done amazing things with mushrooms, and there was a curry-flavored dip that was almost habit-forming. Rebecca was amused to see that French potato chips were so very French that they were practically *pommes souf-flées.*

Barker reached for another cheese puff and asked, "Where are we going to eat, Sue?"

"You're doing fine right here. That's your fourteenth nibble. We can't both be fat. We'd look ridiculous."

"Shall we make Rebecca's first night here atmospheric or elegant?"

"If that means 'Do we go to a bistro?' the answer is no."

"No bistro?" Rebecca asked. "I thought that was the name of the game here."

"It is, and I've stopped playing," Sue said. "I'm through with all those picturesque places. They're for the lady from U-Turn, Arkansas, who thinks she's got the address of a real 'in' spot. 'So-and-so gave me this restaurant,' she says. That's tourist jargon for 'Few Americans know about it.' Well, if few Americans know about it that's because it's inferior. Paris is like any other place. You pay cheap, you eat cheap."

"She hates bistros because they're informal. No maitre d', no captains, nothing fancy. Just a mama-and-papa business with maybe a son or daughter helping out."

"Oh, you make them sound so charming. Tell Rebecca about the cockroaches."

"Now, Sue, that isn't fair. You saw one cockroach in one bistro."

"I know, but I felt he was trying to tell me something. Anyhow, this much is true of all bistros—without the fine, tasty sauces they ladle out so generously you couldn't stand the smell of the meat they serve you. Just like if it wasn't for the magnificent architecture you couldn't stand the smell of Paris itself."

Rebecca glanced at Sue's knitted dress. "Are we elegant enough for a place that uses exterminators?"

"Sure. Paris today is like Los Angeles. You'll see women

75

wearing everything from coronation robes to tailored suits.
The other night we saw a dame in white mink and a beaded
gown and at the next table—" Sue fell silent as she noticed
Mademoiselle in the doorway.

"The children have returned, Madame."

"Thank you," Rebecca said. "Please send them in."

They walked quietly and shyly into the room, going at
once to stand at Rebecca's side. She made the introductions,
glad that Mademoiselle had not waited to see how that little
formality turned out. "You take it from here, Barks. I
haven't forgotten that you were the only American aboard
the *Paris* who spoke French."

To Rebecca's surprise and relief, the children understood
him perfectly. There was a whole series of questions and
answers, then Etienne ran suddenly from the room.

"What's all that about?" Rebecca asked.

"He's going to get their dog so Sue and I can see it."

Ursule now repeated something she had said before.
This time Barker listened, then groaned. "Oh, God, I've
goofed. The dog is allowed only in the kitchen and the
nursery."

But Etienne came back carrying Fifi and, at Barker's
suggestion, placed the dog on Sue's lap.

"I adore poodles," she said, but she had little time to adore
Fifi.

Mademoiselle, very apologetic, reappeared, murmuring
about the children's dinner and their need to prepare themselves for it. She probably counted off exactly ten minutes,
Rebecca thought.

"Those are the most entrancing children I've ever seen,"
Sue said when Ursule and Etienne had departed. "What do
you say we go over to George Five and continue our drinking?"

George the Fifth reminded Rebecca of nothing. It was as

76

though she had never seen the hotel before. Only its name had meaning. The building itself was disturbingly strange. She was annoyed at not feeling any sweet, sad emotion at sight of the lobby through which a young Rebecca had rushed to devour Paris. Of course, this lobby has been re-decorated twenty times since I was here, she thought. But she knew that not paint or plaster and not even remodeling could account for the fact that no memory remained. I willed it so, she thought. I brainwashed myself, and if I hadn't, I'd be a whining, bitter old woman today. I re-member the names of places where Torrey and I went to-gether. Every name. Every place. But seldom the things we did. Seldom the things we said, and never the way I loved him when I was very young.

They had drinks in the bar, Rebecca ordering two to Sue's three and Barker's four. She only finished her first. The bar filled up. There were many people who knew Barker. Even a few who knew Rebecca. All New York and part of Hollywood were drinking at George the Fifth. There were people who had been in London and had seen Torrey. There was a man who said, "Mrs. Winton? Then you must be Vicki Dover's mother." There was a Broad-way star surrounded by her court of fluttering fairies, and she said, "Becky, I'm at the Lancaster. Do call me." And there was a couple who stood at the table smiling uncer-tainly for a moment before the woman said, "You don't know me, Mrs. Winton, but I had to say hello just because we're so far from home. We're your neighbors in New York. We're in Sixteen B, right next door to you."

After a while the Kanes and Rebecca went to a small, silk-lined jewel box where food was served with such ritual and devotion that it was rather like attending a Black Mass. Dinner was excellent, from the Marennes oysters to the luscious *framboise*. The patrons of the restaurant were

77

fascinating. American women in quiet, well-cut clothes. French girls whose bosoms were so flat that their deep décolletage gave them the look of female impersonators. There were dogs in the restaurant: a terrior, a boxer, two poodles exactly like Fifi. One, wearing a tiny rhinestone collar, jumped upon the table and was playfully reprimanded, but permitted to remain till his owner was satisfied that she had drawn sufficient attention.

The Kanes walked Rebecca home through the cold night. The air smelled of trees and thin smoke.

"Here's a cute little neighborhood store, Becky," Barker said. "It's real friendly-looking and right handy for you, too."

She stopped and stared. Christian Dior. Hypnotized by the magic number thirty, she moved toward the building and stood, bemused and wide-eyed, beneath the great name. Sue joined her. In ecstatic silence they gazed into a window that had been emptied for the night. Then slowly they drifted to other empty windows, and making soft, happy sounds, they pressed their noses against the door, hoping to catch a glimpse of something wonderful.

The Kanes left Rebecca in the foyer of the house, declining her offer to search for a bottle of brandy. On tiptoe she went up the stairs. In the corridor she heard a light, pattering sound. She turned and gasped at sight of a small, white apparition.

"Boo!" the little thing said, and was then seized by a fit of giggling.

What was the French for "What are you doing here at this hour in your nightie? You go right back to bed."

And if I knew the French for all that, would I speak it with proper sternness? Could I scold her when she and I both recognize that "Boo" is the code word for "Please find a way for us to know each other"?

Rebecca smiled and put her arm around the child. She was walking her back to the nursery when Mademoiselle, in a blue woolen robe, confronted them.

"This was very naughty of Ursule, Madame. I could scarcely believe it when I heard her laughter. Never before has she left her bed in the night. I know you did not invite it. I know you did not encourage her to—"

"Are you assuring me that I shan't be punished, Mademoiselle? What about Ursule?"

"Surely you can see the necessity for some slight corrective measure."

"Yes. Perhaps you could take dessert away from her at dinner tomorrow evening."

Mademoiselle lowered her eyes and was silent for a long moment. Then, "Who is benefited, Madame, by my making a farce of punishment? Does it increase the children's respect for me? Does it assist in forming their characters?"

Rebecca wanted to laugh. One would think that Ursule's prank was the first step toward debauchery and a ruined life. "It wasn't a very serious naughtiness," she remarked.

Mademoiselle sighed faintly. "As I mentioned earlier, you are the mother of Madame Dover. The child will have no dessert tomorrow evening. With your permission, I bid you good night."

"Good night," Rebecca said. She stooped to hug Ursule. "Good night, Baby."

In her room the fire was burning brightly. The bed had been luxuriously prepared for rest. Across the scarlet quilt lay a nightgown and negligée that the maid had chosen from among Rebecca's belongings. The lights were, of course, unsatisfactorily dim, but the warmth and comfort of the room could not be denied. She felt sleepy and contented. It had all been rather wonderful. The Kanes were absolute dears. She thought of Edouard and of Christian

79

Dior's and of the exquisite restaurant and of her new evaluation of the Eiffel Tower. She thought with special delight of how she had saved Ursule from what may have been a rather stiff punishment. Mademoiselle was just too strict, and the children were such darlings.

God dear, I'm too sleepy to pray tonight. *Vive la France.* Amen.

They entered the village disguised as human beings. They wore the horrifying uniform, but the soldiers were boys in no way extraordinary. The officers were sensible-looking young men. The captain's accent was offensive to French ears, though his grammar was perfect and his vocabulary astonishing to the villagers. The lieutenant could not form a balanced sentence, but he knew many nouns and verbs and had acquired a smattering of the most useful adjectives. Then there was a sergeant who, with disquieting facility, spoke the French of the rural districts. The villagers wondered about him.

Word of the soldiers' approach had preceded them, and the houses were tightly closed when they arrived. Curiosity had not brought a single villager to the square. Not even ambition to establish new business contacts had moved Alphonsine, the whore, to tap upon her window as they had passed her cottage.

Obviously, they were accustomed to cool receptions. For more than an hour they had behaved as though there were no people in the village or, at least, as though no need to meet with them existed. They had separated and walked about in the manner of members of a particularly well-organized guided tour. There had been no shouted orders or methodical groupings. Only a brief convening— ironically, at the base of the ugly piece of sculpture which honored France's war dead, 1914-1918—and then they had spread out in clusters of threes and fours, alert, armed, but neither aggressive nor destructive. From the houses they had been watched as they explored the village. It had been thought that perhaps the invaders would conclude that there was nothing to discover here, nothing to eat, nothing to steal, and that they would pile back into the vehicles that had brought them and go their way.

Some of the soldiers had walked to the top of the hill to gaze admiringly down upon the woods and pastures. Others had appeared interested in the fifteenth-century church and the burial ground where wire wreaths hung in innocent vulgarity upon the simple crosses. There were those soldiers who had looked at the schoolhouse, seeming to regret its emptiness, but the shuttered café and tobacco shop drew more notice and awakened a deeper concern.

Suddenly the sight-seeing had ended. The soldiers had converged upon the public square and had stood at attention listening as the captain gave a swift, low-spoken order. After that had come the sharp knocks upon the villagers' doors and the command to step out into the street for questioning.

Sullenly, with lowered eyes, the villagers obeyed. The women trembled, and sweat rolled down the faces of the men. The captain had seen much sullenness, many eyes that refused to look upon German officers. He had seen an occasional trembling woman before and sometimes a man who sweated or even vomited in terror, but it was not usual. Yet here was an entire village lined up before him without a woman to throw him a brave, black glance of hatred, not a man who faced him with the hard-eyed honesty of those who have nothing to hide.

The captain walked up and down the cobblestoned street and looked long and thoughtfully at these people. Even the tart with pointy little tits peeping through her sleazy blouse had not raised her eyes to count potential customers in the file of soldiers standing wary guard upon the assembled villagers. And, by God, she was trembling as much as the good women who just possibly feared rape. Of what was she afraid? And why had not respectable wives and daughters arranged themselves at a distance from her, as might be expected?

"You," the captain said to the girl. "What's your name?"

"Alphonsine Bergère, sir."

Sir? She had called him "sir." That was remarkable. Ordinarily, from the village slut one received only a mocking eye that said, "You're just a man like any other." Her respect aroused nothing but suspicion. He shot her another quick glance and saw that she was ghastly white.

He selected a man at random. "Who are you?"

"Armand Ribot."

The captain saw soft, unbruised hands. "What do you do for your living?"

"I am the apothecary."

"How old are you?"

"Forty-eight."

The captain made a wild guess. "You have a son with what is jokingly called 'The Resistance.' "

The apothecary shook his head. The captain turned and with his thumb poked at the shoulder of a loose-jawed, loutish-looking fellow. "You, did the apothecary lie? Has he a son with that pack of fools?"

The fellow raised watery gray eyes to the captain's face but made no answer.

"You'll gain little by silence. Did he lie or didn't he?"

There was still no reply. A bony, black-browed woman at the side of the stubborn man clutched his arm and cried, "Speak when you're spoken to. Say that the apothecary is a childless bachelor and that—" Her words ended with a gasp as she was struck across the mouth by the palm of her husband's hand.

The captain waited quietly, allowing time to tell him the feeling of the villagers. Was there approval for the action of the lout? Or was it believed that the wife was a practical woman who had been unjustly punished? He cast a swift look left and right and saw a sudden flutter of hands arranging scarves and reaching for handkerchiefs. He heard small coughs and the clearing of throats. Token gestures for applause and cheers. From the corner of his eye he caught the husband blinking in what could have been acknowledgment of the pantomimed acclaim. It was going to be a difficult village, the captain thought.

He debated the advisability of ordering a dose of rough treatment for the man who had refused to answer. As offences against the Reich were evaluated, his had been commonplace and slight. It was dangerous to initiate a system so stern that even the smallest insubordination drew a penalty. An overly strict occupation officer risked taking on the ridiculous appearance of a peevish, small-minded shop foreman. That was not the picture he wished to present to his company. Still . . .

The lieutenant approached him with the first hastily gathered report. "There are two hundred and seventy-four adults here. In the square, ninety-one children. The village has no doctor or lawyer. The old man with the black glasses has been mayor here for fifty years. He's senile and almost blind. The woman with the deformed back is the schoolteacher. Those persons not now in your presence are the priest, who was not ordered to turn out, and a Madame Du Vair who lives in a rather impressive château. She and her servants were not notified of—"

"Why not?"

"An oversight. The château is not easily seen. It is situated quite a distance from the main road and concealed by trees and shrubbery. An order is on the way to the lady.

There is something else. The girl in the little gathering to your left—the one in tears—has a sick mother who has been bedridden for more than a year. I have withheld permission for the woman to remain at home. I thought you would like to consider which action suits the mood of the village better. We can have soldiers carry the woman here or we can be very sympathetic and—"

"Yes, yes." The captain nodded. "She probably has no use beyond helping us to prove that we are not without compassion." He turned to the weeping girl. "Your mother is ill? What is it that troubles her?"

The girl sobbed and flung her head about in extravagant despair. "I don't know."

The captain was uncertain. Was this an answer conveying only the information that a disease had not been diagnosed? Or was this a conspiracy—momentarily overlooked by the black-browed wife—in which even the insignificant details of village life were to be guarded with unremitting vigilance? He would not bother with that now. He would not permit himself to notice the concentration of the villagers upon the girl as they graded her attitude and performance.

"Well, your mother need not leave her bed," he said. "We would not add to a sick woman's discomfort or trouble her in any way. You may return to her side immediately."

The girl did not even glance at him. She detached herself from the circle in which she had stood and stumbled awkwardly away, still sobbing. The captain refrained from making a sarcastic comment on her failure to offer a word of thanks. Instead, he scanned the faces before him in an effort to determine what effect his kindness had produced. He saw no lessening of apprehension. By this time there should have been a faint sign of recovery. The taut postures of the people ought to have relaxed somewhat. A few words should have passed between the women. The men might have been expected to feel shame for their earlier fear and to begin now to look directly at him. There was nothing of this.

He watched as the French-speaking sergeant proceeded with the listing of names and relationships. He particularly watched Alphonsine Bergère as the sergeant approached her. If she did not raise her eyes in invitation, or at least appraisal, then in this village there was indeed something requiring investigation. And Alphonsine did not raise her eyes.

"Very well," he said, and he realized that with those words he had accepted the fact that here there was more to be dealt with than normal anxiety and hostility. "Very well. Now food must be prepared for my hungry men. There must be—"

"Captain!"

It was the voice of Armand Ribot, the apothecary. It was a thin voice, but it had a certain authority. It would be stupidly self-defeating to silence it, for in another moment it might unwittingly reveal itself as the voice of a leader.

"Captain, you have certainly observed that those who live here are not fat. We have no food beyond that which is needed for survival. It is out of the question for us to feed your soldiers. We have no—"

"I am aware that the feeding of the soldiers will deplete your supplies," the captain said. "You have the problem of keeping yourselves alive. I have the problem of keeping my men alive. In war everyone has problems. Mine are simplified, at the moment, by the fact that I'm in command here. The soldiers will eat."

"What is there for them to eat?"

"Eggs and the chickens that laid the eggs. And don't tell

me that this village has not been breeding rabbits and growing vegetables."

"Very few chickens remain to us, Captain, and the rabbits are dying of some disease and—"

"This is a pointless discussion. In one hour I expect food to be ready. If it is not ready, if it is not thoroughly acceptable, then in one hour and ten minutes everyone now present will have something to regret. Am I understood?"

He looked away from the apothecary. This was no leader. The captain had known that at the mention of the rabbits having "some disease," at the plea that there were "very few chickens." A leader would have a logical name for the disease of the rabbits and he would have given a specific count of the chickens. A false count, of course, but a leader would have made it sound indisputable. The apothecary had spoken only because he had thought it his obligation as an articulate man with more education than the others. A decent fellow, no doubt, this apothecary, but, like all Frenchmen, obsessed with the notion that words could somehow change facts. The soldiers had to eat. What oratory could alter that circumstance?

The captain frowned, chagrined that the identity of the village's chief troublemaker was still unknown. If not the apothecary, then who was the leader here? Well, the answer to that could not be very long in coming. Bumpkin messiahs were never as clever as they supposed themselves to be.

"Are these people to be dismissed now?" the lieutenant asked.

"Yes. I shall seek out the lady in her château. You remain here and permit no lingering on the preparation of food. Force every household to let loose of what it has hoarded. There may be nothing at all in the next village."

The château was not difficult to find once one knew of

its existence. It was, as the lieutenant had said, quite a distance back from the road. Surrounded by a vast park, the tawny limestone building had the appearance of being totally unrelated to the present. The twenty front-facing windows held themselves aloof, with closed shutters sparing them the view of any strangers who might pass through the iron gates. The château's dozen chimneys possessed the dignity of ancient things that are retained not for their picturesque quality but for their usefulness. The captain looked about him, thinking that perhaps kings once had gone to the hunt from here while laughing ladies had played at being country girls. The grounds were short of gardeners now. The trees and lawns had not exactly a neglected air but rather the look of good children who had been told to take care of themselves for a time. Nothing had gone very wrong, but a slight wildness was apparent and there was need for a corrective hand.

In the courtyard a servant was giving his attention to the dusting of a small automobile. He was elderly and slow-moving, and the captain was willing to suppose that the man was not pointedly ignoring him but was simply unaware of his presence.

"Is Madame Du Vair planning a drive?" he inquired.

The servant looked at the captain and at the four soldiers standing behind him, but he gave no answer.

"I spoke to you," the captain said. "And I will have a reply."

The careful dusting stopped. The elderly man fumbled in the wide pocket of his denim apron. He appeared utterly untroubled by the fact that a young corporal had leveled a rifle at him the moment he had reached toward the pocket. He brought forth a small book, dog-eared and stained. It was a French-German dictionary.

A cold rage seized the captain. He was proud of his

French. He knew it to be as good as any foreigner's and he knew that the old bastard had understood him perfectly. The insult was intolerable. Patiently, the servant stood thumbing through the pages of the dictionary and seemed surprised and hurt when the captain slapped it out of his hand.

"Henri, you may go now—assuming, of course, that you have *everyone*'s permission."

The captain turned and saw a lady of perhaps forty-five walking toward him. She wore a plain dark dress and a hat and gloves. A true aristocrat. He could tell by the calm cool of her eyes and the dowdiness of her clothes.

"Your servant is free to go," he said. "You are Madame Du Vair, I take it."

"Yes."

"And you were about to leave?"

"I was about to answer your summons. I was told that everyone had been ordered to gather for questioning in the village. My servants have already left, with the exception of Henri, who would have ridden in my car."

"I am afraid you are all too late. The festivities have ended. I regret that the servants are not here, as it will now fall upon Henri alone to feed these young soldiers of mine."

"Food is scarce," she said.

"Spare me the sorrowful details, Madame. I have heard them in the village. Here they are even more trying. One does not feed servants on air."

"Am I to go back into the house?" she asked him.

"Yes, and I shall go with you. I forgot to mention that Henri will bring me a tray before he serves the men. By the way, where do they go?"

"They follow the bluestone path. Behind the stand of poplars there is a brick walk that leads directly to the kitchen wing."

In German he repeated her words to the soldiers, and they withdrew. Madame Du Vair passed through the arched doorway, and he followed her into a great marble-paved hall ornamented with tapestries and statuary. Priceless articles, he supposed, but futile to covet them. A captain, if the provocation were sufficiently great, could destroy any amount of treasures, but one had to be a general before one could have them lovingly crated and shipped home.

He continued to follow through shadowy corridors and high-ceilinged rooms, rich with portraits and brocades. She brought him at last to a bright little corner of the château where the shutters had been opened to the sunlight. It was a room of flowered materials and fruitwood furniture. Informal and cheerful. This was where she spent her time, he guessed. He saw a sewing basket, a box of stationery and a book concerned with the lives of French saints. He was not asked to sit down, but he did so. Absurd to observe the rules of polite society in view of the fact that he was in the château without invitation.

She removed her hat and stood now slowly drawing off her gloves. Her eyes were a deep blue, he saw, and her hair very black except for a few threads of gray. How severely she dressed her hair. It was brushed straight back, then twisted and pinned into the flat, functional knot usually worn by old ladies. Ah, the aristocrats. What had they that caused a man to stare at a woman who was fifteen years his senior, a woman whose clothes had been painstakingly designed to deflect an ardent glance?

"Have you always lived here?" he asked.

"You know, I quite forgot to tell Henri what he is to do," she said, and left the room.

He went to the window and looked out upon the soft, distant hills and the serenity of sky and golden-green trees.

90

He saw the creations of the château's happier days. The greenhouse, the summer dining room, the ghost of a formal garden. He knew that somewhere there would be stables and kennels and perhaps tennis courts. He was stabbed by sudden envy of people who had lived with such things in childhood, and he left the window and opened the book of French saints. There was writing on the flyleaf. "My gratitude, my admiration and my prayers. Yours in Christ, François."

"Who is François?" he asked.

She had come back into the room and was seated on the sofa, her face turned toward him in readiness for the ordeal.

"My son."

"Is he in this village?"

"Yes."

The captain pondered that, then shook his head. "There was no gentleman among the people I saw."

It was not a question, and she was silent. He prodded his memory. Who, according to the lieutenant, had been absent from the gathering in the cobblestoned street? The sick woman and—oh, that was it. "Your son is the priest, Madame?"

"Yes."

"Really? Did it take much influence to have him sent here?"

"None."

"I see. A young priest just automatically draws comfortable assignment to his native village. In this case, extraordinarily comfortable, considering the château and the servants and, of course, the loving care of his mother."

Madame Du Vair made no response. She gazed out the window at the distant hills.

"I asked you this before. Have you always lived here?"

"No."

"Where then did you live?"

She brought her eyes to rest on his. For a moment he thought that she had decided to answer no further questions; then the reply came. One word. A word spoken quietly, a word not spoken at all until she could pronounce it without emotion. "Paris."

"A magnificent city, Madame. I have recently seen it for the first time."

Her eyes had gone from him. She sat straight and expressionless on the sofa, her white hands quiet in her lap.

"How long have you lived here?"

"Time is a vague thing nowadays," she told him. "I came to the village shortly before the capitulation."

"Your son already had this parish and you wished to be near him. For that reason you purchased the château?"

"I did not purchase it."

He made a careless gesture with his hand. "No matter. You leased it?"

"Not that, either."

"For God's sake, Madame, we are not playing a guessing game. By what arrangements are you living here?"

"The château belongs to a distant relative of mine. I have borrowed it, one might say."

The captain nodded. Naturally. Among such people there would be cousins and aunts who owned châteaux. One had only to think a moment to recall which relative owned which luxurious piece of property near which village. As simple, he thought bitterly, as borrowing a squalid apartment in Dresden for a weekend.

"You are a widow with an only child?"

"No."

"Then where is your husband?"

"I did not deny being a widow."

"You make conversation tedious, Madame. You are a widow and you have more than one child?"

"Yes."

"How many children have you?"

"Two."

"Both sons?"

"Yes."

"What is the name of the other son?"

"Edouard."

"And he is not in the village?"

"No."

"Where is he?"

"I don't know."

"That cannot be true."

"It is true," she said, and rose from the sofa. She walked to a small table and rearranged the silver-gilt objects upon it. Aristocrats, he noted, did not sweat or tremble. When distressed, they fiddled with expensive toys.

"This son of yours—Edouard—how old is he?"

"Twenty," she said.

"Ah, younger than the priest. Possibly a more vigorous type, more physically active, more inclined to be adventurous. Would you say all that, Madame?"

"Yes."

The captain smiled. "Your son is in England, I assume, or in some other hard-pressed part of the world. His commanding officers are men who do not realize what is good for France. What do you say to that, Madame?"

"I say what I said before. I do not know where my son is."

"Very well. We will let that pass. I have other questions for you, now that we have established the fact that—"

Henri came into the room and placed a tray on the table

beside the captain. An omelet, a cup of hot chocolate and a few slices of bread. Insufficient for his needs, the captain thought, but he was suddenly, ridiculously, unwilling to demand a more substantial meal. She would speak of him as a glutton or a pig. He unfolded the dainty, white napkin and busied himself with the omelet.

"So you are a stranger in this village, Madame. Are you becoming acquainted with the inhabitants?"

"Of course."

"Why 'of course'?"

"Because I am a human being. I need the company of other human beings."

"You visit in the homes?"

"I have done so."

"And you make conversation with peasant women?"

"Yes."

"And what has been the main subject of mutual interest?"

"There are many subjects."

"Name three."

"Gardens. Sewing. My son François."

And her son Edouard, he thought. She would have told the villagers romantic stories and painted vivid pictures in their minds. Doubtless she had promised that while brave, determined men like Edouard lived, France was not truly lost.

"And of course the war, Madame. You have discussed that?"

"Yes."

"It would be strange if you had not," he said, gently. "Incidentally, I found your villagers very different from others I have seen. They are more frightened of soldiers, less willing to adjust to the role of conquered people. How would you account for that?"

94

"I cannot compare these villagers with others. I have not your experience."

"True," he agreed. "True."

It had been a beautiful omelet, and, to his surprise, his hunger had been satisfied. Also, delightfully, the omelet had turned out to be a compliment. He learned from the corporal that there had been a huge pot of rabbit stew on the kitchen stove. It was the servants' regular fare, and some had been given to the soldiers. The captain was pleased to believe that Madame Du Vair had thought it too coarse a dish to offer a gentleman.

On the short drive back to the village, he wondered if it really had been she who had unsettled the simple people with fiery appeals to their patriotism. Had she given instructions on how to conduct oneself in the presence of the enemy? Was she responsible for the marked peculiarities of behavior?

"Stop at the church," he said on impulse to his driver.

The historical importance of the church, its architecture and its ancient, childishly wrought statue of the Maid of Orleans held no interest for the captain. He saw only the slender, fair-haired priest who came toward him across the stone floor.

"Good afternoon, Father Du Vair."

"Good afternoon. Do you wish to speak to me?"

"Yes. As a matter of fact, I wished to speak to you earlier, along with your parishioners."

The priest said, "No one told me that. I was preparing children for Holy Communion when two soldiers came and whisked them away."

"The soldiers were courteous to you, Father?"

"They did nothing of which I may complain, but they did not inform me that I was expected to—"

The captain said, "You amaze me, Father. I do not believe that I have ever before met a priest who would permit children to be taken from him by foreign soldiers."

"Do you suggest that I should have fought your armed men?"

The captain smiled thinly. "No. I suggest only that it might have occurred to you that you must somehow remain with the children, that you must follow them, comforting them if need arose and standing in readiness to share whatever fate was in store for them."

The priest reddened. "It did not appear to me that your men intended to harm the children."

"And, of course, they did not harm them. But isn't it strange that I would have felt a deep concern for the little ones while you were content to let them be taken from you? I suppose it's your invincible faith that allowed you to stay here unworried while the children were led away. Even common soldiers were so certain that a priest would follow the children for whom he was responsible that no effort was made to indicate to you that you were wanted outside."

The captain studied the vexed face of the priest. Fine features, a certain elegance of brow, but the man was a fool. He fails to realize that I did not know there were children with him until he mentioned it himself, the captain thought. It was he who handed me the lash with which I stung him.

"I have been to the château. I have had a conversation with your mother."

The priest remained still, but his eyes expressed a brief, chilling comment. Had he dared, he would have said that people can no longer choose their company. But he does not dare, the captain thought.

"We talked at some length of your brother Edouard."

96

"My brother Edouard?" The words were spoken almost in the brittle, high-pitched voice of an adolescent. The priest was aware of that and shamed. He cleared his throat. When he spoke again it was as a man trained to address a congregation. "Our prayers are with Edouard. The state of his soul is our concern. We love him very deeply though his thoughts are not ours, his aims not at all the same."

"Oh, come now," the captain said, benignly. "Aren't you taking his thoughts and aims too seriously? After all, he is very young. Nine, I think your mother said, and working so hard to please his schoolmasters."

So aristocrats *could* sweat. The captain watched Father Du Vair reach into the pocket of his splendidly fashioned cassock. What a beautiful handkerchief he drew out, with what a quivering hand he touched it to his temples.

"Fascinating, this old church, Father. Thoroughly fascinating. I must have my men see it."

He walked to the door and signaled for his guard. "You are needed for nothing in particular," he told the corporal. "You and the others are to wander around this moth-eaten antique, doing no more than displaying yourselves to the Frenchman as impressive symbols of our might."

When he walked back into the church he found that Father Du Vair had seated himself in a rear pew and was perhaps praying. His eyes were closed.

"Well, Father, it is good that you have made yourself comfortable, for we have matters to discuss."

The priest's eyes opened and, for a moment, dwelled in horror upon the soldiers. "What is there to discuss?" he asked, but there was no bite in the question, only anxiety.

"I would like your help or, better said, your opinion. This village rather bewilders me. I will admit that I don't expect conquered Frenchmen to love us, but I sense here a very special problem. I feel that this village is in the toils of the devil." He paused to permit the priest to cross himself. He had wanted to see the man's hands. Yes, they still quivered. "There is a wickedness of some kind afoot here, Father, and I am not accusing you of having spiritually failed these people. I am speaking of more worldly things. We stand ready to bring to all the French a strength and joy, a healthiness of mind and body that they have never known before. We are not going to allow any individual to delay France's great awakening."

He glanced at the priest, who was more composed now, somewhat bemused by having the whole dreaded situation devolve itself into nothing worse than a sort of political campaign speech.

"Father, this village has, in some manner, been led astray, persuaded to trust a false leader. Obviously, there is a leader here. I know it and you know it." He reached out suddenly and clutched the priest's arm. "Now, Father Du Vair, you tell me who that leader is."

The priest gasped but made no other sound. He sat shaking his head and swallowing again and again.

"You are refusing to answer me?"

"No." A deep breath. "I am saying there is no leader."

"But there is. We both know that. Shall I tell you my suspicion? I think the leader is your mother."

"Before God I swear that is not so."

The captain loosened his hold upon the other's arm. "Oh, it is not your mother?"

"No, no."

"Then it must be someone else. Name that person."

The priest uttered a strangled cry. "You will not believe me."

"Why should I doubt the word of a man of God?"

"Because it is a singular thing that has occurred here. I

agree with you, yes; it is typical that in crises people will look for leadership. Here that did not happen."

The captain dug his fingers into the shoulders of the priest and pulled him to his feet. "Then what did happen?"

There was no answer. Father Du Vair leaned weakly against the heavily carved top of the forward pew and pressed the handkerchief against his forehead.

"Father, no delaying tactics will bring to your mind a story that will satisfy me. You may as well speak now. What singular thing happened here? You hinted at it. Now explain."

The priest swallowed hard once more and squared his aching shoulders. "I meant only to say that there is no leader. Simply in concert the village, as though it had but one mind, made its decision. It thought and acted without committee or council. There was never need for discussion. The village, as one heart, one set of nerves, one body, moved toward what it wished to do."

"And what did it wish to do?" the captain asked.

Again there was no answer.

"I understand, Father Du Vair. There was a small plot —mystically agreed upon—that every inhabitant should take a hostile attitude toward the soldiers of the Reich, should try to increase the difficulty of our tasks and make us know we are not welcome. Is that it?"

The priest nodded.

"An inconsequential thing, Father. Almost infantile in its uselessness. But it is interesting that you imply that the entire village was part of this tiny mischief. That, of course, must include you and your mother. Oh, don't bother to reply. It is not important."

Father Du Vair nodded again, and a frail hope began to flicker in his eyes.

The captain reached out and bunched a width of the cassock in his strong hand and dragged the startled priest into the aisle. "Now, suppose you tell me what you and your mother and this entire village are really doing?"

At the priest's moan, the soldiers glanced carelessly toward him. The captain beckoned them to draw slightly closer so that Father Du Vair would be more conscious of their presence.

"Are you ready to speak? And can you do it through your chattering teeth? Try. Tell me. Oh, I advise you to tell me before I discover the truth without your assistance."

For one small second the priest pulled himself to his full height as though for a show of defiance.

The captain pushed him contemptuously toward the soldiers. "They are trained to extract information," he said. "Why should I trouble?"

The priest collapsed, sobbing. He fell upon a bench where he sat with his elbows upon his knees, his face buried in his hands.

"Take him," the captain said.

Father Du Vair raised his head. "Wait!" he cried.

The captain was amused, for he had addressed the men in French. The order had been intended to be understood only by the priest. What a numskull the church had here.

"I am tired of waiting. Speak now."

The priest sighed and for strength looked toward the altar. "There are people hidden here in the village," he said.

"What kind of people?"

"Jews," the priest whispered.

The captain was incredulous. Who could have imagined that? But, yes, of course it was entirely possible. Wasn't it well known that the French were scum without principles or morals? He felt a hot throb of anger, but he contained himself. "Where did they come from?" he asked, evenly.

"Paris."

"Who brought them?"

"They walked. They were starving and weary. For them the journey took very long because it was not safe for them to be seen and—"

"How many are there?"

"Five. It is a man and his wife and three children."

"They are at the château?"

"No."

"Then where are they?"

"In the house of the Ronciers."

"How did the Ronciers gain the high honor of housing the slimy enemies of civilization?"

"Madame Roncier is a midwife, and the Jewish woman is about to give birth."

"Why did they come here? Who were the friends or relatives they sought?"

The priest said, "They knew no one in the village. They had no destination. Fatigue and hunger drew them out of the woods. It was then that the singular thing happened. The village without consultation adopted the family. Food and rest and care were freely given. There was no one who did not feel pity, no one who wanted them to go away."

The captain gazed down upon the wretched priest and he could no longer control his fury. "You stupid accursed French. You do not want to feed soldiers who come offering you a thousand years of peace and decency, but Jews who contaminate society by defiling Christian women and polluting the very air we breathe—those people you welcome and befriend. Well, priest, come with me. I'll give you a lesson you'll never forget."

And now it was in German that he said, "Take him."

The captain strode from the church with his guard be-hind him, the corporal hurrying the priest across the pub-lic square. The lieutenant was alerted by his superior's burn-ing eyes and brought to swift attention the soldiers who were lolling after a reasonably good meal.

"Lieutenant, tell that sergeant who speaks French to drive my car to the château. Have him bring the woman here immediately. There is no time for her to put on a hat or gloves. I want her here at once. Have everyone turn out, including the sick mother of that sniveling girl. Now, priest, which is the house of the Ronciers?"

Half fainting, Father Du Vair led the way. The villagers on the street stared unbelievingly and, as more and more of them were routed from their homes, a murmur arose that was quickly silenced by the soldiers.

The priest paused before a red-roofed cottage. "There," he said and he turned his eyes away.

"Point!" the captain commanded. "Let anyone who is watching see that you have your wits about you and that you can tell which is the house of the Ronciers."

The priest pointed and was then sick in the cobblestoned street, staining his fine cassock.

"Take him back to the square to wait," the captain said. He turned to the lieutenant. "Have the men ready for any-thing. Choose a few of them and go into that house and bring out the Roncier couple and five Jews."

"Five Jews!"

"Yes. They're probably in the cellar."

It took little more than a minute. The Jews came out first. The woman with her enormous stomach. The man biting fiercely at his lower lip. The children had big, wet black eyes. The Ronciers emerged then. The husband bleeding from the mouth and nose. The wife staring stol-idly ahead of her.

"Have them all taken to the square," the captain called.

The lieutenant had a question. "Do we have the Jews watch?"

"No. It wouldn't bother them. Jews have no sympathy. Handle them first. It will accord with something I have in mind concerning the Ronciers."

Surrounded by soldiers, the villagers were forced into the square, then arranged in tightly packed rows against the low-growing lime trees. The captain stood in the center and wheeled slowly, surveying with hatred the faces before him. It galled him that nobody trembled now, nobody sweated. The suspense was over. The worst had happened. The villagers stood in the sun and the silence with their eyes raised to him, and the eyes were filled with loathing.

Two soldiers came into the square hauling a woman in a bedgown. She groaned in misery as she was dropped at the feet of her daughter.

The captain glanced at the Jews. They did not look at him. They looked at each other. The children clung to their mother and she embraced them, but her gaze was locked to her husband's. The captain's glance moved on to the priest, who, in a wild-eyed and demented way, was prattling to a soldier who could not understand him.

And now the automobile drew up and Madame Du Vair was out of it and running across the square. Hatless and gloveless indeed, but with no loss of dignity. She searched out her son and went to him. The captain did not interfere, for the scene could not fail to be interesting.

"François, what has happened?"

The young priest turned from his mother and wept. She looked to the villagers for answer.

"Armand Ribot," the captain ordered, "come forward. You are a man who enjoys the sound of his own voice.

You may tell Madame of her son's service to France."

And the apothecary told. The captain watched Madame Du Vair's face and saw it whiten, but he knew she would not faint and he knew she would not cry. She looked from one villager to another and she was satisfied that the apothecary had not lied and she did not look at her son. She held her shoulders rigidly and took a place in the crowd between Alphonsine Bergère and the daughter of the sick woman, and that was all she did.

The captain signaled to the lieutenant and effaced himself. It was up to others now. The Jews were brought to stand before a wall upon which vines trailed their pretty leaves. And the Jews stood with resignation till they were slaughtered, their blood at first but spattering the stones, then coloring them richly.

The faces of the villagers twisted in agony, and the lieutenant gave the word for the Ronciers to be brought to stand where the Jews had stood. So the Ronciers walked in the blood of the people they had tried to save, and Madame Roncier bent to arrange the skirt of the Jewish woman so that it fell more modestly across her knees.

"Here we will have a slight delay," the captain said to the lieutenant. "After all, there are certain customs to observe." His lips were drawn into a cold smile as he added, "I want to talk to Father Du Vair."

The soldiers brought the priest, and the captain spoke to him softly. "Father, we would not rob you of what must be, at this moment, your dearest wish. Have you an altar boy or bell-ringer who can fetch for you whatever saintly paraphernalia it is that you require? I am going to permit you to administer the last rites to these parishioners of yours who are about to die."

The priest shuddered.

"You hesitate, Father? I cannot imagine why. Please proceed. Attend to the souls of these people. Bring them comforting words which they will welcome since they have so profoundly trusted you."

And the captain watched and the soldiers watched and the entire village watched as the priest walked unsteadily toward the Ronciers. When he reached them he paused and made the sign of the cross, and Madame Roncier spat in his face.

The priest bowed his head before her. "As a man I have earned your scorn," he said. "But I am still a priest. I still hold my holy office, and only at great peril to your soul may you refuse the sacrament which I alone in this company can offer." He addressed Roncier then. "Tell your poor wife to make a good contrition and to prepare herself for grace in eternity. Tell her—"

Roncier shook his head. "What is there to tell her except that you betrayed us?"

Father Du Vair spoke sadly. He said, "You cannot afford now to judge me. You are Roman Catholics and I am your priest."

Madame Roncier stared at him, transfixed, her eyes blazing with sudden excitement, as though he had pointed the road to escape. "I am no longer a Roman Catholic," she said. "Because you are a priest of that faith I want nothing to do with it. Take away your sacraments and your prayers, François Du Vair. I appeal directly to Jesus for salvation of my soul."

"You cannot. If you give up the Holy Church He will not hear you. You will not be a Christian."

"Yes, I die a Christian," she cried. "I die a Protestant." She looked at her husband. "What do you say?"

The man took her hand, and they stood together before the priest, tears glistening in their eyes, new vows on their lips, in grim reminder of a marriage service.

"I guess they have no need of you, Father," the captain said.

The soldiers pulled the shaking priest out of fire range and the Ronciers died as the Jews had died, spilling their blood in the public square. For a full minute the soldiers remained in readiness to deal with any outbreak from the villagers, but there was none. The people stood frozen and stunned. Some stared at the corpses with fixed, glazed expressions. Others turned away, and one would have thought them indifferent had it not been for the fierceness in their eyes.

The lieutenant glanced questioningly at the captain. The captain nodded. "Yes," he said. "Give the order. We still have fifty kilometers to do. I meant only to stop here long enough to feed the men."

The soldiers proceeded on the run to the dusty vehicles. The captain moved more slowly, flinging one last look in the direction of Madame Du Vair. It startled him to find that she was looking at him. Quietly she stood there in her dowdy, dark dress and, through narrowed eyes, regarded him with a curious intensity. What would it take to shatter her? The murder of that consecrated jellyfish? The order that she must now take her place against the vine-covered wall? No. When one considered that even the peasant Ronciers, even the Jews, had not screamed or begged for mercy, one could only seat oneself in the automobile and drive away wondering how the French had happened to lose Paris. Had there been just enough François Du Vairs?

When the soldiers had left, the villagers drew breath and stirred a step or two from the positions they had held. Armand Ribot spoke first. He said, "I suggest that the women all leave the square immediately. A dozen of us men will attend to the burial. Who volunteers? Who will help me to—"

Father Du Vair interrupted, and there was none who did not notice that, with the Germans gone, his voice was more authoritative. "Armand, I wish the women to stay but a little longer. Here in the square where these unfortunate people died we will pray for them. We will have the service directly where—"

"What service, François?" Armand Ribot asked.

And the people heard how Armand had addressed the priest, and they looked at the bodies of the Ronciers, and they were of one mind again, as they had been when the Jews had turned to them for help.

The priest fell back a pace as he sensed the manner in which their thoughts ran. "No, no," he said to them. "You must not. Come. Follow me to the church. I give you my word that at this moment you need confession and atonement more than the dead need prayer. Follow me, I beg of you. It is at terrible risk to your souls that you turn from me and reject your church."

The schoolteacher fastened her gaze upon the body of Madame Roncier. She said, "In this village there is no church of our faith."

And the people nodded their agreement. Some who wore holy medals that had been blessed by Father Du Vair himself removed those medals and threw them to the ground. And suddenly everybody was looking at the mother of the priest.

"My mother," he cried, "in the name of the Holy Mother of us all, speak sense to these poor endangered souls."

But she did not speak to the villagers. She spoke to her son. She said, "None of us are preoccupied with danger. If it were otherwise we would have murdered the strangers ourselves by driving them out of the village. We have grown accustomed to risk."

"You dare not risk your soul."

"You are wrong. I dare."

He looked about him in bewilderment. "You have gone mad. All of you. It is a marvel that in your insanity you have not declared for Judaism."

"We were born Christians," his mother said. "No coward in a cassock is going to rob us of Jesus Christ."

The priest raised his eyes in anguish to the summer sky, then leveled them upon his mother. "Say what torturing words you will, but I tell you there is no alternative to the Holy Faith but destruction."

"Then we are destroyed," the apothecary said. "We want no prayers that can be spoken by you, no sacraments that you can administer. Understand once and for all, we are not Roman Catholics."

"You are mistaken, Armand. You will always be Roman Catholics. As time passes you will find that I have spoken the truth. It would be as impossible for you to be a Protestant as it would be for you to be an Englishman."

Armand Ribot said, "Only that impossible, François? Only that impossible? Let me tell you that since the day of the surrender my heart has been with the English. Do you think I pray for Frenchmen who now fight England in order to deliver ships and weapons safely to Hitler? Do you think I or any decent man owes allegiance to a government that gave us to those swine that walked through here today? This land is German property, a German country, and I renounce it. I choose England."

"Yes, yes," the voices behind him shouted.

"You see, François? By covering only the distance between your church and the cottage of the Ronciers you walked into a village inhabited by English Protestants."

"Well said," the schoolteacher called to him. "Well said, Armand Ribot."

"If the possibility of becoming a Protestant is measured by the possibility of becoming an Englishman, then I shall begin at once to arrange matters. As of now, my name is no longer Ribot. It is England. I am Armand England."

"I salute you," cried the girl with the sick mother. "My name is Churchill, for I know no other English name."

"Help me," Alphonsine Bergère begged. "I know no English name at all. But, yes, of course. There is his given name. I shall be Alphonsine Winston."

"In honor of the king," the black-browed woman suggested to her husband, "we could call ourselves George. Does it satisfy you to be Pierre George?"

"It satisfies me."

The villagers wrinkled their foreheads in thought and they named themselves such things as London and Brighton and Hastings. They did it very solemnly, and Madame Du Vair knew that at first it had been a device for the taunting of François. Now it had deep meaning. All things that had happened in the square that day would be remembered, and the names taken in the presence of the wronged dead would be forever honored. And her mind reached out and touched upon a time when some girl now standing in the square would be an old woman explaining that she had not found a husband because so many men had died in the war. She would add, in the garrulous manner of the aged, that she bore an English name because there had been seven murdered people—no, eight when one remembered the unborn child—and that the ancient church was never used because the village was Protestant.

The sick woman lying on the ground gazed upward. She spoke with difficulty, for she was in pain. "How shall we address you now, Madame Du Vair?"

Madame Du Vair was silent only a moment. "I will answer to the name of Mrs. Dover," she said, and began the walk back to the château. She glanced over her shoulder and saw the women going to their homes and Armand England accepting volunteers for a frightful task. She saw her son moving slowly and alone toward his church, and that was the last time she ever saw him except for one brief encounter in the village street.

It was four days later, and she was returning from a visit to Lucienne Churchill, whose mother had died. François was carrying two books and a haversack. His face was haggard and his haunted eyes sought hers.

"Mother."

She intended to pass, but he plucked at her sleeve and stayed her.

"Mother, I am going away. I don't know where. I don't know what to do."

She waited, cold-eyed and still.

"No one has come to the church. Not for Mass. Not for vespers. Not for confession. I am received nowhere on my parochial rounds. The woman who tended the parish house has not been there since—she has not been there for days. Mother, I've had nothing to eat. No one will give me anything or sell me anything or—"

"Food has been scarcer than ever since the day we fed the Germans," she said.

He looked at her beseechingly. "Mother, I am hungry."

"The Ronciers are not," she reminded him, and pulled her sleeve from his grasp.

Tears flowed weakly down his cheeks. "You never understood. The German captain suspected you of influencing the villagers against him. He might have killed you. Can't you believe that I was trying to save your life?"

She looked at her son for a long moment and then she said, "No."

And as she stood watching him walk down the street toward the edge of the village, she saw Father François Du Vair receive the last and most scorching insult the village had to offer. Alphonsine Winston flashed her rouged smile at him and tapped upon her window.

Torrey said, "It's time to get up," but Rebecca didn't believe him. "Come on," he insisted. "It's eight o'clock."

She felt like crying. A human being had to rest. Of what special material were his flesh and bones that, at this hour, he was already showered and shaved and smelling delightfully of cologne? She squinted painfully at him, and his dressing gown shimmering resplendently in the early sunlight. She thought of claiming a violent headache but he would be unsympathetic. He would say that she had had too much champagne.

"We just went to bed," she said.

"I know. We were fools to stay out so late. Your lingerie woman is due right now and the car is coming at ten. I've sent for coffee and croissants. Jump."

She didn't jump. For a moment, she didn't even move. She lay in bed thinking about the things that made it impossible for one to get a normal night's sleep. What a lot of places there were to see in Paris. And what a lot of drunken Americans. Sort of fun, though, being a drunken American. She remembered weeping because she had no lumps of sugar for the long procession of horses pulling the produce wagons to market. The French drivers had looked politely away, undoubtedly noting that she was a native of a country where it was against the law to buy a drink.

"There's the coffee," Torrey said. He went to the sitting-room door in answer to the knock and was back immediately. "No. It's the woman for the fitting."

"Tell her to sit down. I'll be ready for her in a moment."

Rebecca got out of bed, thinking of the place that had seemed so amusing the night before. A huge, undecorated garret where, if one requested something other than brandy, the waiters shouted aloud the order and the other patrons jeered and stood up for a better look at the stranger. Comforting that one became an old-timer within ten minutes and had jeering privileges which could be used on the next startled American tourist who desired a Scotch highball. Was it there that she had dropped the lighted match on the sawdust floor, thus creating a mild panic? Or had that happened in the crowded dark café next door? She knew there had been no sawdust in Zelli's. Ah, Zelli's, where there were phones and large spangled numbers at each table. How gay and exciting all those tinkling bells had been. Pleasant to remember that she had had five calls from mysterious strangers. As she revolved contentedly under the shower, she wondered about the name of that mad street with all the tremendous electric signs and the Americans wandering in and out of cafés getting drunker and drunker.

Paris was marvelous. It was so full of pretty clothes and luxurious restaurants and piquant diversions. Imagine a respectable wife visiting a brothel and sitting around talking to the girls. Hilarious how the little cross-eyed one with the appendectomy scar had begged her and Helen Patrick to let their husbands go upstairs.

Rebecca and Helen had laughed and laughed, but really they had never expected to be in a brothel. Only by looking around at other American wives in the mirrored parlor could they be sure that this was definitely the thing to do. It was even stylish to say "whore house" instead of brothel, just as it was terribly cute to carry a tin of fifty cigarettes with you for the evening and to wear a white wig and to ask the barman for Centerba or Cana or Solberon. Parisians must find New York very dull, Rebecca thought, as she toweled herself and got into her negligée.

The elderly woman who created such exquisite lingerie was waiting patiently in the sitting room. Rebecca offered her a cup of coffee, but it was declined.

"Well, sorry you won't join me. I simply cannot face the morning without coffee."

"Of course, Madame. Enjoy your breakfast. I offer my apology for being a nuisance to you at this ridiculously early hour. When I arose at five thirty in order to arrive with absolute punctuality, I thought, 'Poor Madame Winton. What a hardship for her.' "

"Oh, I don't mind," Rebecca said, biting into a croissant thick with fresh, creamy butter.

There were a dozen nightgowns, a dozen slips and a dozen pairs of panties. Rebecca had bought expensive undergarments before, but never had they been custom-made and fitted with the care usually reserved for ball gowns. She was delighted with the tiny hooks on the bodice of each nightie, the eye-straining perfection of each small silk loop into which the hooks would slip. She particularly loved the way she looked in the daffodil yellow.

"Show Monsieur," the Frenchwoman suggested.

Rebecca swept into the bedroom and paraded for Torrey as he stood in front of the mirror arranging his tie.

"I wish you could wear that nightgown all the time," he said. "I'm so God-damned sick of seeing knees that a woman in a long, flowing skirt looks like a raving, tearing beauty."

"You mean I'm not *really* a raving, tearing beauty?"

"Get on with the fitting. You haven't all day, you know."

"If you play your cards right, I'll let you be the first to unhook my new yellow nightgown."

"If I play my cards wrong, who'll do it?"

"One of the fellows who called me on the table phone in Zelli's last night."

He said, "You liked that, didn't you?"

"Of course. Don't you take me to those nutty places to have fun?"

He nodded slowly. "But you're not having the kind of fun I hoped you'd have."

"What do you mean?"

"You're enjoying what yokels enjoy, Rebecca. You're not enjoying the yokels."

She laughed and whirled in her daffodil nightgown. "Is that the mail you have there? Anything interesting?"

"Just ads and bills. Go on, finish your fitting."

He did not give her the letter till they were in the automobile. "You would have sat down to read it and we'd never have gotten started."

She tore at the envelope. "It's from Miss Emmett. I hope everything's all right."

"Of course it is. We just heard from Dad yesterday. Everything was perfect then."

Her eyes traveled swiftly over the first page. "Well, everything's not perfect now. Barrett has chickenpox."

"Chickenpox? Has he really?"

"I wonder if Vicki and Juanita will catch it from him? God, what a thing! To be away over here while the children are sick."

"Had we stayed home could you have warded off chickenpox by singing a lullaby?"

"Maybe. There are more mysteries in life than cold people like you ever know about."

"I'm not cold. I just trust Miss Emmett and my father. Moreover, there's not a bloody thing I can do about chickenpox whether I'm in New York or Paris. Is there something you can do?"

"No, but I sure wish your father would call in a pediatrician instead of treating the children himself."

"A pediatrician, when he's one of the greatest medical men in—"

"That's just the point. What experience does he have with chickenpox? He probably underestimates the danger. He'd know how to cope with a big disease but—"

"Be quiet. Your stupidity offends me."

Rebecca stared out the car window. The chauffeur, stoically accepting his destiny, had driven directly into a traffic snarl. Surely he could have seen it from a block's distance. There must have been a way to avoid pushing straight toward the middle of the furious shouting of the drivers and the high-pitched screeching of the automobile horns.

Torrey sank deeply into the cushioned seat and lighted a cigarette. Ordinarily, these Parisian traffic tie-ups amused him, but this one he ignored entirely. She saw that he was not yet finished with her.

"I really think, Rebecca, that you must start while the children are very young to prepare yourself for the time when you won't know whether they are sick or well, happy or miserable. When they're grown they will have illnesses and problems, and though it tears your heart out you'll be no more than a helpless spectator. If you're smart now you can save yourself a great deal of useless agony in the future."

"I know, Torrey. I know."

"You don't know. Mothers never know. They think of having children and somehow they picture dear little boys and girls being around for the rest of their lives. Did you ever know a mother who realized that she has a child for perhaps twelve years and after that she has a person who can't wait to escape from her?"

"Our children won't want to escape. They love us dearly. You must know that. When you walk in the door they leap at you and throw their arms around you and you enjoy it."

"Yes, I enjoy it. Parents are supposed to enjoy their children. Incessant worry destroys that enjoyment."

"You sound as though I spend all my time wringing my hands. For your information, your father thinks I'm a normal, average mother."

"When is he home long enough to make a valid judgment on that point?"

"Oh, he's home."

"When? He comes in to change his clothes and to sleep. He manages about one dinner a week with us. How would he know that you don't have an ounce of common sense where the children are concerned?"

"You know, Torrey, a man raised without a mother—"

"I wasn't raised without a mother."

"You were eight years old when she died, weren't you? I don't consider anyone's raising complete at that age. I was going to say that a man raised without a mother can't possibly know how run-of-the-mill mothers behave."

"I don't care how run-of-the-mill mothers behave. I find run-of-the-mill anything extremely boring. And another thing—I was under the impression that we hired Miss Emmett to save you from becoming an authority on nursery trivia."

"Isn't it natural for me to be interested in—"

"Being interested is different from being obsessed. I'm going to teach you that you can't build a life around kids if it's the last thing I ever do."

Rebecca looked away from him. If she did not argue, she

reasoned, there could be no argument. Somehow the traffic snarl was loosening. Automobiles were detaching themselves from impossible situations and going their way. One had the feeling that the tie-up had been a contrived thing by which monotony was broken and a man had a chance to raise his voice and shake a fist. Perhaps even the gendarmes admitted the need for an occasional angry outburst. They contributed so little to the final unraveling of the knot that one could not help but wonder.

The district to be seen from the car window was bleak and depressing. The narrow streets and squalid old houses would have rat populations outnumbering the human, Rebecca thought, shuddering, but here and there the pitch of a roof or the carving on a grimy doorway stirred the imagination. The people were unattractive. Most Frenchwomen were wide. Most Frenchmen were short. The shops were appalling. All that bread hanging out there for the flies to crawl on. And why were kitchen utensils sold all over the pavement instead of being respectably shelved indoors? Surely none of those people washed the pots and pans before using them. Those houses couldn't have running water.

"There must be a very high mortality rate for children here."

"Oh, my God," Torrey exploded. "Are we going to talk about sick children all day?"

"Torrey, I didn't mean anything about Barrett. Honestly, I wasn't even thinking of Barrett just then."

"Of course not," he said with ponderous sarcasm.

"Go ahead and sneer, if you like. I wasn't thinking of Barrett. Maybe I should think of him. Maybe we should. After all, those children are our responsibility."

"No one could look at my checkbook and doubt it."

"What you spend on them isn't everything."

"No. 'Everything' is giving them one's whole life, and I'll be damned if I'll ever do that. May I tell you something? Adults grow duller and duller with each year devoted to children. And, in the end, the children are adults and find their parents too dull to be companionable. That's the truth, so look to it, my girl."

"I will, Torrey."

Surprisingly, he reached for her hand, and when he spoke it was in gentle, pleading tones. "Listen, sweetheart, we are on our way to battlefields over which I fought—figuratively speaking. My personal battlefields were not quite this close to Paris, but let's look upon it symbolically. We're on our way to something that was mine—not the children's, not yours, but mine. Try to get interested in that. It was a big war, Rebecca, and I was part of it."

And she remembered suddenly how much she loved him. For the first time she realized that it must mean something to a man to visit a battlefield over which he had fought—even if it were only a symbolic battlefield. Suppose she were taking Barrett on an excursion of which he had dreamed? Would she ruin Barrett's day by reminding him that Daddy was ill? No, Barrett would be assured that Daddy was just fine and that the important thing was Barrett and Barrett's day. Why was the father less worthy of consideration than the child?

"What's the name again of that town that was the closest the Germans got to Paris?" she asked.

"Meaux. You'll see it."

She settled herself comfortably in the car. "Yes. Meaux. I must remember that. Wouldn't it have been terrible if the Kaiser had taken Paris?"

"It was nip and tuck for a while there."

"Tell me where you were and what happened."

As he talked, she listened attentively, alert for opportunities to hurl questions at him. Questions, if they were properly placed and voiced with a certain breathlessness, were very pleasing and complimentary. Disgraceful that most women hadn't the slightest notion of what the war had been like for their husbands.

All day long she walked with Torrey, inspecting cannons and graves and shattered trees. They drove to villages that had been destroyed by shelling and not yet completely rebuilt. To everyone encountered on the road Torrey spoke, using his American Expeditionary Forces French. His smile, his magnificent voice and his own amusement at his linguistic failures transformed the strangers into friends. Torrey and Rebecca were taken to see more cannons, graves and shattered trees. One man invited them to his home, where a startled and embarrassed woman was forced to interrupt her cleaning of the chicken coops to bring a glass of wine to her husband's American friends.

Torrey asked every young man where he had fought, and Rebecca heard strange place names and felt herself forgotten as the men remembered war. Torrey unfolded the map he had brought with him, and there was much discussion of rivers and towns and of deeds that had been accomplished on a sunny morning or in the thin, steady rain of an October afternoon. Remarkable how easily dates and locations and deployment of troops were recalled. Inexplicable and sad that every man spoke with a certain wistfulness of the terrible war. One who had lost an arm had seen Torrey's division only a day before he had been wounded, and so they looked upon each other as brothers.

Behind Rebecca stood the chauffeur, content to do no more than keep her in touch with the conversation and fling a word or phrase to Torrey when he floundered. He had been invalided out of the army while fighting the Bulgars at Salonika. He shared no memories with his countrymen who had fought on French soil at the side of Americans. Moreover, he was a Parisian and felt no compulsion to exchange viewpoints with peasants.

Rebecca's attention was leveled not on what was said but on Torrey himself. His laughter rolled readily, his eyes were friendly and interested. With sincere good will he shook the hand of each and every person who approached him. Gallantly he accepted the embrace of a slovenly old woman who said that America had sent an army of heroes. And after a while he remembered Rebecca, and they drove to Soissons and looked at the thirteenth-century Cathedral of Saint-Jean-des-Vignes that had been badly damaged by the Germans.

"Sons of bitches," Torrey said. "You know Thomas à Becket lived in the abbey here for several years."

"I didn't know that. Who was Thomas A. Becket?"

"He was a great character. I'm going to play him some day."

She smiled and felt more comfortable. The man who could look at a war-damaged cathedral and think of Broadway was no stranger to her.

Back to Paris and dinner at Number Five, Rue de Beaujolais. "We are in the arcade of the Palais-Royal, the cradle of the Revolution," Torrey said. "Some of the fiery pamphlets with which Desmoulins ignited the Parisians were printed secretly right here in this restaurant. But before that nasty business Richelieu occupied the—"

"You've been very busy with the guidebook, haven't you, dear?"

"Yes, and I have a riddle for you. What class of person is more ignorant and ridiculous than the guidebook reader? Here's the answer: The person who scoffs at guidebook reading when he himself or she herself is utterly, stupidly

122

unaware of all historical facts. Now, Rebecca, if you can tell me in which year, or even in which century, the French Revolution began I shall consider your scorn for guidebook reading a little less absurd."

"Torrey, I was just babbling. Don't take my remarks so seriously. How could I have scorn for anything you do? I love you."

"I think I would treasure a small token of courtesy above the most extravagant protestations of love. I'd appreciate being treated as you'd treat any other gentleman who was your escort. I was making conversation aimed at heightening your pleasure in this interesting place where some significant history was made. You replied very rudely."

The sullen set of his mouth warned her against prolonging the discussion. "I apologize," she said.

He nodded coolly. "I never refuse a sincere apology," he said, but she felt that he did not like her very much.

He liked her very much in the temples of haute couture. He had selected—after only the briefest consultations with Rebecca—the clothes that should be ordered for her. He had looked at the parading mannequins with no more interest than if they had been animated wax. He had concentrated completely on style and taste and how the cut and color would compliment Rebecca. He had no self-consciousness about riding in the over-cute bird cage of an elevator or stalking through the narrow, cream-tinted halls, which were carpeted in mauve velvet. Rebecca emerged from the proceedings with six gowns, two suits and two sensational coats.

"Torrey, you've spent a fortune on these things."

"Why not? You wear clothes with more élan than anyone I know."

She looked at him doubtfully and waited for the stinger. There was none. "Torrey, you can't mean that I have chic!"

"Just between us two Americans, yes."

He liked her very much at Maxim's, where she glanced at the canvas of the famous undraped female and murmured, "Dear me, American saloon art is catching on all over."

Two couples from the States who had been studying the painting with a respect due to an exhibit in the Louvre now looked at Rebecca. From her smart haircut, her brief little scrap of a dress and the way she handled her cigarette holder they could tell that this was a person who really *knew*. They decided to laugh at the painting.

"You see how easy it is to exercise influence?" Torrey said. "You mold the opinion of generations yet unborn if you say something at the right moment."

He liked her very much at Voisin, where she had the wit to recognize that here was the right moment to say nothing at all. In that ancient and aristocratic restaurant Torrey was delighted to find Frederick and Doris Benson dining daintily upon *noisettes d'agneau*. Rebecca felt no urge to rush toward the Bensons. The Bensons frightened her. She had seen them many times on the stage and sat enthralled. She had met them once and had cowered before the goddess-like grace and wisdom of Doris and the glittering, varicolored brilliance of the Bensons as a couple.

"When did you get here?" Torrey asked.

"This morning. We've been in London," Frederick said. "Sit with us. We'll have a splendid conversational advantage over you while you're feasting and we're postponing our dessert."

Torrey and the Bensons talked of scripts, critics and audiences. Rebecca noticed something wonderful about the Bensons that evening. Though they often looked at her as they spoke, thus acknowledging her presence, never once was either of them cruel enough to ask, "What is your opinion, Rebecca?" To Rebecca their omission of that question was proof of the Bensons' good manners. Lesser people might have smugly pretended that common decency demanded a pause in which the little woman to whom Torrey Winton was married might have an opportunity to make a fool of herself. The Bensons were so highly civilized that they were respectful of well-behaved ignorance.

Torrey liked her at the Louvre because she found Leonardo's "Madonna of the Rocks" more impressive than "Mona Lisa." He only tolerated her in the Tuileries Gardens. She loathed the statues, the stiff artificiality and the gravel walks.

"It pleased queens," he told her, his eyes faintly glazed with disdain.

"Then must I lie and say it pleases me?"

"No, you must not lie. You must cultivate your taste till it is no longer that of a rustic. You must work on your mind till it is capable of appreciating the glory of the Tuileries."

"Oh, shoot," she said, or something very like that.

He liked her very much at the Arc de Triomphe. She gazed into the eternal flame, and they both wept for the Unknown Soldier while Torrey held in his hand his brand-new hat from the establishment of Gélot.

In the Place Vendôme he was very pleased with her because she breathed deeply and ecstatically at the sight of such harmony and perfection.

"Is there really anything in the world so beautiful as this seems to be?" she asked.

He liked her as they strolled beneath the imposing arcades of the Rue de Rivoli. He liked her on the noble Champs-Elysées one day when the city was bright with summer sunlight. He liked her less at the Place de la Concorde.

"I wonder where the guillotine stood. I feel so sad when I think about Marie Antoinette."

"Yes, too bad about that girl," he said, mockingly.

She saw that the mockery was somehow directed at her, but she did not see how she had sparked it. Was he in the mood to play Robespierre?

"I don't believe," she said, "that the poor queen deserved her fate."

"Don't you, dear?" More mockery, and not from Robespierre at all, but from Torrey. "What a little fool you are, agonizing over Marie Antoinette. She was a political figure, Rebecca, a queen."

"She was a woman, wasn't she?"

"Not in any terms that you could understand. It takes great imagination to identify with royalty of past centuries. The philosophy on which those people were raised, the grandeur in which they moved, the fear with which they lived all their lives set them so far apart from anything you could comprehend that your pity is somewhat amusing."

And with sudden shock she realized that had she expressed the thought that queens were conditioned to die at the hands of a mob, Torrey would have looked at her as he was looking at her now and would have called her a fool. She turned her eyes away from him and rearranged her thinking, instructing herself to accept that when Torrey was in a bad humor all things affronted him. Then it was not, she asked herself, that there were times when she bored him almost beyond endurance? No, no, of course not. He was a creature of moods. All artists were. There, now, one could appreciate the incredibly lovely fountain and the marble horses.

She smiled at him. "Could we eat American food tonight, Torrey? I'd love to go to Elza Lee's or the Butler's Pantry for some fried chicken Maryland."

"I have a reservation at Tour d'Argent. I've asked Doris and Frederick to go with us."

"You didn't tell me."

"What difference does that make? You don't have to cook the dinner."

Rebecca did not reply. She thought about clothes and decided to wear a flowered chiffon. A splendid choice, for that was what Doris also selected. The gowns melted softly into the Paris night, and Rebecca, catching a glimpse of herself in a mirror, felt she was no unworthy corner of the stunning foursome.

Monsieur André Terrail, proprietor of Tour d'Argent, came forward hastily as they entered. His joy at sight of the Bensons was tempered by his horror at having no reservation for them. Frederick presented him to Rebecca and Torrey, explaining that Torrey was the host and had reserved the table. Now, in Monsieur Terrail's world, all was well. Yes, indeed, there was a reservation for four and at a very fine table. Would everyone desire *le canard pressé?*

Doris said, "I'd prefer woodcock *flambée* or those darling little ortolans, but it's not the season. I shall have to endure the duck."

The ritual of preparation was almost too much for Rebecca. The carving of an underdone duck was as adroit as successful surgery, and the silver press seemed a bit of culinary elegance inspired by an ancient instrument of torture. Frederick obligingly explained that to the juice extracted from the fowl, crushed raw duck livers would be added along with Madeira, port and champagne and, of course, lemon juice and exotic spices. After that, the heavenly dish would be ready for further cooking.

"Divine," Rebecca said, and thought wistfully of the fried chicken Maryland at the Butler's Pantry. The restaurant was warm, and there was nothing to look at except other people dining on duck. Torrey and the Bensons sat spellbound, enjoying all the wonderful things that were being done for their delight.

It would improve matters if the restaurant were upstairs instead of on street level, Rebecca thought. If this were so, the windows could be opened without passers-by being able to stare at the customers, and one would have a view of Notre-Dame by moonlight. But I guess they don't need anything except ducks to draw a crowd.

And at that moment they were handed little cards telling them how many times the superlative dish had been concocted and the exact number of the duck each guest was on the brink of consuming.

"Good heavens," Doris said, "they've passed the hundred thousand mark."

Rebecca sighed. Obviously, there would never be air, or a view of Notre-Dame. What for?

She became conscious of the fact that Torrey and Frederick were no longer so intent upon the preparation of the food. She looked where they were looking. A young girl had stepped into the restaurant and drawn everyone's attention away from *le canard pressé*. Inexpensively dressed, and wearing at her throat a small golden locket, she rocked the Tour d'Argent. Even Doris stared as the girl advanced into the restaurant. And since none of the four had bothered to glance at her escort they were startled when he paused at their table and said, "What have we here? A band of strolling players?"

"Why, it's Arlen Comstock, gentleman producer," Frederick said, shaking hands. "How are you? I didn't know you were in town."

"I did," Torrey said. "I saw him doing the unforgivable one night last week."

"What's unforgivable in Paris?" Arlen asked.

"I saw you walk out on the Grand Guignol."

"You're right. I did. The Grand Guignol under Choisy's management is not what it was under Maurey's."

"A valid appraisal, no doubt, but neither here nor there," Doris said. "Who's the girl?"

"Her name is Sue Wakefield." Comstock directed his eyes toward the table where the girl already had been seated and was awaiting him. "She happened to be on the ship with me and, so help me God, she's traveling with her father. He's some kind of a spear carrier for a big firm. He wanted to see The Places tonight, so I took her off his hands."

"You're a saint, Arlen," Torrey said. "Imagine making a sacrifice like that for a chance acquaintance."

Comstock grinned and walked to his table. The girl's eyes sparkled as he approached, her smile greeted him as though he'd been away forever.

Torrey said, "It must be Broadway night on the Left Bank. Barker Kane just came in. Do you know him?"

The Bensons shook their heads.

"He's quite a boy. Straight out of some fusty little college and he writes his first play. What is it? Just the hit of last season. *Fellow with a Story*."

"I should say it was a hit." Frederick looked with interest at the tall young man in the doorway.

"Poor Barks. He's standing there like a wooden Indian and being ignored by everybody. I guarantee you that he didn't know he needed a reservation. He's a rube. Someone told him where to get a good meal, and he hurried over in his comfortable sight-seeing suit. I'll have to ask him to sit with us. Do you mind?"

"Not at all," Doris said. "There's always room for a good playwright."

Torrey started to rise from the table, then stopped to laugh. Barker Kane's eyes, searching the room, had fallen upon Sue Wakefield, the girl with the small, golden locket at her throat.

"Oh, that's the facial expression of all time," Torrey said. "Look at that Midwest boy. He's hypnotized. Good God, he's going over to Arlen Comstock's table."

In amazement the Wintons and the Bensons stared as Barker Kane spoke to Comstock, obviously introducing himself. They saw Comstock frown at the stranger, then offer him the minimum smile of acknowledgment. They saw Barker talking on and on, his own smile ingratiating, his attention concentrated on Comstock. They saw Comstock wondering how much longer the young man was going to stand at the table. They saw Comstock forced by good manners into asking Barker to sit down. And finally they saw Comstock present Barker to Sue Wakefield.

"So that's a rube?" Frederick asked.

"Yes, just a simple boy from a fusty college in the Midwest," Doris said.

There was a sudden elegant flurry at the table. Waiters gathered to perform solemnly a dozen exquisite little services. Silver platters gleamed, the fragrance of food intoxicated and a hushed voice announced dramatically, *"Le canard pressé."*

Afterward there was the pilgrimage to Montmartre. Noisy Piel Ou Face. The Russian music at Shéhérazade. Palermo with the best tango orchestra in Paris. Chez Florence owned by the lovely Negress who wore snow-white evening clothes. Fred Payne's bar filled with Britons and

Americans. Le Grand Ecart surprisingly filled with French. It was unbelievable how much the Bensons could drink and still remain distingué, even slightly aloof.

Prostitutes prowling the streets and bars flashed their bad teeth at Frederick and Torrey. From fourteen to forty, the street girls all had dumpy figures and thick, heavy features. They looked unwashed and brutally stupid.

"There are so many brothels in town and so many nude displays in cafés and theaters," Doris said, "that any half-way attractive girl who wants to do something naughty can stay off the streets. These poor monsters can't get into a brothel, nor have they bodies anyone would pay to look at."

"Till I came here I never thought that prostitutes would speak to a man unless he was alone."

"Maybe it's only Americans they approach like this, knowing that American women will laugh it off and American men will—well, look."

Frederick and Torrey were passing out cigarettes and francs to a half dozen frowzy-looking females.

"Why do you suppose men always feel sorry for prostitutes?" Doris asked. "I mean, they never get sentimental about the overburdened chambermaid or the hard-working waitress. Personally, I don't care for prostitutes, and God knows it isn't because I look upon them as competition. Frederick wouldn't think of going to bed with any woman who couldn't discuss Ibsen rather learnedly."

Rebecca thought that might be a slight exaggeration, but it was one way of saying that Frederick had found his marriage altogether perfect.

"Once when we were here," Doris continued, "we looked in on a bordello. Oh, what an arch word that is. Pity it's out of fashion. I expected to be amused, but I wasn't. I saw lots of people chatting and laughing with the girls, but

I was a death's-head at the party. I didn't think it was fun. I could only ponder the economic factors that had brought a girl to that way of life. Surely no one wants to be bought. Surely those girls didn't want to be viewed as curiosities by American ladies from Scarsdale. I didn't enjoy being there, so, after all, maybe I'm sorry for prostitutes, too."

Rebecca examined a wine stain on the tablecloth. Ah, how Torrey would have liked her had she left that mirrored house commenting on economic factors and the indecency of regarding fellow human beings as just another tourist attraction.

She looked at Doris and she said very earnestly, "I know a lot about French furniture." And because she had had too much champagne she would have denied that her remark was wildly irrelevant. "Even if I prefer fried chicken Maryland from the Butler's Pantry and American coffee to anything Montagne can cook, that doesn't mean I'm half-witted. When I was newly married I began to study French furniture. I went to libraries and museums and art galleries and lectures. I read hundreds of books on the subject. I was going to do something sensational for Torrey and his father. I was going to refurnish our house. I bet I know more about French furniture than anybody else in the world who doesn't own any."

Doris patted her hand. "I have a presentiment that this is a sad story," she said.

"You know what happened?"

"Tell me, dear," Doris encouraged, and Rebecca lost her train of thought in contemplation of that wonderful face of Doris's. It was not beautiful, but it became so when the role demanded beauty. The face was not that of a young girl, but it could be. It was not the face of an invalid, but it knew the expression that pain brought to the eyes and it knew that a bitter set of the mouth was a consequence of sweet patience. Rebecca sighed, remembering the parts she had seen Doris play, remembering that Doris could be anything or anybody. What, who was she being now? An actress committing to memory the behavior of a respectable housewife on a binge in Montmartre? Or a woman who could become a friend?

"What happened with your French furniture, Rebecca?"

"Nothing. I never got it. It turned out that my father-in-law loved his Early American. See, Early American didn't look like anything at all to me. I'd been raised with it. I was shocked when I saw it in a rich man's house. I thought that maybe he just didn't know any better, having no woman around to advise him. So I did all this studying up on French furniture so he'd have something he'd be proud of in his house. Then I had a heart-to-heart talk with him. I told him that he had a houseful of plain, ugly stuff that he could possibly sell if he found the kind of people who came to New England in the summertime and bought up all that kind of junk. I said to him, 'Doc—' You know Torrey's father is a doctor?"

"Yes," Doris said, smiling a little. "He's reasonably well known."

"I keep forgetting that. Anyhow, I said to him, 'Doc, let me do the house over for you. I'll make it so gorgeous you wouldn't be ashamed to have anybody come in here.' You should have heard the way he laughed at me. Not nasty, you know. We're very fond of each other, but he sure did laugh. I said, 'Doc, this isn't good enough for a doctor who takes care of millionaires and has his medical opinions written up in thick books and all that. Why, my mother's cleaning woman has stuff like this in her house.' You know what he said?"

"No. What?"

"He said, 'Sounds like I'd better go look at that cleaning woman's house.' "

"Did he?"

"He certainly did. One month later he went up there and bought every stick of furniture she had, including some I didn't know was stored in the cellar. After that I gave up the idea of French furniture and concentrated on something else. I learned how to manage the house and the servants, and now our place could be photographed any day in the week, it's so perfect. From basement to attic it shines, but I don't think Torrey or Doc notices."

A man with a happy smile and a slight stagger jolted the table and paused to apologize. His glazed eyes widened at sight of Doris. "Aren't you—aren't you Doris Benson, the actress?"

Doris simpered prettily. "My name's Mabel Hooper. Do I really look like an actress?"

"Well, for a moment there I thought sure that—but I can see now . . . Sorry. Awfully sorry." His bewildered glance fell on Frederick. "Drunker than I thought," he murmured, and wandered away.

Rebecca said, "You had an idea that this was going to be a sad story, and it really is, but not about the furniture. While Doc was up in New England he called on my mother. They'd never met before. He had only to look at her to know that she was a sick woman. Doc insisted on bringing her back to New York with him, but she only lived a month or so. He couldn't save her. She'd been slowly dying for a couple of years and I'd never noticed. Kids hardly ever notice their mothers. Did you know that, Doris?"

Frederick leaned across the table and said, "Torrey has suggested onion soup at Les Halles. Do you suppose you

134

could stop chattering long enough to consider his proposition?"

"Have I been chattering a great deal?" Doris asked in hurt surprise. "Perhaps I've had too much to drink, though I shouldn't have thought so. As to the onion soup, you know I can never resist it. Let's go to Pied de Mouton. I adore the place."

Pied de Mouton was so crowded with dinner-jacketed gentlemen and ladies in flowered chiffon that there wasn't a seat to be had. Torrey led the way through the market between mountains of lettuce heads and pyramids of plumed carrots. The others followed, shaking fish scales from their shoes and trying to avoid contact with slaughtered bullocks hanging in bloody rows. Muscular women unloaded wagons of butter, cheese and eggs while screeching invectives directed at assistants who moved slowly or drivers whose horses edged too near the egg crates. Through the noise and bustling confusion visitors from Siam, San Francisco and Savoie strolled calmly, stopping under the sharp, naked lights to admire fruit as fresh as the morning and vegetables more colorful than anything the flower women had to offer.

Torrey found a peculiar little low-ceilinged restaurant which still had room for four. The soup was delicious, though the place was hot and stank evilly. A lady wearing a diamond choker three inches wide was nibbling on chips fried in donkey fat, while her escort handled a pig's foot as though it were a lollipop.

"You know," Doris said suddenly, "this is all rather disgusting."

They left the restaurant and the market and tiptoed into a Paris that had turned dove-blue and silver. A beautiful Paris, where here and there shutters were swinging wide to whatever the day might bring.

"Good night," Doris said. "That is, if it really is the end of the evening."

Frederick glanced at his watch. "It's after five, dear."

"Then is it time for coffee?"

"No. It's time for sleep. Good night, Wintons."

"Good night, Bensons."

As Doris and Frederick walked into the Ritz, Rebecca observed that Doris's elegance was not subject to normal deterioration. Dispiritedly Rebecca leaned back in the car. "When Doris gets all made up with her hair all combed and everything, I'll bet that Frederick varnishes her from head to toe so she'll stay kempt indefinitely."

" 'Kempt' is an archaic word," Torrey said, sternly. "And you don't need any varnishing."

She sat up straight and didn't feel the least bit tired. She could have rushed over to Tour d'Argent and begun the date with the Bensons all over again because this was an evening on which he had evidently liked her tremendously.

But there was never a time in Paris when he liked her as much as when he became ill. At the outset she didn't guess how ill he was. He said he had had a restless night and that perhaps he was getting a bad cold. He said he didn't want any breakfast and he telephoned Paul Patrick and canceled arrangements to go to the race track. After that, he threw himself on the divan in the sitting room and did not even glance at the Paris edition of the *Herald Tribune*.

Rebecca walked over and peered at him, recalling that he had complained of chills the evening before, had scarcely touched his dinner and, for the first time, had dismissed the chauffeur at an early hour. He certainly didn't look well, and summer colds were so miserable.

"What about lunch, sweetheart? Shall I have soup sent up? Or a breast of chicken or something like that?"

He shook his head.

It was a chance to have the sort of luncheon she really enjoyed. She dressed and walked up to Sherry's on the Rond-Point, leaving a glass of water, the newspaper and the telephone close to Torrey.

Oh, how wonderful was Sherry's coffee and rich cream, the tasty waffles with Vermont syrup and, for dessert, chocolate layer cake straight out of an American's dream. Where else in Paris could you get a meal like that for only six dollars and forty cents?

Torrey was still on the divan when she returned. "How are you now, dearest?" she asked him.

He didn't reply. He coughed. It was a deep, frightening cough, and it seemed to hurt him. She placed her hand upon his forehead. He was burning, his eyes were too bright and shiny, and on this warm sunlit day his body quivered with chill. She was terrified by the way he looked as he lay there. She ran into the bedroom and pulled the coverlet from the bed. As she placed it over Torrey she realized that her action was formal acknowledgment that illness had moved into the suite at George the Fifth.

She went to the telephone and spoke to the concierge. "Mr. Winton is not feeling well. Can you send a doctor—one who speaks English?"

"Yes, Madame. I will telephone you at what hour to expect him."

"I need him now."

"I will do my best, Madame."

She drew a chair up close to Torrey and sat down. He opened his eyes and stretched his hand out to her.

"I love you," she whispered.

He smiled and closed his eyes again. Through the afternoon he dozed, awakening from time to time to cough harrowingly. Twice more she called the concierge, who assured her that the doctor had Mr. Winton's name on his list and certainly would arrive soon.

It was almost five o'clock when he came. A gaunt, unsmiling man. It was clear that he had much experience and little patience with Americans who were ill in high-priced hotel suites.

"What were your husband's dietary indiscretions last evening? Oysters and whisky? Or simply whisky with no food at all?"

Rebecca said, "He didn't drink and hardly ate." And she could not refrain from adding, "Please don't write a prescription till you've seen him."

He followed her through the foyer, quickening his step as he heard Torrey cough. Solemnly, he bent over the divan and spoke a few words which Rebecca guessed had no purpose other than to establish that the patient was conscious. The doctor slipped a thermometer in Torrey's mouth, removed the pajama coat and began the stethoscopic examination. It took less time than Rebecca had expected.

"Madame, your husband has pneumonia," the doctor said, managing to convey in his tone something that sounded very much like an apology. "He must go to the hospital and at once."

"The hospital!"

"Yes. He cannot be properly cared for in a hotel."

"Do we know that for a fact?"

"Oh, indeed, Madame, we know that for a fact."

In desperation she asked a hopeless question. "Is it possible to telephone New York from here?"

"I regret that we are still a few years away from that convenience. Also, I should say that there is no time for cabled messages back and forth. I presume that you will want a private room for your husband at the American Hospital."

"*American* Hospital?" It was a black moment, but he had spoken a shining word.

"Yes. American. Excellent. Do you give me permission to engage the room?"

There was only this man, this stranger, to trust, so she must trust him completely. And she must find a way to steady her voice and her trembling hands. The decisions were hers to make, the course hers to determine. Who could save Torrey if, by foolish temporizing, she failed him?

"Of course, call the hospital. Will he need an ambulance?"

"We can take a blanket from here and let him lie down on the back seat of an automobile. You will have to rent a large, comfortable one. I have only a small—"

"We have a limousine. Please tell the phone girl that our chauffeur is needed and, yes, I want a private room for my husband and I want private nurses."

She left him with the phone and flew into the bedroom. She packed a suitcase with several pairs of pajamas, a dressing gown, slippers, razor, soap, cologne and the latest copy of the *Literary Digest*. She took a blanket and a pillow from the bottom drawer of the bureau, put on her hat, made certain that she had money in her purse, and found a fresh pair of gloves.

The doctor said, "Inquiry has revealed that the hotel has a wheel chair. I have arranged for it to be sent up so that we can get Mr. Winton out of the hotel as painlessly as possible."

Rebecca sat on the floor of the car and held Torrey's hand on the way to the hospital. She bolstered him at sudden stops and whenever he opened his eyes she smiled at him. The hospital was in Neuilly, a suburb north of the Bois, and the ride seemed interminable.

The doctor had arrived a few minutes before them at

the hospital, and he had an attendant with him at the receiving entrance.

"Go get your dinner," Rebecca told the chauffeur. "Then come back here and wait, please. I don't know how long I'll be."

Torrey was placed in another wheel chair. The attendant took charge of him. Rebecca followed, with the doctor walking silently beside her. The private room was very large and very clean. A plump brown-haired nurse, who could be nothing in the world but a New Englander, was tightening a sheet on the bed. She said a brief "good evening," and without quite knowing how it had happened, Rebecca suddenly found herself alone in the corridor with a closed door separating her from Torrey. For a moment she thought there had been a mistake. Surely the door would open and the doctor would say, "My apologies, Madame. Do come in." But there were no apologies, and she remained alone.

The plump New Englander had no word when she suddenly appeared. She hurried away and returned with a towel-covered tray of clinking objects, and the door was closed again. Rebecca walked and walked up and down, trying to rouse an interest in the things she saw. The "Do Not Enter" signs in two languages. The solarium for visitors who had wearied themselves with anxiety. The wilted flowers set outside a door to be flung away by someone less noble than a nurse.

She walked and walked, telling herself that this was not the time to cry, not the place to despair. And at last the doctor came out of Torrey's room.

"I have made a more thorough examination, Madame. There was nothing to learn that I did not know before. Your husband is now under treatment, and I shall see him again at perhaps nine or ten o'clock tonight. There is nothing you can do, so I suggest that you go back to your hotel immediately."

"May I see my husband?"

"He is better left undisturbed."

She was still at the hospital when the doctor returned at ten fifteen that night. And at half past seven in the morning she was there again, although the doctor had not yet arrived. There was a different nurse on duty. A frail, flaxen-haired girl with a southern accent.

"According to the chart there hasn't been what you'd really call a change."

And that was the pattern of Paris in the days that followed. Leaving the hospital after the doctor's night call and back at the hospital before the doctor's morning rounds. No change. Your husband's a very sick man. We're doing all we can, Madame.

Every night when she reached the hotel there were messages. Mrs. Frederick Benson called. Mr. Barker Kane called. Exhausted, she would fall upon the bed and weep. Sometimes she would remember that she had not eaten. Every night she cabled Doc. He had made contact with a prominent Parisian physician, who had hurried to Torrey's bedside, thus antagonizing the doctor of record on the case.

"Am I to understand, Madame, that you have not faith in me?"

"Doctor, you are to understand that I'm not up to soothing anyone's hurt feelings right now. Nothing matters except my husband's recovery. Just put the cost of the insult on your bill and write a nasty letter to my father-in-law."

On the fourth night the phone rang as Rebecca lay weeping. With hands gone suddenly icy she clutched the receiver.

Doris Benson said, "I know I haven't awakened you because I rang only fifteen minutes ago and you were still out."

Rebecca was so relieved that it was not the hospital on the line that she could only sob.

Doris said, "Why haven't you called me?"

"There hasn't been any time for seeing people, Doris. Torrey is—Torrey is very ill."

"Of course he's very ill. What do you suppose I've been calling about? The paper reports on his condition daily, and we've telephoned the hospital, but I wanted to talk to you. Now, what is it that we can do?"

"You're very kind, but there's really nothing. He has nurses and—"

"I was talking about you. What can we do for you? Do they feed you at the hospital?"

"Oh, I eat. It was very nice of you to call, Doris. Thank you. Thank you very much."

At six o'clock next evening the Bensons located her in the solarium at the hospital. She wanted to run when she saw them. God, how could they dream that she would be able to make conversation? How could people be so insensitive as to believe that she could be "cheered up" or diverted by false jollity?

Frederick said, "We're not going to be a nuisance to you, I hope. Little Red Riding Hood here had an idea, and she packed her basket and—"

They had brought fried chicken Maryland from the Butler's Pantry and American coffee in a thermos bottle. And because they were the Bensons they neither pulled long faces nor smiled too much. They asked for the latest report on Torrey. They stood for a silent moment tuning themselves to her need and then, picking up the signal, they blew her a kiss and went away.

On the sixth day Torrey showed signs of improvement.

That night the doctors told her he was out of danger. She sent the good news to Doc and called the Bensons. Then she remembered the messages from Barker Kane. He was not in his room, but he telephoned later.

"Rebecca, this is what I've been wanting to talk to you about. I imagine that you'll want to take Torrey home as soon as he's able to travel. I thought you might like to have me on the ship with you. You might feel more at ease if you and Torrey have a friend aboard. How about it?"

"Why, that would be wonderful, but of course I don't know yet on what date we could sail. I'd hate to mess you up with delays or indefinite information or—"

"I'm just here awaiting your command. If it weren't for my determination to take you and Torrey home I'd have sailed last Thursday. My girl sailed then."

"Your girl?"

"Oh, you don't know about her, do you? I met her through Arlen Comstock. With any luck, I'm going to marry her. She's promised to think about it."

They sailed on the *Paris*, not so elegant as the *Ile de France*, but comfortable and solicitous of a convalescent. Torrey rested most of the time, content to have Rebecca at his side or to play an occasional game of chess with Barker Kane.

"I wanted to take you to Versailles, Rebecca. That will have to wait for another time."

She bent and kissed him. "Yes, darling, and that's really a good thing. I'll tell you why. I'm going to improve myself. I haven't been the wife you really need, Torrey. In a way, I've let you down. I'm going to gather some knowledge about history and architecture and art and—oh, just about everything."

He gazed at her affectionately. "Don't change, Becky, my love, I beg of you. You're perfect just as you are."

"I won't really change. I'll just read and observe and use whatever brains God gave me. Then some day you'll say, 'You know, Rebecca, you've become a remarkable person. I really enjoy talking to you.' "

And he actually did say something of that sort to her one afternoon, but by then they had been divorced for more than five years.

*R*ebecca, *after* an hour of riding in the back seat of Vicki's car, was still impressed by the chic appointments and the elegant hush of the motor. The children sat on either side of her, not yet recovered from disappointment. They had begged Mademoiselle to take the station wagon, saying that its many windows provided a fuller view of the countryside. Mademoiselle had replied that Mama's beautiful automobile was more suited to the occasion. Mademoiselle had translated for plaintiffs and defendant, and Rebecca had made no comment. She was constantly amazed at the compulsive rage for small deceptions. Clearly, the children wanted the station wagon because their little poodle was not permitted in Vicki's car. Just as clearly, Mademoiselle wanted Vicki's car because her opportunities to drive that handsome automobile were few.

People are rarely candid, Rebecca thought. To whom would I admit that I am nervous about meeting Edouard's mother? Why should I be nervous? She is only a woman who was once my daughter's mother-in-law. My daughter has had other mothers-in-law. The first was quite nice, as I remember, and the second was more than a little mad, poor thing. But Mrs. Dover, now. Why do I feel like a child being brought to the principal's office? I haven't done anything. It was Vicki who hurt Edouard, not I. I am not responsible for Vicki. In no way am I responsible for Vicki.

She stared out the window at the sky and decided it was the most depressing shade of gray she had ever seen. She thought of airline advertisements that urged one to see

Paris after the crowds had left. Did they ever say exactly why the crowds had left? Did they ever mention that if you liked the wild, bleak weather of the Scotch moors you'd love Paris in autumn? No, of course not. The best-kept secret in the world was the atrocious climate of northern France.

Purposefully she looked away from the dismal skies and smiled down at Ursule. "I love you," she said, knowing that the meaning must be guessed by the tone color in which she had wrapped it.

Ursule purred, and she and Etienne moved closer to Rebecca as if for warmth. Though there are many kinds of warmth, Rebecca immediately thought of the least poetic.

"Mademoiselle, do you think the children are cold?"

"No, I do not think so. Their coats are heavy, and it would be very uncomfortable in here with the heater functioning. The temperature is certainly not less than five degrees."

Rebecca was shocked.

"Centigrade," Mademoiselle added.

"Oh." How much would five degrees be in American weather? "The cold here is very penetrating."

Mademoiselle said, "But one has one's furs."

Except that Mademoiselle had no furs, and Rebecca realized that once again she had irritated the young woman. She must apologize from an oblique angle. She could scarcely say that she regretted a governess's inability to buy mink.

"I'm afraid I am rather tiresome, Mademoiselle, with my frequent criticism of your weather. I would like to say that I rarely have a good word for my own. New York is always too cold or too hot or too dry or too rainy to please me. You must mark it all down to an old lady's habit of complaining and pay no attention."

"As you say, Madame."

Remarkable how Mademoiselle, using no more than a correct and routine phrase, could be so bitterly insulting.

Ursule jumped suddenly from the seat and began chattering to Etienne. The two pointed and shouted, and Rebecca caught her breath at sight of the Forest of Fontainebleau dazzling in its autumnal brilliance, the golden trees rising in bold rebellion against the gloom of the day.

"Do we drive through the forest?" she asked.

"No, Madame, but at least you have caught a glimpse of our ancient trees in their blaze of glory."

And Rebecca did not mention that she was from New England, where trees gone mad by the touch of autumn were no novelty. She did not mention it because also in New England there were people who designed clothes, and it would be foolish to speak of them when the subject was Givenchy or Balenciaga.

Rebecca sat back in the car. The edge of the forest had been skirted and the bone-chilling grayness of the day returned. She thought again of Mrs. Dover. Will I be left alone with her at any time? Will she speak of Vicki and force me to defend my daughter? And just how would I defend Vicki? When a woman has a son such as Edouard and he takes a wife who— God, how she must hate Vicki. What can I say to Mrs. Dover if Vicki's name is raised? Why have I come here? It's such a stupidly unnatural thing to do.

"This is the town, Madame," Mademoiselle said.

Rebecca saw an antique trinket that was a railway station. She saw the town through which Mademoiselle was driving very slowly. Rebecca had the feeling that Mademoiselle and the town were both terribly amused at the tourist who expected to find a simple village. Here was a bookshop with its window display of not only the latest

147

French publications but also the best sellers from the American lists. A grocery as sophisticated and no doubt as expensive as its counterparts in Paris. One caught sight of fine teas and spices and delicately wrapped fruits in artistic arrangements. A haughty stationery shop with exquisite wares. What sort of people lived here? Well, probably the same sort who lived in Westchester County or in certain communities of Connecticut. Rebecca felt more satisfied, now that she had figured that out. Of course. The town was exactly like dozens she had seen except—except that this town had a castle.

"Francis the First," Mademoiselle murmured.

So it was never really that easy. There were no interchangeables. This was not merely a French Westchester County. No matter how close you came, no matter how certain you were, there was no way to overcome the feeling that here was another world. Only a fool would think, even briefly, that a block of smart shops was the key to understanding. The key was up there in the moldering castle. Only the unimaginative could believe that a child who fitted the sixteenth century into his picnics and walks had not a different philosophy from one who thought time had begun when Mommy brought him home from the hospital.

The car had rolled away from the town now, passing fine homes and beautiful gardens, and suddenly there were tall, iron gates and a mirrorlike pool with swans upon it. There was an eighteenth-century manor house, and Rebecca recognized it all from the descriptions Vicki had given when Edouard had been new and exciting to her.

"It is here that Mrs. Dover lives," Mademoiselle said.

The front door opened, and Edouard came toward them. The children screamed their delight at sight of him and were promptly silenced by Mademoiselle. She added a few more words, and Rebecca guessed the meaning, for the children walked sedately though they longed to run. Rebecca glanced at Edouard and was surprised to see him nod approvingly as he watched Ursule and Etienne approach him with childish dignity. Rebecca was not at all certain that the curbing of natural impulses was beneficial. It could lead, she thought, to dreadful repressions later in life.

Edouard kissed his children fondly, then turned to welcome Rebecca. What charm he possessed. Playful gallantries for her and exactly the right note of affability for Mademoiselle. And how striking a figure he was in his leisure clothes. The black pull-over sweater, the charcoal-gray slacks. Rebecca suddenly thought of Fallon McKee, and the taste of bitterness was in her throat as she was led into the house to meet Edouard's mother.

Mrs. Dover. I must remember. Not Madame Dover. Mrs. Dover. Mrs. Dover had a slim figure, snow-white hair and deep blue eyes. There was no gaiety about her, no attempt to play at youthfulness. Yet though age had been accepted without protest, there was no fragility or weakness. A strange thought occurred to Rebecca: I am not as old as she is, but she will be here to say that she is sorry when Edouard reports that I have died.

The introductions concluded, the ladies sat together on a green velvet sofa and the children were brought to Mrs. Dover. She kissed them and then they stood before her, not dreaming to seat themselves since they had not been invited to do so. Ah, this other world in which a grandmother did not reach out to cuddle such adorable children, but instead quizzed them earnestly as though they were applicants for positions in her household. And the fact that the eyes of Ursule and Etienne were filled with eagerness and affection as they spoke answered no questions for Rebecca. How did they know to love this grandmother who was so preoccupied with rules of conduct? What made their smiles so sweet as they looked back at her when they had been dismissed?

"They appear to be in splendid health, Edouard." Mrs. Dover spoke in English, and Rebecca felt certain that this was a courtesy rather than a custom. "And they are learning their lessons well. Mademoiselle is a fine girl. A very fine girl." She turned to Rebecca. "Are you contented with the little ones? Or have they distressing flaws which I have not observed?"

Rebecca smiled. "They are absolute angels."

Mrs. Dover said, "We share a precious treasure, Mrs. Winton. No other woman in the world can be grandmother to Ursule and Etienne. Only you and I were so favored."

Edouard sighed. "And to think that when I was young you never noticed how handsome and brilliant and noble I was."

"How do you know that I did not notice?" his mother asked him. "A child's mind should not be stuffed with ideas that will encourage conceit any more than his stomach should be stuffed with sweetmeats that will invite an illness. But enough about children. Are you enjoying Paris, Mrs. Winton? Have you seen it before?"

"I am enjoying Paris tremendously. It is my second visit. The other was many years ago."

"How do you think the buildings look, now that they have been scrubbed with such energetic fervor that the patina has been removed, leaving us with a city of glaring white vulgarity?"

Edouard rescued Rebecca from the dangers of replying to the question. "Mother, the patina that was removed is spelled g-r-i-m-e. Even the would-be obstructionists are beginning to admit that Paris needed a good scrubbing."

Mrs. Dover argued the point, and for a minute or two Rebecca was free to smile politely while paying no attention at all to what was said. There was even an opportunity to admire the room in which she sat. She noted the Louis Fourteenth gilded wood clock above the fireplace, the armchairs that were certainly covered in Beauvais tapestry, the Jacob console, the magnificent carpet woven by long-dead craftsmen. The furnishings were innocent of self-consciousness in their antiquity. Rebecca surmised it was because they had not been "collected" but had merely been moved from the home of one relative to another as well-loved household possessions. And she sat quietly, considering the gilded wood clock, and from beyond the windows she heard the laughter and the prattle of the children as they fed the swans. And it seemed to her that the clock was fondly aware of Ursule and Etienne though uncertain regarding the century. There had been so many noons and so many children.

Edouard had brought the conversation around to sightseeing and now offered it back to Rebecca. "Shall I have the pleasure of taking you to Versailles one day, Madame? And perhaps you would like to see Malmaison. Ladies are always fascinated by the Empress Josephine legends."

"Mrs. Winton might also be interested in some aspects of your work, Edouard. Perhaps not the factory, but surely the atelier."

They talked then of design and production of fabrics, which had been the passion and the wealth of Edouard's paternal line for three hundred years. Lavish brocades and cut velvets, satin embroidered with garden implements, damasks embellished with golden bees, fine linen, paisley and plaid, cottons printed with *chinoiserie*. Toile depicting balloon ascensions, earthquakes, archaeological discoveries and South Sea harbors. A modern history of France seen through the eyes of the fabric makers. And how exciting Edouard made it all seem.

"Oh, I do want to visit the atelier," Rebecca said, "but also the factory."

"Really? You wouldn't be bored?"

"Bored? Of course not."

Edouard looked at her thoughtfully, almost broodingly. "I fear that once I have begun, I talk too much about fabrics."

Mrs. Dover smiled. "Your father spoke of little else. It was very difficult for me, Mrs. Winton, because in my family there were no enthusiasms except horses and gardens. My parents never understood my husband's devotion to business. In the beginning they were determined that no 'yard goods merchant' would have their daughter, and I do not believe there was ever a cordial conversation between my husband and my father till my first son was born."

Her first son? Rebecca wondered if a question was in order. Why had she always thought of Edouard as an only child? Where was the other . . . Suddenly the story Vicki had told came to mind, or at least fragments of the story. The older son had been a priest and the Nazis had marched into his village and . . . She could not recall the details, but somehow it had all resulted in the family taking a new name and a new faith. What was it the older son had done? When Vicki had recounted the story it had dealt with people unknown to Rebecca. Now, sitting beside Mrs. Dover, speculating on the misdeed of Edouard's brother, Rebecca wished she had listened more closely to Vicki.

Her thoughts were interrupted by the announcement that dinner was served. The large meal of Sunday came early in the day, Edouard explained. No one knew why. It was simply the custom.

"And we are very informal," Mrs. Dover added.

The informality was represented by decanters of both red and white wine awaiting one's pleasure on table instead of being ceremoniously poured by the butler. The atmosphere of the dining room with its Directoire furnishings and dark paneling was far from casual. The heavy crystal and silver, the splendid lace tablecloth, all caused Rebecca to conjecture what glorious display was made for the formal occasions.

What Edouard had called the large meal of Sunday turned out to be a very large meal indeed. It began with a clear soup, which was reasonable enough. After that came sea perch served with hollandaise. Delicious. Rebecca was then ready for dessert, but, instead, sweetbreads and spinach arrived. Well, that was not too much, providing a light dessert had been planned. She was jarred by the revelation that the end of dinner was not yet in sight. The main course was still to be faced. When the leg of mutton was placed before Edouard for carving she toyed with the idea of confessing that she was already overfed. She held her silence. In this other world, the most courteous of refusals might constitute a criticism of the food or even an insult to the traditions of the household.

"Madame, do you prefer thin slices or the more usual cut?" Edouard asked.

"Thin, please," Rebecca said, faintly.

Mrs. Dover glanced at her. "Edouard, I believe that you would serve Mrs. Winton best if you sliced so thinly that there was no meat at all upon her plate. Personally, I have eaten all that I intend to eat and our guest may feel the same."

Edouard looked questioningly at Rebecca and his mother. "Neither of you is hungry?" he asked in amazement.

"Not since the sea perch, dear son. Dinners are geared to the appetites of men. Didn't you know that?"

Later, camembert cheese and fruit were placed upon the table, but to be regarded no more importantly than the lettuce leaves beneath a stuffed tomato. Dessert was *bombe glacée,* and sweet champagne was served with it.

"A fine dinner, Mother," Edouard said, as they moved back to the living room.

"Your pleasure is mine, Edouard, but I number among my friends no lady who would not rather have an omelet on a Sunday afternoon. If I did not fear the judgment of servants, I would reduce most of my meals to one simple course and dessert—except on the occasions when you are visiting me."

There was much talk of food then. The American menu as opposed to the French, diets, supermarkets. At table there had been discussion of Parisian shops. Mrs. Dover frequently read New York newspapers and she had commented that for present-day American women there was nothing to be had in Paris that was not available in New York except the thrill of shopping in Paris. Now she spoke as vehemently of frozen dinners, ready-mixes and pizzas.

"All symbols of decay. Dread harbingers of a world in which there will be nothing but what there was in the beginning—a need to fill the stomach and an animal-like indifference to what substance stills the hunger pangs. Eating has always been a necessity, but a highly developed civilization gave it charm and sociability. Now we are on our way back to prehistoric man, who knew nothing of taste in any sense of the word."

Edouard said, "In many ways, the world is better than it was fifty years ago."

"No, dear. Only the promises are better."

Edouard smiled at Rebecca and got to his feet. "I hope you ladies can spare me for a brief time. I should like to take a walk with my children."

And now she was alone with Mrs. Dover. Wouldn't it be natural for the mother of Edouard to sigh and to remark sadly that he adored his children and that separation from them was a tragedy? After that, an acid comment on Vicki could so easily follow. Follow? No, it would be an integral part of any remark concerning Edouard's unhappiness.

What shall I say in answer? Can I agree that it is a tragedy and treat the whole matter objectively, as though I were not acquainted with the woman who deserted Edouard?

She was conscious that the deep blue eyes were fixed upon her, studying her. She turned to face whatever it was that Mrs. Dover wished to say. For a moment they looked at each other, and then Mrs. Dover asked, "So you were in Paris long ago? Where did you stay?"

"George the Fifth."

"A lovely hotel. I remember when it was being built. It was quite a favorite of Americans, wasn't it?"

"Oh, yes. It still is. I was there with some American friends the other evening, but they happen to be living at the Plaza-Athénée."

"Ah, the romantic, luxurious Plaza-Athénée. It was there, you know, that Mata Hari was captured."

They spoke of restaurants that Rebecca remembered. A few, though they had been sumptuous, were unknown to Mrs. Dover. Rebecca guessed that they had been either American haunts or had attracted the racier type of Parisian.

"Those days after the First World War were so happy," Mrs. Dover said. "My husband had come home safely, and we believed that there would be no more wars. Of course, he did not live to see the second one."

"My husband was also in the first, but I did not know him then."

"You were fortunate. You did not experience the terrible waiting and worrying. And your son is just the right age to have missed all your country's involvements, isn't he?"

"For a time I thought he would have to go to Korea."

"But he did not. I am happy for you. During the Second World War, Edouard was with what I think you called the Free French. But of course you have heard about all that."

Rebecca nodded. Who would have told her of Edouard's war record? Only Vicki. So they were both thinking of Vicki now. Rebecca waited, and presently Mrs. Dover spoke again. She spoke of the sad days of the First World War when she had superstitiously avoided setting foot upon the Avenue Montaigne because its former name had been Avenue of Widows.

And at last Rebecca realized that under no circumstances would Vicki's name be mentioned. Here was something to remember about Mrs. Dover. This was not a woman who would vengefully refuse to meet Vicki's mother. And this was not a woman who would receive Vicki's mother in order to review the heartaches Vicki had caused. This was a woman who in some tragic manner had been separated from a son and she did not speak of that either, not even on a dreary Sunday afternoon when she sat with another old lady on a green velvet sofa and talked about the past.

All the way back to Paris Rebecca sat very still in Vicki's automobile. She thought about Mrs. Dover and the things of which Mrs. Dover would not speak.

At the house there was a message that Mrs. Kane had telephoned. Rebecca called her at once.

"We're going to wander around Montmartre tomorrow. We thought maybe you'd like to wander with us."

"What time?"

"What difference? Montmartre's been sitting up there a long time. It'll wait for us."

"I'm busy from eleven to one. That's why I asked."

"We could go any time. Or would you rather make it Tuesday?"

"Sue, I'm going to be busy every day from eleven to one."

"Doing what, for God's sake?"

"It's a secret."

"At our age there aren't any secrets."

"Too true, and I'll probably break down and tell you the whole thing, but not on the phone. I just arrranged for it on Friday. Tomorrow will be my first day."

"First day of what?"

Rebecca said, "I might tell you tomorrow."

But Sue did not ask again, and Rebecca kept her secret as they walked about Montmartre on a cloudy afternoon. The Place du Tertre was, as advertised, filled with artists and their canvases. Bright streaks of color against the melancholy day. One smiled encouragingly and was immediately quoted the rock-bottom price on a painting of Sacré-Coeur.

They stood looking at the white Byzantine dome that had become, along with windmills and buxom models, a trade-mark of Montmartre. On all sides of them tourists with cameras dangling forlornly from around their turned-up collars were also gazing pensively at Sacré-Coeur. Would the sun ever come out? And was Sacré-Coeur as worthy of flashlight bulbs as Notre-Dame?

Rebecca peered in the windows of small art galleries and she noticed cafés whose names did not make her think of dead artists. She thought of Torrey. Lapin Agile. Mère Catherine. She had been in those places. She remembered riding in taxis up the steep streets. But everyone had been laughing then, and now it was going to rain.

There was a pastry shop, and Barker hurried her and Sue into it. They drank dreadful coffee and ate delicious croissants. They talked to an old woman who claimed to have known Renoir and Cézanne and, of course, Utrillo and his famous mother.

Sue set a mean little trap. "You modeled for them all, no doubt."

"Utrillo was a painter of landscapes," the old woman answered, waspishly. "And I did not say I had modeled for any of them."

Barker gave her ten francs because she was a spirited woman with good sense. She had wrapped her croissant in a paper napkin to be taken home and eaten at the hour of her choice.

Outside, the rain fell sadly on Montmartre. The Place du Tertre was deserted, and Rebecca wondered to what shelters the artists had retreated. Hugging their canvases protectively, they had run to . . . To where? She found she could not even imagine. She fancied that a younger person, even though a stranger to Montmartre, might have guessed something of the habits of those who painted in the square.

"You sighed," Sue said.

"Yes. I feel terribly old."

"That's what comes from being in Montmartre on a rainy day. It's really a very spooky place, you know."

"Only we used to laugh like crazy here," Rebecca said.

Barker nodded. "I remember. Maybe we should have dinner at Maxim's tonight. Would you like to do that, Becky?"

"Thanks. I'm tempted, but I have a dozen letters to write and—"

"Okay. I was just trying to cheer you up."

"Woe to the woman who can be cheered by nothing less than a dinner at Maxim's." Rebecca gazed across the trays of pastry set invitingly in the showcase. Odd, how the white dome of Sacré-Coeur gained no majesty even with the theatricality of a stormy sky behind it. It simply looked wet and shiny and rather like the most pretentious building on the grounds of a world's fair.

"Do you think we'll get a cab?" Sue asked. The question sounded a note of loneliness and anxiety, as though Sue feared that they were doomed to live and die here in the Montmartre rain.

They found a taxi without any trouble at all, and the Kanes dropped Rebecca off, promising to telephone within a day or two.

Rebecca waved to them and entered the house. She went directly to the nursery. Even in so short a time, it had become a pleasant habit to kiss the children good-bye when leaving and, during their waking hours, to kiss them again upon returning.

Mademoiselle was knitting. The wool upon which she worked was as somber-colored as the afternoon. Oughtn't Frenchwomen eschew knitting? It was such a nasty reminder of how their ancestors had busied themselves in the minutes between guillotinings. Etienne abandoned his toy soldiers to run to Rebecca. Ursule raised a tearstained face.

"What's the matter with her?" Rebecca asked.

"There has been a small unpleasantness." Mademoiselle counted six stitches and laid her knitting aside. "Please observe the dressing gown she is wearing."

It was a bright-red quilted cotton, ankle-length and adorable on Ursule.

"It was a birthday gift to her many months ago. She has worn it infrequently. Today it suddenly became the center of importance, and she now wishes to wear it downstairs to dinner."

Rebecca smiled disarmingly at Mademoiselle. "And you are opposed to her doing that?"

"Madame, one does not wear a dressing gown to dinner."

"Not even once? Not on a rainy evening, Mademoiselle, when the gay color and the informality would make the dinner hour almost a festive occasion?"

Mademoiselle's lips tightened in the way that had become quite familiar to Rebecca. "It is my desire to please both you and the child, but, unfortunately, she has made it impossible for me to yield to her whim. She did not accept my ruling gracefully, Madame, but made strong protest."

"Do you mean that there is never a time when 'strong protest' is proper?"

"I mean that strong protest cannot become a habitual response to each and every order. It is irrational when used on trivialities. It must be reserved for matters of principle."

Rebecca said, "To the child this could seem a matter of principle."

"If it does, Madame, then her values need very diligent attention. She must not grow up unable to note the specific differences between a caprice and a crusade."

Rebecca smiled again. The children were watching, and they must not suppose that Mademoiselle was being criticized or lectured. "You are such an intelligent person that I don't think you will be vexed by my saying that you are, perhaps, too serious. Would you question yourself a little on that point? You see, to my mind, the child wearing her red dressing gown to dinner would be a bit of harmless fun. Just think, Mademoiselle, at this moment you would have a bright and happy nursery had you said yes instead of no when she made her original request."

"Ah, yes, Madame, *at this moment* the nursery would be filled with peace and good cheer. May I tell you that I am not a baby sitter? I am a teacher and, please God, a builder of character."

"We disagree on methods," Rebecca said.

"I regret that, Madame."

Somehow Ursule sensed that the two women had no more to say to each other. She crept close to them and worked her small hand into Rebecca's. When she spoke, her voice was heart-wringingly beseeching, but Mademoiselle was unmoved. She responded coolly.

"What does she want, Mademoiselle?"

"She wants you to stay in here and listen to records on her phonograph. I told her you have other things to do."

Rebecca nodded. "That will be easier for everyone." Reluctantly she detached herself from Ursule and left the nursery. The child cried out in disappointment, but Rebecca continued along the corridor to her own room. She must not, she would not create an impossible situation between herself and Mademoiselle. But how inflexible the woman was. Poor little Ursule. Rebecca remembered how different things had been in the nursery presided over by Miss Emmett. One could have said to Miss Emmett, "She's going to be allowed to wear her red dressing gown to dinner as a special reward for having been such a good girl yesterday. Surely that's fair enough, isn't it, Miss Emmett?" And Miss Emmett would have replied, "Oh, yes. I completely forgot what a good girl she was yesterday. Of

course she gets to wear her red dressing gown to dinner."
As simply as that everything had been put right in the
pleasant nursery Rebecca remembered. A pity that Mademoiselle mistrusted anything that wasn't painful and difficult.

And, God, how I hate those lonesome dinners downstairs. Why does everything have to be so bloody pomp-
ous? Wouldn't it be marvelous if I could eat with the children in their dining room? Or what joy if Mademoiselle
were human. I could pop in and say, "Let's have trays for
everybody tonight in the nursery. We'll all wear dressing
gowns."

There was some contentment to be had from the bright
fire in her bedroom. Rebecca hung up her coat, then seated
herself at the desk. From her purse she drew a slim book
and a pad still in the stationer's wrapper. Very seriously she
began to write.

*J'ai un crayon. Je prends un livre. J'ouvre mon livre. J'écris. Le
crayon. Le livre. Le papier. La plume. Qu'est-ce que c'est? C'est la
chaise. Non, ce n'est pas la chaise, mais la table.*

How surprised the children would be when suddenly
one day she turned to them and said, "*Une pendule est plus
grand qu'une montre.*" Or, "*Parmi les insectes, il y a le ver
à soie, la mouche et le moustique.*"

She must really get out of the habit of glancing at the
back pages of the book. Actually, there was nothing exciting to see there. The people who wrote these things for be-
ginners were very unimaginative. When, in the history of
the world, had it ever been necessary to tell anyone that a
clock was larger than a watch? Who cared that the insect
kingdom included the silkworm, the fly and the mosquito?
Why in the back of the book—or even in the first lesson—
wasn't one taught to say, "My darlings, I have made a tre-

mendous effort to learn a few words in your language so that you will know I love you"?

Un arbre. Une boîte. Un chapeau. Une étoile. Un oiseau. Un panier. Un poisson. Une souris.

The gentleman who was her instructor had been so terribly honest.

"Of course, you know, Madame, that one does not acquire a foreign language once one is beyond the years which nature provided for study and learning."

"You mean I can't learn enough to communicate with French members of my own family?"

"I said only that one cannot acquire a foreign language. I wish to avoid your suffering disappointment if you have the notion that you can develop a fine accent, a complete knowledge of idioms and an ear for the language on all status levels. This is an impossibility, Madame. However, you can learn hundreds of words and phrases that will make for conversation in your home. You and your family must resign yourselves to the fact that always you will speak with an American accent. You have come to French too late, Madame."

"I know."

"You will not always be understood, nor will you always understand."

"All right."

"Just so you are aware of the problem, Madame, and do not expect too much of yourself or of me."

La maison. Le jardin. Le parapluie. La porte. Je parle. Je dois. J'espère. Je voudrais.

How dull that I turned out to be the kind of grandmother who wants to communicate with the children. Quelle bourgeoise!

And in the gloomy weeks of autumn she courted Paris

lovingly because it was that other world to which her grandchildren belonged. She studied meters and liters and kilograms and livres. She learned to convert Fahrenheit to centigrade and discovered that from the Concorde gate of the Tuileries to the eastern façade of the Louvre—around fountains and the Arc du Carrousel—was not five-eighths of a mile but just over a thousand meters. She found all this so fascinating that for hours she could put from her mind the thought that her only mail had been from the Bensons and Jennie Frost. Barrett and Juanita, one could easily imagine, were busy and had nothing of moment to say. But one might have expected some word from Vicki. Surely she was in touch with Mademoiselle, inquiring as to the well-being of her children. Rebecca could not bring herself to ask Mademoiselle if there was correspondence with Madame Dover. And had there been tender little notes for Ursule and Etienne? Picture post cards perhaps? Or, in the letters sent to Mademoiselle, an affectionate message for the little ones? Or had there been nothing?

After her daily lessons Rebecca took questing walks, her dazzled gaze wandering across monuments from which sprang forth bell towers, domes and slender spires. She came to know a score of parks, gardens, squares and esplanades. She looked in shop windows and remembered to think, "*On achète des robes dans un magasin.*" She shivered in the cold and was delighted to find herself thinking quite naturally, "*J'ai froid.*"

The shops were an eternal mystery. What hours did they keep? Who knew at what time they would open or close? By what clock did they conduct business? She walked through the Flea Market in the rain. Perseverance might lead to some magnificent bargains, but that was a game for other people to play. She strolled the Ile Saint-Louis and the Ile de la Cité. She looked at Notre-Dame by daylight. *La église. Tiens! Quelle église!* She stood wide-eyed before the wonderful old houses on the Rue Chanoinesse. She bought a guidebook and found that there was more to Paris than she could ever hope to explore, and so she limited herself to the possible.

Edouard took her to dinner on several occasions. There was the restaurant of incomparable luxury where the roof suddenly, unexpectedly rolled back to clear the room of smoke. A quick flash of cold stars, a touch of frigid wind, and the roof was in place again, the air clear and fresh. And there was the genuinely regal food and service of the restaurant set in a neighborhood of dark, crooked alleys. One dined at preposterous expense and then, dashing back to the car through the chill night, one noticed wretched little cafés with names like Martinique and Guadeloupe. One heard Caribbean music and saw freezing, homesick Negroes who had dreamed that Paris would be sunny.

With Edouard she saw Malmaison and Versailles. For him she regretted that he had so much time to give to her. Where was the lady who, instead of his ex-mother-in-law, should be touring his factory and atelier? Or, at least, where was the girl who would make his life too exciting to waste a moment of it in the company of old women?

With the Kanes Rebecca went many places. Because Tour d'Argent held romantic memories for Barker and Sue, she suggested that they go there alone.

"But you were practically with us the night I met Barks," Sue protested.

"I remember," Rebecca said. "I remember vaguely."

And she sat in the Tour d'Argent that was nothing like the Tour d'Argent she had known. She smiled at the Kanes and drank champagne with them, and all the while she was busying her mind with the objects on the table.

La fourchette. Le couteau. La cuiller. La serviette. Le sel. Le poivre.
Le beurre. Le verre de vin.

She listened as the waiters spoke to each other. She did
not understand a word. With envy she looked at Barker.
There was no justice. Of what use was French to a man
who had no grandchildren?

Stubbornly she went back to the instructor next day and
took another lesson, and she took another lesson the day
after that as well and the day after that. And one morning Sue called to say, "You'll never guess what! Christian
Dior has Christmas decorations up! Come on over and
look."

The decorations were incredibly elegant. An imposing
display of opulence and beauty. The trees and candles and
wreaths all had the originality and subtlety of other Dior
creations. Sue and Rebecca hesitated only a second before
plunging into the Christmas splendor. Surely never before
had there been such negligées, such sweaters and gloves
and scarves and such mountains of lovely fancies for the
dressing table, the breakfast tray or the bath or bar. And
the men's department! What miracles of perfection in
texture and cut.

"I'm not going to buy a thing till I've made my list," Rebecca said. "It's not safe. Everything is too gorgeous."

There was no question but that the Christmas madness
had arrived. The streets and shops all over the city were
suddenly densely crowded. Were Dior's decorations the
signal that it was now appropriate to mark the birth of the
Infant Jesus? Overnight the department stores blossomed
with imports of the world, and in advertisements everything from pheasants to airplanes was pronounced the truly
ideal gift.

Packages from New York began to arrive. Some were
placed in Rebecca's room. Others went to the nursery and

were hidden away by Mademoiselle. And at last, there was a letter from Vicki.

Mother dear,

Forgive me for not writing. It's been so difficult to get around to it. I have thought of telephoning, but the large difference in time makes it almost impossible to catch a convenient hour for both you and me. I have never found New York as wildly demanding as it is this season. I have been going everywhere. Tremendous dinner parties and late gatherings have left me with little energy and practically no spare moments.

I'm sorry to say that I have not been able to use your pretty apartment. Since the building has no restaurant from which my breakfast could be sent and no maid service I have had to make other arrangements. Flower says that you let Lottie go visit her sister in Memphis while you are away. I took it for granted that Lottie would be here to work for me. I wish we had discussed the matter. I don't want to hire just anybody and it would be almost impossible to get a superior person for a temporary job. As you can see by the stationery, I've moved into the least obnoxious hotel. I hate them all, but anything's better than fixing one's own breakfast.

I hope you are enjoying your stay with the children. Aren't they lambs? I'm afraid I've neglected them as I've neglected you, but the thought that you three are together has consoled me. I know they must adore you. My thoughts and my love have been with you all. There are packages on the way to you and the small darlings. I hope you have a wonderful Christmas with them.

I don't know any more about when I'm returning than I did in the beginning. The play seems to be in wonderful shape and if you hear from Barrett to the contrary, don't believe him. He came to two rehearsals because he was graciously invited, not as a coach but as my brother. No one wanted his professional opinion, but it was given, and with dire predictions. It strikes me that he knows less than nothing about the theater and I told him so. Consequently we are not speaking to each other now. But that's neither here nor there. The play goes to Boston for tryouts and perhaps to New Haven as well if further rewriting is necessary.

All my love and Merry Christmas, Mother dear. I will try to write more often.

V.

Rebecca thought of Vicki sharing with Fallon McKee the long, tedious hours of on-the-road tryouts. She thought of Edouard, of the children who were his and Vicki's, of the house that had been furnished exactly as Vicki wanted it. She thought of the ancient ballad of the fine lady who had chosen to follow the raggle-taggle gypsies. Incredible what people did with their lives.

And suppose the play is a success? How long am I expected to stay here? She couldn't have thought that I would stay indefinitely, like through the run of a smash hit. We never spoke of that. I didn't tell her that Lottie had respectfully declined to work for Miss Vicki. And she didn't tell me that I was to hold the fort for months and months. And what if McKee's movie contract swings into action when the play closes?

Rebecca stared down at the letter. Just how long would Vicki stay away from her children?

La lettre. La mère. Les enfants. La maison. La femme. L'homme. Quel dommage. Très triste.

Surely Vicki will come back to Paris, if only for a visit. Right after the Broadway opening she might come. But suppose she doesn't? Dare I tell her that she has given McKee no chance to yearn for her, no need to pursue her and no reason for marrying her?

Rebecca placed the letter in her drawer and glanced out the window. A heavy rain was falling. It looked cold and dangerous. What was the French word for "influenza"? Actually, she did not need to take her lesson in such weather. The instructor did not come to the school just for her. But there was still time to decide.

She walked down the corridor to the nursery. Ursule and Etienne were standing, each at a different window, gazing out in the classically despondent pose of housebound children on a rainy day.

Mademoiselle said, "As you observe, we are bored and woebegone. Yesterday we concluded our autumn studies very successfully and today we were to have celebrated the beginning of the holiday season. I had thought to take the children to the Musée Grévin. They like the magician and the distorting mirrors."

Ursule walked away from the window and with a deep sigh of ennui threw herself upon the blue corduroy couch. Etienne permitted the curtain to fall back in place. He seated himself beside Ursule as though conscious that together they presented a more heartbreaking tableau of desolation.

This is the moment, Rebecca thought. A tremendous wave of stage fright swept over her. Her tongue fastened itself to the roof of her mouth, and she could feel her heart pounding. But she spoke. She said, "*J'ai une surprise pour toi.*"

Mademoiselle glanced at her sharply, but for a moment the children were concerned only with the surprise, not with the language used to announce it. They looked at her eagerly. What surprise?

"*J'étudie le français,*" Rebecca continued, trembling nervously. "*Je vais à l'école parce que je voudrais parler à toi.*" Was there a plural for "*toi*"? And what on earth was it? She fixed her eyes midway between the children so in case she was using an exclusive pronoun all might still be well. "*Est-ce que tu peux me comprendre?*"

Ursule leaped from the couch. "*J'ai compris,*" she cried. "*Grandmère! J'ai compris.*"

She flung her arms around Rebecca and suddenly Etienne realized that he, too, had understood, and he came running and shouting. And the children listened as Rebecca told hesitantly and, she feared, rather ungrammatically, how she had longed to speak to them. They urged her to say more and they laughed at the way she pronounced a word and they shrugged in mystification at the meaning of another. They had so many things they wanted to tell her, and a dozen times Rebecca begged them to speak more slowly, but, for a beginning, it was very good indeed.

"*Je suis heureuse*," Ursule said, looking with shining eyes at Rebecca.

And Rebecca was also happy. The children brought cushions and sat at her feet and asked if she knew any stories.

"I know many stories but I have not enough French to tell them to you." Ah, *quelle joie*, the nervousness was gone, and she had remembered that the plural of "*toi*" was "*vous*." Pleasantly astonished as the unfamiliar words came to mind and lips, she continued, "When I was a child I had a dog. Perhaps I can say something of him."

She said that the dog was big and not at all like Fifi. He had hated baths and he had barked a great deal. He had been very lovable though troublesome. And there had been a cat.

The children had forgotten that it was raining. They were fascinated by this grandmother from America who had learned to speak to them, and they were delighted by the game she invented.

"My cat was—now, you say colors and other things about her. I'll tell you when you are right."

And the children called out the French words for black, white, gray, soft, big, small, good, naughty. The competition was so exciting that their voices grew loud and shrill, and Rebecca, who had been blissfully unconscious of everything but her success, all at once remembered the presence of Mademoiselle. She turned with the intention of apologizing for the small commotion she had caused and she found Mademoiselle's eyes fixed earnestly upon her.

"You have worked very hard for this, Madame," Mademoiselle said. "We will permit nothing to destroy your pleasure."

Rebecca caught her breath in amazement. It was indeed another world, a world in which one never knew what to expect of the people who lived in it. Gratefully she smiled at Mademoiselle and felt courageous enough to address the Académie Française.

"*Quand j'étais enfant,*" she said to the children, "*je montais à cheval.*" Her audience was eager to hear more. What was amusing about those rides on poor old Black Prince? Nothing really. One would have to improvise. "*Comment dit-on,*" she asked airily of Mademoiselle, " 'I was always falling off'?"

Mademoiselle spoke the words, and the children giggled. What was the horse's name? Where did she keep him? Did she ride him to school? What did he eat?

"*Œufs,*" Rebecca said.

The children were startled. The horse ate eggs! Why did he eat eggs?

"Because I don't know how to say 'oats' in French," Rebecca admitted.

That was hilarious. The children screamed with laughter when Mademoiselle explained. Rebecca thought it might be just the right moment to leave. She got up from her chair, promising to return later in the day.

"*Je voudrais bien écouter les disques,*" she said.

Ursule ran immediately to select the records she would play for Grandmère directly after luncheon.

Rebecca walked to her room and sat down before the fire. After only a moment she moved to another chair. Then, with careful attention to the slant of the rain, she opened a window. It was the first time since she had come to Paris that she did not need the comfort of the fire.

$\mathcal{T}$*he letter arrived* special delivery at the brownstone house while Rebecca was interviewing a laundress whose references were most impressive.

"I hope the agency explained to you that the work is very heavy here. There are three children, two of them girls, and you know what that means in terms of fussy ironing. Then there is my husband, who is extremely particular about his shirts." She glanced at the postmark on the letter. Bermuda. Bermuda? How odd. "And *I'm* very particular about my good tablecloths and napkins and the bed linen and, of course, my lingerie." He must have written the letter on the boat, then found himself unexpectedly docking at Bermuda, and had mailed it from there. "I will tell you frankly, this is a hard job. I wouldn't want you to take it without realizing that. On the bright side, you would be given a very comfortable room and three excellent meals a day. And, as you know, the wages are above average." But why would he write a letter on the boat or mail it in Bermuda? A letter couldn't travel any faster than a person. If the letter was here, why wasn't he? "Suppose you go back to the kitchen and let the cook give you a cup of tea while you're thinking the matter over."

The letter seemed to throb in her hand as Rebecca hurried to the privacy of her bedroom.

Rebecca dear,

I dislike such threadbare lines as, "This is a difficult letter to write," but, by God, it is a difficult letter. I want you to know it was as painful to write as it will be to read. I told you I was coming back on a freighter because I was exhausted from doing a play and making a movie at the same time. I told you that London audiences had drained my vitality, that British movie making was as maddening as the Hollywood brand, that the social life of a great ship would finish me off, and that I needed the restful hours and informality of the freighter. The truth is that I needed the long, quiet voyage for only one purpose, and that was to think hard and carefully. I docked at Bermuda yesterday with my thinking concluded. I shall remain here until you and I have settled matters by letter and can meet without indulging in conversations that would range from tedious to heartbreaking and back again.

Rebecca, I want a divorce. That's a shock, isn't it? I'm sorry. You are thinking, "What a coward he is to write about it instead of facing me." I am not a coward, Rebecca. Truly I am not. I considered coming home to explain in person, but I did not see what either of us would gain by that empty gesture. Surely you would not be happier for having heard me say the words with which I began this paragraph.

I do not believe I was ever intended to marry. I find marriage an unreasonable arrangement which imposes most unnatural restraints. And now you are thinking of one restraint and one only. Very well. I will admit I have not been faithful during these last few years. But will you believe me when I say that fidelity is not what I consider the most irksome clause in the contract? If it were, I would not ask for a divorce. I would do what millions of men all over the world do. I would have my affairs and continue the pretense of being a fine family man. But, Rebecca, I am not all physical. There is a me who detests marriage because, though you are beautiful and sweet, the institution of marriage has made it impossible for me to delight in your company or to tingle with interest at what you might say next. Is that brutal? Forgive me. I am trying to explain. A wife is a woman whose opinions are too well known to make conversation stimulating. Everything about one's wife becomes predictable, and though she may be admirable and—I suppose—even brilliant, the familiarity of marriage makes it impossible for her to say anything that she has not said before. She has become a commonplace creature because she has given herself and her viewpoints and her small rages and her merry smiles and her trite phrases and all the rest forever. And "forever" is a word that turns all things stale.

Now, as to our particular marriage—I find no fault with you, Rebecca, that I would not in time find with any other woman. Do not ask yourself how you lost my love. There is no such thing as love. It is an emotion invented by poets when the world thought itself civilized and demanded a genteel label under which lust or greed or convenience could be marketed as products of unquestioned purity and value. The intelligent person who speaks of love today means, "I would rather be with you than with anyone else." Very fine, except that at that point marriage seems a good idea, and then follows all the agonizing boredom that need never have happened. Oh, Rebecca, how I would have hurried to New York if you were no more than a phone number in a small, very private book. And if there is a more bitter commentary to make on marriage, I don't know what it could be.

I hope you will go to Reno. The laws of New York would, I think, create a distasteful situation for you. However, if you want to bring suit there, I will admit my guilt. As a matter of fact, I have already done so in another part of this letter. It seems to me that for the sake of the children you would prefer Reno. I am sure you would rather have them ponder the sin of evil temper than of adultery.

This seems to be the time to reply to the unhappy, bewildered question that is now presenting itself to you. "How can he do this to the children?" Do what, Rebecca? I have not been the kind of father who took them to the zoo or played "catch" with them or provided any philosophical guides to living. I am fond of my children and I will see them often. To be housed under the same roof with them is not essential to my happiness or theirs and does not make for one long, joyous holiday. I do not find children interesting or challenging or unfailingly adorable. I would, however, do a great deal for my children. I would give my life to protect them, but I will never give it in small, piddling ways, inch by inch, in the unprofitable business of being "good old Dad." Couples who go on living together for the sake of the children proceed on the theory that the children are more important than Father and Mother. Why are they? Why? I don't feel that I have less right to happiness than my children have. In siring them I don't see that I have forfeited the privilege of choosing what I shall do with the years ahead. I think it insane to sacrifice any part of one's life for people who will soon grow up and regard with complete indifference the matter of whether or not their parents were divorced.

You will hate everything I have said here. I regret that. Rebecca, let me hear from you.

Torrey

Dear Torrey,

You may not feel the weight of obligations and responsibilities, but I do. And it may surprise you to find out that I am not speaking of the children. I am speaking of you. I am your wife, and among the things that I owe you is an earnest effort to make you happy and to prevent you, when possible, from doing foolish things that you will be sorry for having done. Believe me, it would be very easy right now to creep apologetically out of your life and to let you have your way. I have pride, and therefore I would like to move with dignity out of your way, but there are more important things than pride. One of them is your future happiness. I will not let our marriage be destroyed by a passing whim of yours.

I know of course what's going on with you. You have been working ten weeks with Camilla Sheildstone in her marvelous London and you have become wildly infatuated with her. In spite of the offhand things you say about love I would bet that at this very moment you fancy yourself in love wih Camilla. You want to marry her. That's the truth, isn't it? I'm not as unimaginative as you think, Torrey. I understand how you could go mad about Camilla. She is gorgeous and clever and world-famous. If a person can refrain from spouting moral issues—and I can—there is no possible way to blame you for finding Camilla desirable.

I don't expect you to see it now, but please believe that it would be stupid to wreck our marriage for the few months of happiness that you and Camilla would have together. Torrey, I think you must understand how sincere I am by the fact that I have not exploded over the calm way you mentioned your infidelities. That hurt, but I shall make nothing of it, now or ever. I want to stand by you till this affair has worn itself out. Is Camilla with you in Bermuda? Was the freighter sort of a romantic, forbidden honeymoon? I can understand. Honestly, Torrey, I can understand and I can forgive when it's all over.

Please try to see that I have chosen the hard but sensible way to face this thing. I don't like the feeling of being unwanted, and if I yielded to impulse the divorce proceedings would begin tomorrow. Our marriage is too important for that, Torrey. I am going somehow to weather this thing out. When you recover from your delirium you will be glad I was stubborn and that I permitted common sense to control me.

Torrey, we have built a life together that is worth preserving. It isn't perfect. But has anyone done much better than we have? Do a lot more thinking, dear, and come home when you're ready.

Rebecca

P.S. If your poor father were living, what do you think he would say about all this?

Rebecca,

I am absolutely shaking with fury as I write this. How can you be such a shallow, silly, empty-headed fool? Did you read the letter I so carefully wrote or did you just glance at it? Don't you understand English? I hate the idea of marriage. Is that clear? Your brave, muddleheaded reply straight from a Bertha M. Clay novel almost drove me out of my mind. I do not fancy myself in love with Camilla Sheildstone. I do not want to marry Camilla Sheildstone. Camilla Sheildstone is a splendid actress and in her "marvelous London" she is almost as famous for her acting as for her lesbianism. Does that answer your question about her being here with me? Does it suggest that perhaps we didn't have a "romantic forbidden honeymoon" on the freighter? Good God, what trouble I went to in my futile attempt to reveal something of my thinking to you. There isn't anybody I want to marry now or at any time. If I can extricate myself from the marriage I have, there will be no other, I assure you.

Let me have another go at this in simpler and perhaps harsher words. I am fed to the teeth with marriage. I don't want to eat all my meals with any one person for the rest of my life. I don't want to listen to any one person talk and talk about things I've heard before and in which I have no interest. I'm through with getting married. Do you follow me so far? Maybe the fact that I'm an actor makes me more aware than the average man of how deathly dull reality is. I don't know. I only know that marriage is oppressive and that I can stand no more of it. For God's sake, try to believe that no woman is taking me away from you. I wouldn't walk into this trap a second time. Read the other letter over again. If necessary, have it read to you by some intelligent person.

Torrey

P.S. If my poor father were living he would say nothing about all this. He had enough sense to realize that a man does not pull up his roots unless his roots are strangling him.

Torrey,

No doubt you were drinking when you wrote that second letter. I like to think that you are unaware of how insulting it was. To proceed in our discussion with some degree of sense I must mention that I do not believe your being an actor can be considered an excuse for your behavior. After all, Frederick Benson is an actor, and there are those who even rank him as just about the best actor around. He does not find married life oppressive. If you want to say that Doris is more interesting than I, I will agree with

177

you. But so far you have only blamed marriage for your unhappiness.

I am remaining firm in the conviction that whatever is troubling you is a passing thing and that you must have time to recover from it. One doesn't rush into divorce without giving a lot of thought to it. With time, you may have a change of heart. If you do not, we will cross that bridge when we reach it. For now, I am going to do nothing.

Rebecca

Rebecca,

So you are going to do nothing. I might have expected that you wouldn't be bright enough to accept the facts and act on them with determination and a show of graciousness. Actually, if you are so enthusiastic about marriage I should think that you'd be anxious to have the divorce over while you're still beautiful and youngish. If you wait for my "change of heart" you could still be waiting when you're eighty. I will tell you now, Rebecca, that though you might cling like adhesive tape to the idea of being married to me, I am never going to live with you again. I am simply not going to continue the dreary tedium of life as it has been. We're finished, Rebecca. Do you understand that?

As to Frederick Benson: I admire him greatly but I doubt that anyone among the truly knowing considers him "just about the best actor around." Frederick is talented and very persuasive, but I wouldn't mention him in the top three. Be that as it may, his marriage is not like anyone else's. He and Doris work together. They talk of nothing except the theater and have a partnership that seems to delight both of them in every department of living. If you are thinking that I would have cherished you forever had you been a great actress like Doris I can only say that you still are missing the whole point. Marriage is not for me. I will not live within the bounds of it again even if you never divorce me. I am serious. You had better begin to believe that I am, because when I return to New York I intend to take an apartment. You will have so much explaining to do that you will find it tiresome.

Rebecca, face it. The marriage is over.

Torrey

She went to Reno and lived at a luxury ranch house and played cards with other women. When the card-playing palled, they knitted and talked about the husbands they were divorcing. Rebecca didn't want to talk about Torrey, but he was no shadowy "my husband," no vague unknown. The women were interested in Torrey, and one could be coolly withdrawn for only so long. After that, one would be left to oneself, and loneliness was so new that she was afraid of it.

Rebecca talked of Torrey and she enlivened an hour, here and there, with gossip and anecdotes of the theater. The divorce, she said, was by mutual agreement. There were several women who believed her. There were some who did not listen. They had no need for gossip or knitting or card-playing. They were the elite, the ladies who had asked their sorrowing husbands to step aside. They were high-spirited and patronizing. They were on the long-distance lines night and day. They received flowers, gifts, thick letters and telegrams.

For those who had no heartbroken husbands, no impatient lovers, days were very long in Reno. The nights were longer. One went to the movies in the hotel bus or risked a few dollars in the casinos. There were slot machines for the moments when blackjack came perilously close to arousing thought. It was better not to think. From thinking, people had been known to die.

Rebecca cried a lot and wrote jolly letters to the children. She participated mindlessly in the diversions organized by the management: the covered wagon ride, the outdoor pancake breakfast. She watched the square dancing and the rodeo and went back to stand in front of a slot machine, pulling the lever and waiting for the result without interest, like a vacant-eyed zombi.

She met a man at the side of the pool. A local man. A doctor. It was a Sunday morning, and he had come to breakfast with the Crowells, who owned the ranch and were his longtime friends. He was a big man, with black hair just beginning to gray. He had amiably inquisitive eyes and skin toughened by wind and sun. Perfect Hollywood type-casting for the Western doctor, she thought, as she acknowledged the introduction. He would be strong, silent and fearless. She smiled at him, wondering if he really were a doctor. Perhaps, like the covered wagon, he was atmosphere kept on hand to amuse the guests.

He had been a widower for just over a year. He had a son and daughter, both away at college. He had not grown accustomed to living alone, he confessed. He didn't know what to do with the hours in which nobody needed him. And after a while he was drawn into wider conversation, and Rebecca went to her bungalow and sent post cards to the children.

On Wednesday she received a letter addressed to Mrs. Torrie Winton. It came from town, so she supposed it was from her lawyer. But wouldn't one expect him to know how her husband spelled his name? The letter wasn't from her lawyer.

Dear Mrs. Winton,
    The Crowells are coming to my place for dinner on Friday evening. I'd be so pleased if you would come with them. . . .

His place was also a ranch house, not much smaller than that which the Crowells used for a hotel. He, too, had bungalows on the property. Recently built, he explained. The kids might like to bring Eastern friends home with them and the bedrooms in the house weren't very stylish. He and Iola had been planning on remodeling and refurnishing for years. Now he probably would never get around to it. Building the bungalows hadn't been like doing the house over. No memories involved.

Rebecca had accepted the invitation because she was tired of her fellow guests at the Crowells'. She was tired of the constant discussions of alimony and settlements. And, of course, to be asked had been balm on a painful wound.

"You're the only woman he's noticed since Iola died," Mrs. Crowell had said on the drive.

Rebecca had been charmed by the homely compliment. Western movies weren't as silly as she had judged them to be. There really was an honesty and goodness about the West, a simplicity of relationship that produced in the Crowells unquestioning approval of a stranger who had found favor with their friend. She had looked at the full moon sailing through the Nevada night and she had played that the Crowells were neighbor folk bringing the lonely widower his mail-order bride.

Now the Indians will come riding down upon us, but the chief's son will have been raised as foster brother to the doctor, and Mrs. Crowell will say to him, "Shame on you, Beaver Tooth, for riding in vengeance through the night with your people instead of bringing enlightenment to them." That would cause Beaver Tooth to slink away in shame.

They saw no Indians at all, but Chinese were rather plentiful.

"His family has always had Chinese servants," Mrs. Crowell said. "They keep passing their jobs on to relatives, you know, when they decide to go back to China."

The dinner was tolerable. The doctor's Chinese servants would not have been in demand in the mansions of San Francisco. They were very well placed right here in the uncompetitive life of easy-going Reno. The doctor was a host in the old-fashioned, hospitable style: Take more. Oh, that's not enough. Don't go away hungry. Rebecca was touched by his innocence in believing that nowhere was there better food than right here at his table. She was delighted with his remarks to a patient on the telephone.

"Now, this is the thing, Joe. You've been sick long enough to know whether you're sicker than usual or just kind of low in your mind. If you're sicker than usual, I'll sure come right over, but if you're just low in your mind, then turn on the radio and forget your troubles, because I have Dan and Betsy Crowell here and a lovely lady from New York."

Oh, he was sweet and funny and real, and the West was exactly like the movies said it was. It was uncomplicated and guileless, with truths that could be depended upon eternally. Were Western movies popular because there were still people who longed for plain statements of right and wrong? A person could look at the doctor and have no doubt as to the man he was. This was a land free from affectation and chicanery. She had to tell these Nevadans how much she loved their country and when she did, their geniality reached out to envelop her in warmth and contentment.

"You've never been West before, Mrs. Winton?" the doctor asked her.

"Not really. Southern California isn't at all the big, wide West."

"Oh, you were to Southern California?"

"Yes. With my husband."

The doctor thought that over briefly, then in his fine straightforward way he asked, "What business is Mr. Winton in?"

Rebecca stared at him. "Mr. Winton's an actor," she said.

"Is he? That's interesting. I've met several actors. They come up here on vacations, you know. Fine fellows, a lot of them."

She smiled and nodded and noticed for the first time that in one of his front teeth there was a gold filling. Unbelievable.

Mrs. Crowell said, "Torrey Winton is a very famous actor. He made one picture in Hollywood and that's considered a classic. Only he hated Hollywood and won't go back at any price." She looked at Rebecca. "Isn't that true?"

Rebecca said that it was.

The doctor was abashed and apologetic. "Guess I'm a big lunkhead, but I don't know much about artistic things. Now, Iola would have heard of him. She kept up with everything. I just don't have the time."

Rebecca had learned long ago that everybody had the time for things they really wanted to do. Had Iola really kept up with everything? Or did he mean that she had read fan magazines?

A Chinese boy brought a huge box of chocolates and handed it to the doctor.

"Good fellow. I almost forgot." He took the lid off the box and admired the arrangement inside. "Looks nice. Do you care for candy, Mrs. Winton? Well, go ahead and just help yourself when you feel like it." He placed the box on the table before her and beamed. "That goes for you, too, Betsy. How about a drink, Dan?"

Ladies never drank in Western movies. Only the dancehall girls drank, but they had hearts of gold and often willingly died by a bullet intended for the hero. Rebecca thought longingly of a sip of brandy. Really, it was just a little too much that he had never noticed at the Crowells' that ladies could drink and still be ladies.

Twice after that evening he again invited her to dinner. Once he mentioned that he'd like to take her to the grand dining room of the hotel in town. She said she thought she had caught cold. The second time was to be a repeat of the Crowells at his house and he hoped she would come. She said she had a great many important letters to write.

And after a while her divorce was granted, and she went

back to New York and reported that the Crowells' guest ranch had been quite good but, God, what a miserable wasteland the West was.

"The people live like characters in a Western movie. Nobody knows what goes on in the outside world."

Sue Kane asked, "Were there any men at the guest ranch waiting for divorces?"

"No. That happens very rarely. Most men are too busy to sit around Reno."

She shuddered. "You mean just women were there?"

What a child she was. After almost eight years of marriage she still thought of life as though it were a boarding-school dance. No men equaled no fun in Sue's figuring. But did anyone's figuring total out to a different answer?

"Just women," Rebecca said. "It was as ghastly as you imagine. Oh, I did meet one man."

Barker turned interestedly at that and waited. Sue wanted the man described.

Rebecca said, "He was big and sweet and artless as all outdoors. He did everything but call me 'ma'am.' "

"Was he a cowboy?"

"No, dear, he was a doctor—and a widower. He lived in a large and rather dusty house and though he didn't quite say 'Come and get it' when dinner was announced, that sort of sets the tone."

"Oh, perfectly. I can just see him and his house. He had pictures of horses all over and chandeliers made from wagon wheels and—"

Barker said, "Wait a minute. Let's not make fun of this fellow." He looked closely at Rebecca. "What was wrong with him, Becky?"

She smiled. "Nothing, Barks. He was a darling. And so unspoiled by reading or anything like that. He asked me what business Torrey Winton was in."

"Not really! He must have been clowning," Sue said.

"That's what I thought at first. But, no, he was very sincere. He'd never heard of Torrey."

Barker frowned at Rebecca. "I bet you liked the doctor right up to that moment."

"I'd only seen the man twice. Incidentally, that's all I ever saw him."

"And maybe that's too bad, Becky."

"What do you want me to do? Jump on a train and go right back to Reno? Listen, to make even a friendship work people have to have something in common."

"They don't have to have Torrey Winton in common, do they?"

Rebecca grinned. "Everybody's concerned about my future happiness. But does anybody go out and find me a four-bedroom apartment with lots of closets? No. My friends are just too romantic. I don't need a new husband. I need a new real-estate agent."

In due course Rebecca found an apartment and moved out of the brownstone house. The apartment had the required number of bedrooms and a good address. Miss Emmett was very brave about her room, though it was small and she did not care for the wallpaper pattern. The room assigned to Juanita and Vicki had no space for shelves, and Barrett was annoyed that a vast accumulation of games, puzzles and oddments had to be accommodated in his room. There was no place for a servant to sleep, so everyone had to grow accustomed to a stranger named Arthura who cooked, kept things tidy, and went home after dinner.

The children were beastly to Arthura, but one had to make allowances for the traumatic effects of the divorce. Juanita had taken it very emotionally. The two younger ones had not wept or asked searching questions, but surely their rudeness to Miss Emmett and their selfish disregard of responsibilities were manifestations of inner torments.

"You're going to learn to pick your clothes up off the floor and put away things you've taken out, because I'm not going to do it for you," Arthura told them. "Maybe you used to have a million servants, but it's just me now."

Rebecca wondered if Miss Emmett could be prevailed upon to carry back to the kitchen such objects as Coke bottles and fruit peelings and discarded candy wrappers that infuriated Arthura when she encountered them in the living room. It would be lovely if Miss Emmett would somehow persuade the children to attend to these chores themselves, but that was out of the question. It was years since Miss Emmett had given a firm order or exercised any form of discipline. Strange, because in earlier days Rebecca had had to say a dozen times a week, "Good heavens, Miss Emmett, try to remember that they're only babies."

She found herself going to Jennie Frost with all her problems. One couldn't burden one's lawyer with every small perplexity, but there were no rules against consulting his wife.

Jennie said, "Sure, Juanita has been hurt by the divorce. She's the sensitive one. It hasn't bothered the others, Rebecca. Between your adoring permissiveness and Torrey's notion that kids are for laughs, Vicki and Barrett have always been . . . well, they've always been . . . What's the affectionate word for 'monsters'?"

"Jennie, really, they're darlings, but the domestic crisis has definitely put a mark upon them. I want to be lenient and sympathetic, but still—"

"Be lenient and sympathetic with poor Arthura. She's working herself to death for you. Get an extra girl to give her a hand."

"Why, I couldn't afford that."

"Oh, stop. Bill told you that you can afford anything

you want. He was prepared to be tough with Torrey on the settlement, but Torrey gave you damned near everything he had."

"Just the same, I have to be careful. Whatever I have has to last forever, you know. I can't earn a living, and there'll be no more money coming in and—"

Jennie hooted. "Except from stocks and bonds and the rentals on some of Doc's properties. The trouble with you is that you never handled money before. You don't know whether you're rich or poor. Let me be the first to tell you that you're not poor."

"You're the second. Bill made a big speech about my finances when I turned down the apartment that I liked better than the one I took."

"You were silly to turn that lovely place down."

"But the price was wicked. What I have is expensive enough."

"Oh, Becky, wake up. You haven't a worry in the world. Spend your money, give your kids a good belting, and be happy ever after."

"Happy, Jennie?"

"So okay, you're still in love with Torrey Winton. Learn to live with it. It won't get worse and it may get better."

Twice that month Rebecca saw Torrey, once by accident. She was in the Stork Club with the Bensons and Mel Gardner, who had produced *Husband to Cornelia*. Torrey was sitting beside an elderly, fox-faced woman whose white hair had been rinsed in blossom pink. Rebecca recognized her from photographs in newspapers and magazines. She was Anna Pemberton Mayce, a best-selling author whose latest novel was so momentous that Torrey had consented to return once more to Hollywood to star in the screen version.

Rebecca watched him for some time as he and Miss

Mayce talked. She was reminded of the day Torrey had taken her to the battlefields outside Paris. He had talked to strangers with that same rapt concentration that had never been given to her. She remembered that she had felt deserted and forgotten. But it hadn't been true—not then.

Torrey's eyes strayed at last to surrounding tables, and he saw her. He spoke a brief apology to his guest and came to stand for a moment at Rebecca's side. He brought his wonderful smile and a bright word for everyone, and then he was gone again.

There was no way to accept that he belonged at that other table, that he would not return to sit with her and their old friends, and that this was the way life would be for as long as life lasted.

The following week she met him for luncheon.

"Was there anything special you wanted to talk about, Torrey?"

"Of course not," he said, reproachfully. "I just want to keep in touch with you."

She led the conversation to what she judged as safe ground. The new plays, Barker Kane's winning of the Pulitzer prize, Torrey's projected trip to Hollywood.

"Would you believe Miss Mayce is almost seventy?" he asked her. "She has the most brilliant, most dynamic mind imaginable. We talked of what the screen writer must do with the book and of how flawless the casting must be and of a dozen other relevant matters."

Rebecca smiled at him. "Illustration Number One: Freedom is not necessarily a pretty young girl in the bedroom."

He nodded. "That's what I wanted you to understand all along, Becky dear. More often freedom is a strictly professional conversation that would bore one's wife, or it's a bridge game that unexpectedly continues till dawn. It can even be a walk down Fifth Avenue at three o'clock in the morning with explanations to no one, or it can be a sudden impulse to eat spaghetti at Rocco's instead of feeling duty-bound to go home for dinner."

She felt herself possessed by a sudden hard, cold anger. "May I remind you that freedom is always gained because someone else was willing to lie down and die?"

He looked at her with sour displeasure. "You didn't die for my freedom, Rebecca. You are very much alive and you're a hell of a lot better off financially than I am."

"Oh, lucky me."

"At least you don't have to work in Hollywood. Why do you think I took that deal?"

"Because Miss Mayce wrote a part that will be great for you."

"And because I need the money."

"Do you think you were overcharged for the use of my services?"

"I set the price myself. I thought if it were high enough it would cure you of self-pity. But nothing helps, does it, Rebecca? You're determined to make a career of your sad, sad story."

"You're without mercy."

"No, only without patience toward your attitude. You see, I happen to think that marrying me brought you a very good life. Had I dropped dead last winter you would now be speaking of all the marvelous things I did for you. But I didn't drop dead, so I'm a bastard. Nothing I ever did for you counts. I cheated you of a widow's veil and you'll never forgive me for that."

"I'm not even going to answer."

"Of course not. You can't answer. I understand you, Rebecca. You want a nice, clean-cut bitter sorrow, and all I want is to meet you occasionally for lunch at Twenty-One."

"Do you really believe that we can meet and talk naturally and act like old friends?"

"Yes."

"Then I had better tell you that I have no old friends who wouldn't have asked me an hour ago how the children are."

"I know how the children are. I spoke to Miss Emmett this morning. Didn't she tell you that I'm visiting them on Sunday?"

"I haven't seen Miss Emmett today. I was at the hairdresser's." He had caught her off balance. She had responded without thinking and she felt her face grow hot with the anguish of having revealed that before meeting him she had rushed to have her hair done.

He made nothing of it. He said, "She mentioned a new school. What's the story on that?"

"Vicki made friends with a child in our building who goes to a school that sounds a lot less stuffy than Mrs. Fielding's. Vicki wanted to change over, so I let her. I want her to be happy."

"I just wondered."

"You never wondered about schooling before."

"Frankly, I was searching for conversational material for Sunday's visit. A Sunday father has to have something to talk about. Would you like more coffee?"

"I guess not."

"Then it must be time to go." He turned to signal the waiter.

Rebecca wished she had accepted the second cup of coffee. Now he would settle her in a taxi, smile at her, and walk away. She could have delayed the moment.

She said, "Oh, speaking of school—I'm taking courses in American history and music appreciation."

"Are you really? That's wonderful." He had the waiter's attention now. He glanced at his bill and signed it. He helped Rebecca with her coat, and they left the restaurant. "Will I see you on Sunday?"

"No. I'm sorry. Good luck to you in Hollywood."

"Thank you. Do you need a cab?"

She said that she did.

How had it all come to this? How could you have a marriage, a home and three children with a man, and then drive away from him in a taxicab without even asking who would pack his clothes or where he would be living in Hollywood?

She turned and through the rear window looked back at Torrey. A few steps from the restaurant he had encountered someone he knew. She saw him standing, bold and glorious, laughing in the sunlight.

Here was something worth considering, she thought: Again and again she had told God Himself that she loved Torrey Winton and because she had not feared or hesitated to tell Him, she knew it was the truth. She loved Torrey tenderly, devotedly, passionately. Why, then, did it torture her to see him happy?

Flower lay on Zoltan's bed and thought about Barrett Winton. Zoltan was rewriting a scene which would be placed in rehearsal in the morning. Soon she would be called upon to translate it, type it several times, and deliver the new version to the director, the producer, the leading lady and to the star, Mr. Barrett Winton. The leading lady, she decided, could just possibly be offered a carbon. That would save some time and effort.

There was a happy nervousness inside of her as she thought of going to Barrett Winton's apartment. She would see where he lived and how he lived. She would see him. It was an hour now since today's rehearsal had ended. An hour since she had spoken to him. The moment the scene was out of the typewriter she would leap into a taxi and— No. She would make her other stops first, keeping alive the pleasure of anticipation. Besides, there was a chance that Barrett might invite her in for a drink, and she would be more at ease if she had already attended to everything else. She cautioned herself against disappointment. In all likelihood Barrett would simply take the pages, thank her, and say good night. He thought of her as Zoltan's secretary. And, of course, she was Zoltan's secretary—but she was more.

When the play had been accepted for Broadway production she had mentioned to Zoltan that translators were given respectful credit for their work. Zoltan had smiled at her. "Sweetheart, be sensible. Your name is not as good for our purposes as my cousin's name. Who are you? A secretary. Who is my cousin? A professor of ancient history at the university."

"But translation is an art in itself. He couldn't have done this."

"So who will know? I like that a professor did the translation. We gain no dignity with a secretary's biography in the program notes. And if you are thinking of money, my darling, you know what I have is yours always, especially when I am dead. You can be patient. You are very young and I am an old man."

Flower had said no more, though she knew that even if the play were a tremendous success Zoltan would not buy her so much as a coat with a fur collar. As for rewarding her in his will—why, Zoltan had never married because he begrudged every penny spent on anyone but his widowed sister, her daughters and the children of those daughters. Flower knew what names would be in his will, and it was a matter of indifference to her. As the child of fifth-rate opera singers she had never known luxury or dreamed of security. She had dreamed only of graduating from a secretarial school so that her father would stop telling her that convents had been invented to save big, awkward girls from becoming perpetual burdens to their parents.

She had been Zoltan's secretary for six months when, on a jaunt to one of the film festivals, he had discovered that her English was admirably fluent. He already knew that her French, German and Italian were perfect and that the languages of eastern Europe were those of her childhood. Her facility with English set him to remembering a half-finished play that he had once thought could find favor with an American producer. Sometime during the completion of the last act Flower became Zoltan's mistress, but the only thing that surprised her was that a New York producer actually signed a contract for the play. She had considered it shamefully derivative. It had a fantasy theme, and the premise was that a modern-day Olympics swimmer is transported back into the world of ancient Greece. Entertaining, perhaps, but scarcely original. The play would provide an opportunity to see New York, and Flower regarded that as its chief asset.

She looked across the hotel room at Zoltan as he sat working out the new dialogue. He was a meaty man with a thick thatch of yellow-gray hair. He could not have been appealing in youth, she thought. But always he had been clever. Not brilliant. Clever. In the past she had philosophically recognized that a young girl who is not pretty cannot be demanding, and she had, with good common sense, evaluated the importance of all they had brought to each other. She was an excellent secretary and a youthful, agreeable bedmate who did not expect gifts or excursions to expensive places. He was a figure of some distinction in the European theater, and through his activities her life was enriched. She enjoyed the mechanics of play construction and the novelty of belonging, more or less, to some man. The arrangement had been practical and satisfactory enough till she had seen Barrett Winton.

Now, lying on Zoltan's bed, the sight of Zoltan sickened her. She thought of getting up and going to her own room, but her dress was drip-drying in Zoltan's shower, and she could not walk across the hall in her bra and petticoat. It had seemed such a good idea, coming in from the hot and dirty streets, to wash that comfortable sleeveless dress so it would be fresh for the evening. She had thought to nap while it was drying, while Zoltan was working, but now she was not in the mood for a nap. She wanted to think about Barrett Winton.

Strange, that she had not been in love before. She had credited her steely self-discipline for the unconcern with which she had gazed upon young, good-looking men she could not have. She knew now that they had not really interested her. With Barrett it was different. Everything about him interested her: what he said, what he wore, what he did. She had even stared fascinatedly at his mother, who had come by the theater at a lunch break to carry him off to some snobbish restaurant. What a life that woman had had, Flower thought enviously. She had been the wife of the fabulous Torrey Winton. But, of course, she had had the advantage of being beautiful. Even now, at her age, the mark of beauty remained upon her, so that men as young as the producer and the director spoke charmingly to her and looked at her with wistful resignation, accepting that in their part of the century there existed nothing quite as wonderful as she had been.

Flower wished she knew why Barrett's parents had been divorced. Neither had married again. She had made inquiries. All things that had to do with Barrett were significant. And now she was thinking of something she did not care to think about. The quality of Barrett's performance. He played with considerable poignancy, considerable theatrical effectiveness, but only spottily. Up to now there had been no vigorous, consistent building of character. Well, but this took time. It was what rehearsals were for. He would develop the role magnificently before the week was out.

Still, it was frightening to hear the director bestowing praise upon a mere worthy intent. In the absence of actual accomplishment a director perhaps could do no more than implant confidence in an actor and pray that something sturdy and fine would grow. Of course, that would be done only when a director was convinced that the actor was giving all he had to give. With Barrett it was different. He was still in the process of experimenting with the possibilities of the role. A solid characterization would evolve, and then he and the director, working together, would polish and hone till something spectacularly keen emerged. Had Barrett sensed yet that a vital simplicity would be—

"I think I have a better scene here now," Zoltan said. "Come read it."

Flower left the bed and walked over to the writing table. She picked up the penciled pages and read them attentively. Zoltan watched her. He liked to observe her reactions as she read. He strained forward, waiting for a smile or a flutter of an eyelid. At last she looked up from the scene.

"Who do you suppose they—the people at the theater—think does the translations of these new scenes?" she asked. "Do you imagine that they think you have your cousin, the professor, in the typewriter case?"

Zoltan frowned. "How is it? How is the scene?"

"Much as it was before. I told you what the director requested. He said to me and I explained to you that he hoped for a note of sincerity from the girl."

"I changed her speeches."

"Not meaningfully."

"So you are a playwright and a critic now?"

"You asked my opinion."

"Out of courtesy. Translate it and type it. It is very good."

It was even better after Flower had translated it. She called at the director's apartment first, and he asked her to wait while he read the new dialogue. He introduced Flower to his wife, and the two women sat on a terrace and smiled at each other and at the East River for an agonizing fifteen minutes. Once the hot weather had been mentioned, there was little else to say.

The director liked what he had read. "Tell Zoltan it's great. I've never worked before with a fellow I couldn't

197

talk to, but he's caught my meaning. I guess I have you to thank for that."

"Zoltan is very perceptive," she said.

"He really got just what I think the scene needed. There's a certain tenderness now, a certain believability . . ." He fell silent and stood looking thoughtfully at Flower. "It's just great," he said.

She went to the producer's apartment next. A servant accepted the envelope. Norah lived in a hotel and she was not in her room, so her envelope was left at the desk. And then it was time to take the last envelope to Barrett.

Barrett had chosen an apartment building old enough to offer spacious rooms and a sort of autumnal elegance to its tenants. Flower was pleased at this evidence of his good taste. The Negro man who admitted her seated her in the living room among some very nice pieces of furniture and a great many books. He disappeared and, after a moment, returned and asked her to step into the dining room.

Barrett was still at table and he had guests. Flower saw a middle-aged couple and a young girl with glistening black hair and sharp nails that glittered like flame points in the candlelight.

"Very kind of you to come," Barrett said. "I thought perhaps you'd have coffee with us."

He and the other gentleman were standing and smiling at her. She was overwhelmed by this show of good manners. Why had Barrett not simply ordered his man to take the envelope from her? Why? Because Barrett was rare and wonderful and blessed with the kindly impulses of a young prince. That was why.

The introductions were interesting. Mr. and Mrs. Barker Kane. Wait till she told Zoltan of meeting Barker Kane, the American playwright Zoltan most admired. The black-haired girl was Judith Foster, the darling of the mandarin set with her records and night-club appearances.

Flower drank coffee and wondered if Barrett were sleeping with Judith Foster. But why did that matter? The only thing that would be useful to know was the answer to this: Were they in love with each other or were they in love with sleeping together? That was always the most important question.

When Flower left, Barrett walked to the door with her.

"I hope you will like Zoltan's new conception of the scene," she said.

"I'm sure I will." She was almost out the door when he stopped her. "Wait a minute. May I ask you something?"

"Of course."

"Is Zoltan satisfied with the way I'm developing the character?"

He spoke with no more intensity than any conscientious actor might, but she saw the terror in his eyes. She saw that he was aware that a playwright may furnish a splendid script and the director conceive the perfect interpretation, but that, in the end, the starlit glimmer that hypnotized an audience must be radiated by the actor.

She said, "Zoltan has said nothing, so he must be pleased."

"Well, is that his way? Does he usually speak only if he is disappointed or—"

"You must remember that Zoltan has never before sat at rehearsals where he did not understand what was being said." She was ashamed to have offered such flimsy assurance, but he did not seem to notice. He had something he wished to say.

"You know, this is a more difficult character to play than most people would realize. It's a gimmicky thing, a trick that has to be negotiated with uncommon skill."

She nodded. "Yes, you have described it exactly. I knew yesterday that you understood, when you said if it were played lightly the meaning would be lost and that if it were played too heavily it would become comic strip. There is a deceptive frosting of nonsense on a very profound story, and you have observed that. So the key to how it must be played is happily in your possession."

He smiled and gave her a friendly hug. "I'm a constant, worry-type actor," he said. "But you've made me feel better. Thanks."

And though he was lost and casting aimlessly about for the way to play his part, he had shown her how to play hers. He had spoken to her trustingly, had thrown his arm carelessly about her, and he had taken the good, big girl in the drip-dry dress as his friend.

After that, she watched him even more carefully at rehearsals and she watched how the director dealt with him. She weighed the gentle, good-natured suggestions that were offered to Barrett against the sharp, sometimes sarcastic remarks that were thrown at the man who played the second lead. It was clear which actor had been judged capable of improving his performance.

Sometimes the director sat beside Flower as a scene was being played, and on his face she saw doubt and discouragement. He would speak to her. "Ask Zoltan if he will give Barrett a different line there. I think the one he has is too subtle." Or, "Explain to Zoltan that we need as much sympathy as we can get for our character. Ask him to take out the 'fallen warrior' speech. Americans might not recognize its irony."

Flower knew what the director was saying. Barrett could not reach an audience, could not establish that mystic rapport which enables a spectator to experience the emotions of the artist so vividly that there is no possibility of misunderstanding. And yet Barrett's technical skill was undeniable. He was master of a fine proficiency from which, when he needed fire, there flew only chill sparks of intelligence.

Flower reflected bitterly on the incident of Norah approaching Barrett during a cigarette break to ask, "What's the matter with the message bit? I feel I'm doing something wrong."

"Yes," Barrett told her. "You're just holding out your hand as though the boy were delivering the evening paper. Everybody who receives a personal message has some concern, or at least interest, as to its contents. Now, since you are thinking nothing, naturally your eyes are showing nothing, and there is no reason for me to hurry to you. The crossover becomes just a stage maneuver without any validity."

And when the scene was played again, Barrett's eagerness to be at the girl's side as she read the message seemed completely logical. Flower sighed. He could not have brought forth anything as arresting and provocative as the tiny glint of misgiving that had fluttered in Norah's eyes at sight of that message. But he had known what was required. He could explain what was required. He could not do what was required.

She had gathered by now the complete history of Barrett Winton's theatrical career. He had taken two years of training with a highly regarded drama coach, then had done summer theater followed by a tour in a national company. After that, he had been guest star playing Romeo with a very fancy group of big names who were wealthy enough to spend time improving the public taste. Flower thought it almost too precious that the exquisite Frederick and Doris Benson had played minor roles to Barrett's Romeo. From that experience he had gone to Broadway and had been in five plays. This was his first starring role, if one discounted Romeo. Flower had read his reviews. He had been rated as low as "adequate" and as high as "pleasing." A narrow range, again if one discounted Romeo. Here, one could read that "Mr. Winton has a nice talent but he has set himself a task reserved for genius." Or, "Barrett Winton is handsome and young. If he has other qualifications for playing Romeo they have escaped my notice." Or, "Mr. Winton is so splendid that one is dazzled by the dream of what he will accomplish when more experienced."

And Flower sat day after day in the theater at Zoltan's side and she watched Barrett Winton's rehearsals. And all of her that was mother wanted to weep and all of her that was huntress quivered in anticipation.

She brought him coffee and she counted how many cigarettes he smoked so that she would know when his beautiful gold case was almost empty. Sometimes he came down from the stage to study the work of others as they played a scene. She would go sit beside him, manufacturing a question from Zoltan. Did Barrett think the new curtain speech was stronger? Did Barrett feel that the Olympic-torch bit was too solemn now? Always he would stop looking at the actors up on the stage and turn to her with desperate, whispered questions of his own. How did his performance look to her? Had Zoltan said anything? Anything at all? Could she get Zoltan to join him in his argument about the swim trunks?

"There's no reason why I couldn't be wearing a bathrobe." Barrett glanced annoyedly toward the director. "He says the character wouldn't think of grabbing a bathrobe at that moment. I say that if I have to play in trunks the whole damned scene will suffer. People in the audience will be asking each other, 'Who does he think he is? Mr. America?' "

"Actually, Barrett, since you have such a fine physique you should not object to—"

"Well, I do object. Will you just ask Zoltan to vote for the bathrobe? Oh, one more thing. Would Zoltan give me a line when Andutius exits? I don't care what the line is. It's just awkward that I don't even say good-bye."

The director was quite willing to humor Zoltan. If the playwright believed that the script was enhanced by a few additional words, that was perfectly acceptable. However, he was troubled by the idea of the bathrobe.

"I've sort of banked on serving up our hero practically nude," he said. "We haven't got much else going for us, you know."

Flower did not smile at his coarse little joke. She was aware that he was turning something over in his mind.

"Look, Flower, we're in trouble, and I think Zoltan should know it. Barrett just isn't making it, and here's what we must consider: the reorientation of the entire play, so that the power of it is divided between Norah and Phil. I don't know how I could convince Barrett to stay after the heart had been taken out of him, but I'm a pretty good salesman. I want you to tell all this to Zoltan so he can be thinking it over, then tonight you two come up to my apartment and we'll have a good talk about it."

Flower said, "Yes, I will tell him. I will tell him right now." She stood still and silent for a moment. "I will tell him," she said again.

She walked to a seat in the third row where Zoltan was devouring a candy bar. She dropped down beside him and said, "I have something very important to say. Please listen carefully." With a sidelong glance she made certain that the director would be eagerly watching Zoltan's initial reception of the proposition. "Zoltan, I have not been feeling well. This morning I went to a doctor. There will have to be tests and further examinations. He said I may be seriously ill."

Zoltan gazed at her in open-mouthed horror.

"Actually my life may be in danger."

Zoltan gasped and dropped the candy bar.

"I have to go into the hospital this evening, and it may be that I shall not come out alive."

Zoltan's face twisted in anguish.

"Don't speak," she said. "Please, for a moment, say nothing and do not reach for my hand. I could not endure a sentimental gesture. Just let us sit here quietly together. Think deeply, my love, of all that we have been to each other."

Zoltan thought deeply. His eyes blinked emotionally at her through the thick lenses that were always smeared with finger marks. He looked stricken and confused.

So far, so good. Now! "I don't know why I should lie to you," she said, briskly. "None of what I've just said is true. The fact is that I'm tired of this whole business of rehearsals and translations. You work me too hard, and I'm going to leave you. I want my plane ticket from you right now. I'm going home tonight."

Zoltan let out an angry roar and jumped from his seat into the aisle. The actors stopped their idle conversations and turned to stare. The director began moving swiftly toward Flower between the upturned seats.

"You wring my heart with a cruel, vicious lie," Zoltan shouted, "then you calmly tell me you're leaving me. Well, you can't do it. I will call the police. I will tell them you are crazy. They will put you in an asylum for the insane. You cannot go. You cannot go home until I take you there."

"Please," she said, softly. "It is harmful for you to get so infuriated."

"Don't talk to me, you blackmailing bitch. And don't

think you're going to leave me. I won't give you your plane ticket and I won't give you a penny. You'll stay right here and do what you're told."

He was bellowing now and his face had crimsoned frighteningly. Flower placed her hand on his arm, but he shook it off. She looked at the director piteously.

"He was deeply shocked and saddened by your pessimism," she whispered. "Then when I outlined your suggestion regarding major script changes—well, this is the result. He's enraged."

"Now you ask strangers for help," Zoltan cried, throwing a venomous glance at the director. "If he gives you any money, I'll sue him. You told him you did the translation, didn't you? Maybe you told him you wrote the play!"

He stood trembling with fury. The director spoke soothingly, "Zoltan, Zoltan." But Zoltan only glared at him.

Flower said, "Please go away. I'm afraid no more can be mentioned of your ideas."

The director shook his head wearily. "Tell him to forget the whole thing. I don't want him to have a stroke."

"Yes, he's severely shaken. He said that he does not want a commercial success at the cost of his integrity. He says the purity of the play's structure must not be violated so that you may redistribute speeches to those you consider the most deserving actors."

The cast was still leveling its attention upon Zoltan, who stood breathing hard and muttering angrily.

"Just try to calm him down," the director said. He turned to the actors then, giving them his most charming, most boyish grin. "Quit wondering, kids," he said. "We'll never know what that was all about. Back to work. Let's have scene three."

Flower edged close to Zoltan and murmured, "Sit down,

my love. Please let me talk to you. I was only teasing. I would never leave you. Forgive your foolish girl for upsetting you."

"Shut your stupid mouth," he said. "There's a rehearsal in progress."

"But I must talk to you. Come to the lobby with me for a few minutes. I must explain or I shall be useless for the rest of the day. How can I concentrate on anything when I know I have wounded you?"

And with a sinking heart the director observed Zoltan leaving the theater. That's all I needed, he thought. A feud with the playwright.

In the lobby Flower slipped her arm through Zoltan's and gazed at him prayerfully. "Forgive me, darling, forgive me. It was all a woman's trick. I have felt neglected since we have been here. You are so absorbed in the play that I have felt unloved. I have brooded, and today I could stand my doubts no more. I had to test your love. I expected you to weep when I said I was dying. You did not weep. Then I threatened to leave and you became furious."

"You're an idiot," he said, not unkindly.

"I know. All women in love are idiots." She spoke then of the director. "He was an innocent bystander. He was not, I assure you, my champion. He admires you greatly. Will you shake hands with him? It is the only way an American can tell that he is liked."

They went back to their seats then, and the director was comforted by the sight of them. At the next break Flower approached him and said, "Zoltan does not wish any ill will to exist. He asks that you shake hands with him. This will signify that he has forgotten your shattering suggestions and that you will never urge them upon him."

"Oh, I'll take the Boy Scouts' oath."

So the two men shook hands and smiled at each other, and Flower laughed aloud. This was from joy at the reconciliation, she explained, and the director was rather surprised that she was that emotional. Afterward she went out and fetched a carton of iced coffee for Barrett. He looked so warm and tired.

"I read the 'dignity of wealth' speech differently that last time. Did you notice?"

"I noticed."

"Did you like it better?"

"I think that question should be addressed to the director."

"Please tell me how the speech sounded."

"It had a good ring, but he will stop you if you continue to read it that way."

"He'll stop me? Why? Wait. Don't answer. I know why. It's because when it's delivered that strongly it can't be topped and will take the edge off the exit speech. Right?"

"Right."

He looked at her with a sort of astonished respect. "How did you know that?"

She shrugged. "I have some theater knowledge."

"Yes, you have. When can I buy you a drink to even up on all your thoughtful cartons of coffee and packs of cigarettes?"

"Tonight."

"Great."

"I will be in my room at the hotel after half past ten. You call on the phone and I will come right down."

He took her to a small, rather elegant bar where a well-tailored young man sat at a piano and furnished the theme music for memories and regrets. They talked about the play and about theater in general. They drank iced gin with a splash of quinine water, and the hour grew very late.

"The theater," Flower said, "has inspired more devotion than any other trivial thing in the world."

"The theater is trivial?"

"Of course, and do not tell me of the pleasure it has brought to countless millions. The same can be said for roller coasters or even chewing gum."

"I imagined you to be a person who loved the theater."

"I intend, in one way or another, to be associated with it all my life. I do love the theater, but not blindly. Never will I give my time, energy or thought exclusively to the theater. It is not worthy of consuming one's complete being."

"It isn't a question of worthiness."

"Yes, everything on earth is a question of worthiness. Really, do you think that to love the theater means denying oneself long walks in the country and reading quietly beside a fireplace and perhaps painting a picture or building a very large doghouse for one's favorite Dalmatian?"

He grinned at her. "You're my favorite Dalmatian."

"I'm not Dalmatian at all. I just happen to have been placed in a school in Zara for a year, and I like those lovely spotted animals that are called Dalmatians. Some day I shall own several of them, and I shall be an authority on the theater, and I shall walk and read and paint. One uses the theater if one can. One does not die for the theater. My God, what a lot I must have drunk to babble on like this."

Barrett lighted a cigarette and narrowed his eyes at her through the smoke. "I am considering the idea of buying you a spotted dog. However, I shall expect in return some of your expert knowledge on theater. For a starter I shall ask: What the hell is the matter with me? I'm no more solid than I was on the first day of rehearsal."

"Nonsense," she said. "You have come a long way since then."

"Don't kid me. I need help." He set his glass down in precisely the same wet ring it had occupied before he had raised it. He said, "I think I should have kicked this show during the first week of rehearsal. It's a little late to do it now."

"You must not even think of it."

He looked at her coolly. "Why not? Why must I continue the misery if the theater is so trivial?"

"Because *you* are not trivial. You could not do an irresponsible thing like that and live with it. You would be tortured by the knowledge that you had forsaken the producer and the director and Zoltan and the actors and all the people who trusted you. In the end, it would kill you to remember what you had done."

"You've got to be a witch," he said. "You just know too much."

She smiled at him. "Walk me home, please. I am outrageously full of gin."

"But you have not told me why I'm not comfortable in this play."

"Have you ever been comfortable in a play, Barrett?"

He stared down at the shiny black table where the lights of the bar were reflected in muted blue abstracts. The well-tailored young man at the piano played "Dancing in the Dark," and there was a sadness in the elegant little bar.

"No," Barrett said. "I have never been. Why is that? Tell me."

"Not now. Not tonight. It is not a thing I would say when I have been drinking because it may be a thing I would not say if I were sober. Do you understand?"

"I understand that there is something you can tell me."

"I am not sure that I can tell you. Please take me back to the hotel."

She did not sleep that night. She thought of Barrett. She knew what he had seen across the small table in the bar. A girl no one but Zoltan had ever desired, and Zoltan's reasons had not been entirely erotic. But I have offered Barrett something that no one else ever thought he needed. Women have assumed that, as Torrey Winton's son, he is strong and secure. I am the first who has bothered to notice that this is not true, and he is aware of me. This far I have come. He will call for me tonight. Or tomorrow night at the latest. He will not rest till he hears what I have to say.

At breakfast she was very cross with Zoltan, and it was a bad day at rehearsal. Norah had been for a fitting and hated her costumes. She told Flower that she doubted the authenticity of the Grecian designs and that Zoltan had better look carefully at the sketches. When this message was relayed to him, Zoltan said that he trusted the producer to hire a reputable costumer and that he refused to argue with anyone about women's clothes.

Somewhere in the discussion of what was to be worn by whom in which scene the director remarked that he still wasn't sold on the idea of Barrett wearing a bathrobe over the swim trunks.

"Zoltan insists on the bathrobe," Flower said.

"He insists, does he?" The director, she noted, was not in a very good mood himself that morning. "I don't remember, young lady, that the Dramatists' Guild contract gives a playwright any power to control the costuming."

"I control the costuming when it comes to that bathrobe," Barrett said. "I'll wear it or, by God, you'll get yourself another boy."

Something grim and disagreeable flickered in the eyes of the director, but Flower spoke before he did.

"I grant you that perhaps the playwright cannot control the costuming, but please, I beg of you, do not make an issue of it today. Zoltan is convinced that the bathrobe should be worn. And he was so sick all last night that I hope you will not upset him this morning."

"Oh, for Christ's sake." The director walked away, mumbling that he would never again touch a show that didn't come fully equipped with a young, healthy playwright who spoke English.

All day long there were nervous little arguments and tense moments of indecision.

The stage manager winked at Flower. "Everybody's putting on their New Haven shudders," he said. "At this point people always think they're connected with a turkey."

"Well, the odds are, aren't they?"

"Oh, sure," he said, cheerfully. "But you have to figure it this way: It isn't your money. And what would you rather be doing with your time?"

"So," Zoltan said when Flower rejoined him, "you failed with the star, so you'll try for the stage manager now."

"It gives me much pleasure to see that you are jealous of me, but you are the one who taught me that the success of a play often depends on keeping the star happy. For that reason I have catered to Barrett Winton and made an errand girl of myself. As usual, I expect no gratitude from you. As for the stage manager—this one happens to know many things concerning the art and subtlety of the theater. For instance, he has just said something to me which is worthy of your consideration."

Zoltan smiled indulgently. "Perhaps then you will tell me what he has said."

"Yes. He said that he hopes Mr. Winton wears a bathrobe and does not appear in the second scene wearing only swim trunks."

"Oh, my God, what do I care what anybody wears? Costumes are for somebody else to worry about."

"Not if a story point or a characterization you have worked for is involved. The stage manager suggested that if our character walks into a press conference almost naked then he is not the shy, retiring fellow that you have been at such pains to delineate in the rest of the play."

Zoltan's fat lips puckered thoughtfully. He squinted his eyes in the effort to get a better look at this keen young stage manager.

"Zoltan, he is right. This particular piece of costuming could injure the delicate characterization you so brilliantly created. Even the Dramatists' Guild would agree, I think." On her pad she drew a swift sketch of a terry-cloth bathrobe. "Put your name under this, Zoltan, so the director will know what it is that you demand in the scene."

When she met Barrett that evening she was able to say that the matter of the bathrobe was settled. They walked through the hot, sticky summer night to the small bar and sat listening to the pensive piano and drinking their chilled gin.

"What was it you could not say last night to me?"

She said, "Something that perhaps I should not say tonight, but I have thought it over and decided you should know. It is simply this: An actor—and my discourse deals only with actors and not with large-bosomed girls or ex-truck drivers who make a living in the entertainment world—an actor needs many blessings. Among such blessings are inventiveness, imagination and practiced taste. The actor needs a fine voice, intensive training, authority of bearing, a sharp mind and a respectable education. You are asking yourself if, in my opinion, you lack any of these requisites. The answer is no. You have them all. Then why have you never been comfortable in this or any other role? I will tell you. You lack what every actor must have. Euphemistically it is called 'star quality.' I will tell you it is plain, unvarnished conceit."

The piano played "Where or When," and Barrett Winton looked across the table at a big girl with a high-bridged nose and the eyes of a Tatar.

"Barrett," she said softly, "never have you read a part and believed you could play it better than any other man alive. Never have you accepted a role without wondering if it were offered you because you are Torrey Winton's son. Never has your play failed without your suspecting that you harmed it. Are these things not true?"

He could not speak. He nodded, and the blue lights of the bar glittered in his wet eyes.

"You have not the self-esteem that convinces an actor and his audience that he is second to none. Conceit alone is contemptible and useless, but when it has been added to ability and a long list of other tremendous values, then it becomes the master power. Your father has it. Every actor whose name is remembered has had it. You possess every element of theater greatness, but you do not believe you are great."

"No, I don't," he said, and he smiled sadly.

"And I am not telling you that you must believe it or that you can believe it. This is not a pep talk or a sermon or a lecture. I am but making a statement of what I know about you, Barrett Winton."

He sat studying his hands as he tore a pack of matches to pieces. And presently he walked her back to the hotel.

Then all of a sudden it was New Haven. Zoltan was displeased with the sets. Norah's wig for the Grecian scenes hadn't arrived. The director was suffering from a bad cold. The producer was disturbed by a report that the New York advance sale on tickets was very unsatisfactory. A

213

member of the cast who played a modern-day sports writer and a slave in ancient Athens had been in an automobile accident and was hospitalized. The stage manager stepped into the small dual role. Phil was shaken by this substitution, claiming that the stage manager's face was essentially comic and that he, Phil, ran the danger of having his most powerful scene punctuated by chuckles from the audience.

It was a dreary dress rehearsal without verve or pace. Norah had a speech in a Grecian scene that began, "Oh, fearful night of menace . . ."

The director flinched.

The rehearsal limped to an end at a quarter past one in the morning. The director, with a sore throat and a rising fever, addressed the company from his seat in the orchestra. "Go get some sleep. Be back here at two this afternoon. We're going to work on this right up to curtain time."

"I don't believe we have a success," Zoltan said, as he and Flower left the theater.

She didn't reply. Her mind was on Barrett. She had watched only him. Her eyes had burned with pitying tears. His attempt to infuse warmth into the character of the Olympics swimmer had been heartbreaking. His final effort to give his Grecian scenes a heroic quality without alienating the sympathy of mere humans in the audience fell with deathly emptiness, reaching neither heroes nor commonplace men. Flower had suffered torments for him, though she had known that a successful Barrett Winton was a man who would not remember her name.

The show closed in New Haven after one performance. The local theatrical coverage had been merciless in its treatment of Barrett. The New York publications that had sent reviewers to the opening scorned to print more than a line or two, but in each case the brief report included a sneering judgment of the star. Even so, the show might have come into New York as scheduled. It was a shock to producer, director, playwright and cast to learn that Barrett Winton was ill, too ill for even a second performance in New Haven.

In the dark early hours while others had slept, Flower had been awake. She had left her room and walked upstairs. In her nightgown and pink cotton kimono she had moved stealthily along the hotel corridor till she had come to the door she sought. She had turned the knob and the door had opened.

Barrett was lying on the bed, a half bottle of whisky on the table, the newspapers strewn upon the floor. His gaze rested upon her without surprise.

She lay down beside him and took him in her arms. He wept, and she held him close. She told him to trust her, to borrow strength from her, and to believe that no one had ever cared for him as she cared. She promised that acting was not all, and she reminded him that one must not die for the theater. She assured him that he would not have to face the company again or play another performance. She would answer all questions and deal with all problems. She urged him to depend on her because there was nothing she would not and could not do for him.

She stopped talking then and placed her mouth upon his. It was, she thought, an oversimplification to say that all needs were one; still it would be a great mistake to let him suppose that there was any need with which she was unfamiliar.

$\mathcal{T}$*he tall, polite* Negro stood listening, chauffeur cap in hand, as she told him that she did not have the key to the Potter place.

"My mother's not here right now. She uses the parlor for her office and she has lots of keys there, but I don't know which belongs to what."

"I see."

She gazed past him, admiring the automobile under the trees near the Morelands' house. It was black, and it looked both expensive and mysterious. It would be an adventure just to get a closer look at it and at its passengers.

"I'll go explain," she said, and flew through the crisp, golden leaves that were ankle-deep in the front yard. The chauffeur walked sedately behind her.

The automobile had a New York license and there was a mountain of luggage piled upon its roof. Four people sat waiting. She told them that her name was Rebecca and that she was the real-estate lady's daughter. She stared at the people in the automobile. They stared at her.

They saw a slender girl with bronze-flecked eyes and thick braids of glossy black hair coiled crown-shape on a lovely head. Mouth, soft and very red. Dark eyebrows sweeping gently upward in narrow, graceful wings.

She saw a Negro woman in a fine broadcloth coat and, at the woman's side, a bearded, blue-eyed Viking who held upon his lap two frolicsome terrier pups. As she stared, the man who had rung the bell climbed, chauffeur's cap and all, into the rear seat. Rebecca's eyes wandered forward to a fat female of advanced age whose white hair was short and wind-tossed. The female was smoking a cigarette, and though this was worthy of note, it was the driver of the car who captured Rebecca's attention. He was a young man, dark-eyed and yellow-haired, and it seemed to her that if he were neither king nor god then all standards must be revised to accommodate the fact that a man could be more beautiful than a lion.

The white-haired woman spoke, and her voice was astonishing because it was like melted gold, a heavenly contralto that could not have been expected to issue from that shapeless flesh. "I claim the privilege of a wayfarer," she said. She opened the car door and with surprising agility moved her great bulk into the roadway and stood with a commanding eye fixed upon Rebecca.

Rebecca did not understand immediately, but when she did, she led the woman into the house, watched her lumber up the stairs, and listened to the melodious voice complaining that, in today's world, consideration was shown only to automobiles. "No stop since Boston. If gasoline is not required, one simply travels on forever with no thought of human comfort."

Rebecca knew she should have darted upstairs ahead of the visitor and gotten one of those small, embroidered hand towels out of the linen chest. She also knew that good manners decreed her waiting patiently for the woman to come downstairs, but she hastened back to the automobile.

"The dogs are so cute," she said.

The Viking smiled at her and spilled the terriers upon the ground. He pulled himself out of the back seat and with long strides moved vigorously up the hill toward the main square, the dogs jumping and yapping in delight.

"Are they his or yours?" Rebecca asked the handsome young man.

"They're his."

"Oh, I just wondered."

"Don't you know where you could telephone your mother?"

"No." She had a sudden inspiration. "Why don't you come in the house and wait? I'd make some tea. Or maybe you'd like cider. The cider is really awfully good and—"

And at that moment Mother's shabby little car turned the Moreland corner. Simultaneously, the large figure of the white-haired woman emerged from the house. Mother's eyes indicated no puzzlement. Mother was rarely puzzled.

She said, "I'll get your key. Come along, Rebecca." And as they covered the few steps to the doorway, "What were you doing out at their automobile?"

"Apologizing that you weren't here."

"Nothing to apologize for. They were supposed to arrive late in the evening."

Rebecca watched from the window as Mother, Potter key firmly in hand, marched back to the strangers. She would instruct them to follow her. They didn't know where the Potter place was. It always amazed Rebecca when people rented a high-priced house without ever having bothered to look at it. Did they have deep faith in real-estate agents or a royal indifference to cost? She saw the big man and his dogs hurry to the automobile, and then everyone drove away. She returned to peeling potatoes and onions and preparing the grinder to receive what was left of Sunday's roast.

By the time Mother walked into the kitchen, dinner preparations were completed. She had not taken off her coat and she stood resting her thin shoulders against the wall. She said, "Don't you try cooking that hash. You always dry it out. I'm going to throw myself on the bed for a while and you wait with the cooking till I come down. It's too early to eat anyhow."

"I know. I was just getting things ready. Mother, why on earth do people rent a house here at this time of year?"

"It's only for two months. They want peace and quiet."

"Who are they?"

Mother's face hardened. "They're tenants, and don't ask any more questions. I've been on the go since six this morning." She walked away, shaking off the old brown coat as she went.

Why was she always so tired? Was it really hard work to ride around in a car and talk to people about real estate? Mother didn't stand on her feet all day like women in stores and she didn't do any housework. Rebecca always washed the dishes and made the beds, and one day a week Mrs. Hill came in to scrub the kitchen and bathroom and sweep the carpets. At night Mother did nothing but play solitaire.

I could do what she does all day and go dancing every evening, Rebecca thought. But there wasn't much opportunity for dancing. Talk was that in Boston there were places where the dancing never stopped. If I marry Norman, I'll get him to take me to Boston for the honeymoon. She thought about the new tenant in the Potter place. You wouldn't even have to ask a man like that to take you to Boston for the honeymoon. He'd think of it himself.

Norman came over about eight o'clock. He always came over about eight o'clock. He had a healthy complexion and good teeth, and he worked in the hardware store. Mother approved of Norman because he was in a hurry to get married. She had discouraged Norman's less serious-minded rivals by spreading word that Rebecca was practically engaged to him. This relieved Norman of competition and infuriated Rebecca.

220

Tonight, however, Norman was very interesting. "That fellow you rented the Potter place to—you know what he does for a living?"

Mother nodded. "He's an actor," she said.

Rebecca caught her breath. "An actor!"

Norman said, "That's what he is, all right. The chauffeur and cook came into the store just before we closed. Seems like she can't use anything much that other tenants have been using. She bought pots and pans and knives and strainers and all kinds of things, just as though no cooking's been done up there for years. Anyhow, I got talking to the chauffeur. He told me his boss is an actor."

"An actor!" Rebecca said again.

Mother looked at her chillingly. "Yes, an actor. What's so fine about that? It's just a way of making a living like anything else."

"That's right," Norman agreed. "There's a fellow with him who writes books, and he's going to start writing one while he's here. It's all about the South Seas and he's been there and knows everything about how the natives live and their ideas and habits and things like that."

Mother took her pack of cards from the office desk and went upstairs.

"Did the chauffeur tell you about the fat old woman, Norman?" Rebecca asked. "Who is she?"

A frown puckered Norman's smooth forehead. "I didn't quite get on to what he was saying about her. He mentioned that they had a lady with them, and then, you know, just so I wouldn't get a wrong impression, he said she was elderly. He said she was a coach. I don't know why he called her that. I just don't know."

"A coach?"

"That's what he said. Real strange people, I guess, the

whole bunch of them." Norman slid closer to her on the sofa. "Would you give me a little kiss, Rebecca?"

She gave him a little kiss. "What's the actor's name?"

"The chauffeur told me, but I forget. I'll find out for you. I'll find out everything about them that you want to know."

It seemed very odd to Rebecca that a man who claimed to love her knew so little about her. Did he really think that she would wait quietly for him to bring her scraps of information concerning such fascinating arrivals?

It was a long walk up to the Potter place. Rebecca paid scant attention to the flaming autumn trees as she walked. She had other matters on her mind. On all the Thursdays that Mother had gone to Allenville to check her listings she had never come home before six o'clock. Could full reliance be placed on this pattern? If so, then it was safe to accept an invitation to sit down and stay awhile. Would she see him? Would he be neighborly? It occurred to her that he might offer a drink. Actors lived dissolute lives. So did writers. Probably the trunk of their automobile had been packed with whisky. Or perhaps they had heard that old Mr. Driscoll sold it to the summer people when he got to know them well. No reason why he shouldn't sell it to autumn people. In any case, she would not accept a drink, no matter how they teased or pleaded. And how was she going to explain this visit? Mother was sure to be pretty grim about it, but the silver lining to Mother's constant weariness was her recent disinclination to scold or lecture.

The Potter house was large and Victorian, with pretentious turrets, towers and a hysterical superabundance of bay windows. It had five acres of land planted in stately trees and gardens. Mrs. Potter was always willing to rent it and would do so on a few days' notice, taking herself off very contentedly to some unnamed destination. Mother had never failed to find a summer tenant for the house, and Rebecca thought that perhaps now October was coming into style.

The door was opened by the chauffeur, who was wearing a black alpaca coat and looking very much like a butler today. He greeted her courteously.

"Hello," she said. "I've been sent up to see if everything's quite satisfactory."

"Oh, yes, Miss. Everything's just fine. Just fine."

"I don't suppose you'd mind my taking a look around the house."

"No, not at all. You go right ahead." He waited a moment, then smiled and closed the door.

She could have cried. It had been a mistake to use the word "around." The man had taken it to mean that she wished to inspect the surrounding acreage. She stood crestfallen and irresolute. Was there nothing to do but begin the long walk home?

She heard the thin barking of the terrier pups and she walked toward it across the lawn. The bearded Viking was leaning against a tree, watching her approach.

"Hello, pretty girl," he said.

She decided to be brisk and businesslike. "We've not had dogs here before. You won't let them destroy the planting, I hope."

"Don't you worry about anything," he said. "I'm going to replace those two oak trees they knocked down this morning."

She was startled. Oak trees? The little puppies?

He said, "They just wagged their tails, but unfortunately they were closer to the trees than they realized and— crash!"

She stared at him. "What really happened to the trees?" she demanded, sharply. "You can't tell me that those little puppies—"

"No, I can see that I can't tell you anything that would be fun to believe. I can see that right away. You're very earnest people up here. Very earnest."

"Oh, not always. We like jokes but—"

"But they mustn't be about death, religion or property." He paused to consider what he had said. "I'll take that back. I imagine that it's just property that's really sacred."

She was horrified. "Well, if you think we laugh at death and religion, you are very much in error."

He stood looking at her. "Incredible," he murmured. "Absolutely incredible." He whistled to the puppies then, and walked away.

These people were even more extraordinary than she had suspected. And they were outrageously rude. The servant had closed the door in her face. A guest was insufferably insulting. The host, if she encountered him, would no doubt aim a shotgun at her.

Idly she strolled past the old carriage house and what, long ago, had been the housekeeper's cottage. She could always say that she had been asked to report on whether or not passing motorists were littering the edge of the Potter place with bottles and rubbish.

She paused to listen. She was certain that she had heard a voice. Cautiously she moved toward a stand of maples and peered through them at a most curious sight. The white-haired woman was sitting on a tree stump. Her eyes were closed, her head tilted. She wore a black cape over her massive body, and on her lap she held a soup plate which she was using for an ash tray. It was heaped with cigarette stubs. At a great distance from her stood the beautiful young man, and he was speaking. Speaking to the white-haired woman? Impossible. He was saying such strange words. What could they mean? Why, he was acting, Rebecca realized with a shiver of delight. Acting. She made herself as invisible as she could among the maples and she tried not to breathe.

"If I may trust the flattering truth of sleep,
My dreams presage some joyful news at hand.
My bosom's lord sits lightly—"

"I told you to make me hear you," the woman said.
"Aren't you hearing me?"
"Yes, but you have raised your voice. I can hear any fool if he speaks loudly enough."

"And all this day an unaccustomed spirit
Lifts me above the ground with cheerful thoughts."

The woman shifted her weight on the tree stump. "Forget the dramatic values, please. We are, at the moment, working for projection and diction. Into 'Ah, me, how sweet is love' now, and I want it sublimely pianissimo. Don't forget that if you are able to gladden my ear here, under the conditions that I have set for you, you will have achieved something that will be part of you forever. You will force spectators in the farthermost balconies of the world's theaters to declare that you are without equal. Worth working for, wouldn't you say? Now make me hear it. Almost a whisper, boy, but make me hear it."

"Ah, me, how sweet is love itself possessed
When but love's shadows are so rich in joy!"

The woman, her eyes glowing, rose majestically from the tree stump, the soup plate splintering to death at her feet. Astonishingly, she said not a word, but strode toward the house, her head high, and a small, proud smile upon her lips.

The young man watched her out of sight, then turned and walked directly toward the place where Rebecca stood. "Excusable once," he said. "But don't make a habit of it."

She moved nervously from behind the maples. Her voice was shaky and very low. "I'm sorry. I just happened to—"

"Don't be sly and deceitful. You came to observe. Just don't do it again. You are trespassing, you know."

"Trespassing! Why, I've been a friend of Mrs. Potter's all my life. She came to the high school when I graduated. She—"

The young man said, "I'm overwhelmed by Mrs. Potter's interest in you. A pity that by renting the place to me she forfeited your right to visit at will. Inquire of that good businesswoman, your mother, if you have license to rove freely across these grounds during my tenancy."

Rebecca looked squarely into his eyes and said, "You and your friends and your servants are the nastiest people I've ever met."

She knew that vexation had flooded her face with the high color she detested. It did not help any to have the wind suddenly loose a drift of scarlet leaves that swirled about her, accenting the redness of her cheeks. In annoyance she swept a bright leaf from her black hair and thought that it must have been an exceedingly awkward gesture, for the young man was gazing at her fixedly.

"You could be a nuisance in more ways than one," he said.

"Oh, don't worry. I'm going."

She walked purposefully toward the back road and was surprised to find him following.

"This is a beautiful part of the country," he said. "And I suppose you know all the spectacular things there are to see. I'm inclined to forgive you for trespassing and spying. You look to me as though you would be the perfect guide for the visitor to New England."

"Do I?"

"I'm working very diligently, but I could find the time for a drive, if you could."

She said, "I don't go driving with strangers, and you mustn't skip any of your work for me. You'd only be disappointed."

He laughed lightly. "I think I have a disappointment for you. You misunderstood me."

"Misunderstood you?" She stopped walking to give him her full and angry attention. "Do you think I can't recognize the regular everyday thing that's in your mind? You weren't the one to discover that I'm a girl, you know. People right here noticed that some time ago. I've been invited to go driving before. Don't tell me I misunderstood you."

"All right. Then perhaps you misunderstood yourself. What do you think brought you up here today?"

It was a fair question. She tried to answer. "I don't know that I can tell you now. I wanted to talk to you, yes, but I didn't want to . . . I didn't expect that you'd be . . . well, like lots of other fellows. You looked so shining and so exciting and different from ordinary people."

He turned his glance away from her but not before she had seen that in some strange manner she had hurt him. When he spoke, his voice was soft and rather sad. He said, "I ask your pardon. It's true that you did not misunderstand me."

"No harm done."

"Oh, yes, Rebecca. Much harm. Please don't go away till I've had a chance to repair it. Your forgiveness would mean a great deal to me. A very great deal."

"Why?"

"I'm not quite certain why. I only know that if you held a good opinion of me I would be happier than I am at this moment."

She gazed at him in wonderment, because in the brilliant October sunlight, where there was no opportunity for deception or cunning, he had somehow produced magic. He had made her believe that it was she who was shining and exciting and different from ordinary people.

"What's your name?" she asked him.

"Torrey."

"Are you really an actor or is she just teaching you to be one?"

"I'm an actor, and she's helping me to be a better one."

"Oh. Well, I guess I'd better go now."

"Can't you stay and have lunch with us? I'd take you home afterward."

"Would you really?" she asked, eagerly. Then with sudden dismay, "No, I'd better walk. People would see me in your automobile." The bronze-flecked eyes had sobered but now brimmed with laughter as she reached a final decision. "This may not be very flattering, but I just can't resist riding in that big New York automobile of yours. What difference does it make if people see me?"

Mother thought it made quite a difference. She had shortened her day in Allenville and was lying on the couch in the parlor-office when Rebecca came in.

"So you went looking for a bad reputation, did you? Well, they're easy to find. You'll get yourself talked about all right, if that's what you want."

"People always talk. I don't care what they say when I know I've done nothing wrong."

"Maybe you don't care, but I do. And Norman will care. If they talk enough, he won't marry you."

"He'll marry me, Mother."

"Oh, will he? Not when you have a bellyful of trouble he won't."

Rebecca was appalled at her mother's coarseness, though Mother half apologized for it. "Strong words are sometimes necessary. I just have to get you settled and off my mind. Norman's a good boy, and I don't want you to risk losing him. The actor can mean lots of misery if you're not careful."

"Mother, he's very nice and gentlemanly and—and, if it's any comfort to you, he knows I'm not the giddy kind."

"You've already had occasion to tell him that, have you?"

Rebecca said, "It's a thing every girl lets a man know pretty quick. You'd have liked him if you'd seen how he behaved after that. He was respectful and friendly and—"

"And a whole lot smarter than you. He knows now that it's going to take a little longer. You're no hurry-up tumble, so he'll have to have patience. He'll give you lots of respect and friendliness right up to the time you trust him so much that anything he wants to do is all right."

"Mother!"

"I know what I'm talking about. Don't forget I was a young widow. I discovered that your father had been just about the only decent man for miles around. Fine men are rare, and I never met a second one. I stayed a widow, a respectable widow, but I heard all the fancy words men speak when they want a woman."

"I've heard the fancy words, too, and you'd be surprised to know who in this town—"

"I wouldn't be surprised. I've been telling you to watch out ever since you were fourteen. You're a beautiful girl and you're a temptation to ordinary men, just the same as you are to men like Torrey Winton. I don't care how many actresses or society women or anything else he's seen, he's never set his eyes on anybody better-looking than you."

"Do you honestly think that's true?"

"Of course it's true, and he won't rest till he's tried every trick he knows. I'm telling you that I don't want you to see him again. I want you to let Norman know tonight that you're willing to get married immediately."

Rebecca went over and sat on the couch beside her mother. "I can't marry Norman. I've never been in love with him and—"

"He's in love with you. That's enough to make sure you'll always have protection and support and a good life."

"Do you want me to lie to Norman? Do you want me to say I love him? Right now I can't get Torrey out of my thoughts."

"You stupid, silly child. You hardly know that actor."

"Still I can't think of anything else but the way he looks and talks and—"

"Think about the way he'll light out of here as soon as his lease is up. And he'll never give you another thought, either."

"Why should that be, if I'm so beautiful?"

"Because his father is a very wealthy man. Remember, I had to check references for the Potter house. Sons of wealthy men marry girls with money or some kind of important background."

"Oh, I didn't believe for a moment that Torrey Winton would marry me."

"And even if he says he will, go right on not believing it. Men often promise marriage but forget the promise right after the damage is done."

"There's not going to be any damage, Mother, but . . . but I'm not going to stop seeing Torrey."

"What do you mean, you're not?"

"I'm going to drive with him to Trillington tomorrow to see the old burial grounds."

"I've given you an order, Rebecca."

"I'm very sorry, but I'm not going to obey it."

Mother turned her face away and began to cry. Rebecca was not particularly troubled by that. Mothers were always carrying on about something.

What really troubled her was a puzzling proposition arising from the well-known fact that if a girl gave herself to a man he certainly would never marry her. This was perfectly clear, correct and obvious, but if she withheld herself and he did marry her, how could she ever be sure that he sincerely loved her? Wasn't there a danger that a tantalized man could become confused and not know love from desire? A thing like that could make for unhappiness in later years.

It was consoling to realize, after a few minutes of hard thinking, that she had invented a problem that could never exist. Doubts and unhappiness were the results of misconduct. From unswerving rectitude flowed nothing but assurance and bliss.

They sat in the Italian restaurant on Rue Mirabeau and ate *scampi fritti* and talked about going to La Grande Séverine on New Year's Eve.

"If we can get a reservation," Rebecca said.

"We can," Barker assured her. "Paris hasn't been taken over yet by computers in dinner jackets. In New York I couldn't guarantee to get us a table in my own apartment, but here I'm still as important as Big Business."

Sue said, "Oh, you manage to get attention in New York. New York's not so bad. It's just that suddenly you've turned into a Francophile. Had I known you were going to do that I'd have stayed home."

"Think what you'd have missed."

"Yes, I'd have missed spending Christmas in a hotel room."

"You didn't spend Christmas in a hotel room. We were Rebecca's guests, and that was quite a dinner they put on over at that little place where she's staying."

"It wasn't really an old-fashioned Christmas."

Rebecca looked hurt. "You mean in your childhood it wasn't traditional at your house to have *jambon de Lorraine en croûte* for Christmas dinner? Why, we always had that or *noisettes de veau Toulousaine*."

"We always had *lapin* Iowa," Barker said. "That is, if my father was lucky enough to shoot a *lapin*. However, my little fat wife thinks in terms of holly wreaths and roast turkey. I think holidays make her homesick."

"You're damned right they do," Sue said. "On Christmas a person shouldn't be in a foreign country."

"Of course not, honey. Christmas is an American holiday, like Fourth of July."

"Well, I know it's not an American holiday but—"

"But you get lonely for the reports on traffic accidents and rapes and murders, don't you? It's the true American spirit you miss. I understand. Just yesterday I was walking around Place Vendôme and I thought to myself how lacking it was in inspiration. Not one Parisian had had the initiative to chalk up a filthy word anywhere, and there wasn't a single bit of evidence that the French know even basic vandalism. After all we've done for them, too."

Sue made an elaborate point of not replying, and Rebecca saw how things were with the Kanes. There had been small arguments, quiet resentments. Sue had had enough of Paris. Enough. Not yet too much. When it was too much Sue would weep and Barker would take her home.

"Let's go to the movies," Rebecca suggested. "I hear something marvelous opened at—oh, speaking of openings, there's a big one tonight, but not within walking distance. Fallon McKee makes his Broadway debut a few hours from now."

"How does the show look? Have you heard?"

"Yes, I've heard from Barrett that it's incredibly bad. I've heard from Vicki that it's incredibly marvelous, and I've heard from Doris Benson that it's a dear little play."

Sue said, "Doris makes the most murderous pronouncements sound perfectly darling. I don't feel like going to the movies. Let's take a stroll and have coffee later on."

It was an early night. Rebecca was in bed by ten thirty, straining her eyes over American magazines she had bought at Le Drug Store. She never knew just when she fell asleep, but when she awakened the miserly bulb on her bed table

234

was still aglow. The telephone in Vicki's room was ringing. It was a wrong number, of course. Everyone knew Vicki was out of the country. She glanced at the clock. Not quite seven. The servants were evidently still sleeping, but in any case they would not hear Vicki's phone. It was a separate number with no extensions. Even Mademoiselle on the far side of the corridor would not hear it. Surely it would stop ringing soon. It did not stop, and all at once Rebecca knew that it would not stop because the call was for her. Why, of course, it would be Vicki herself, so charged with excitement over McKee's opening that she had forgotten the time difference. Rebecca threw her dressing gown around her and rushed to Vicki's room.

It was not Vicki calling. It was Juanita.

"Mother?" The voice was sharp and urgent. Rebecca reached out a hand to steady herself. She clutched the bedpost and fought the shivering dread that had seized her.

"What's happened, Juanita?"

There was a dreadful moment of silence. Then, "Vicki. She—she's in the hospital. They just took her. I don't know yet how bad it is, but it's rough, very rough. Forgive me, but I don't know how to make it easy on you. I'm so rattled and—"

"Go on. Tell me. Tell me."

Juanita spoke swiftly, tonelessly, as though that were a way to rob the words of meaning. "She took sleeping pills. In McKee's apartment. She left a note. The police have it. McKee found her on his bed when he got home and called them. Then he called Barrett. McKee hasn't been seeing her, but she still had a key to his—"

"What do you mean, he hasn't been seeing her?"

"He broke off with her. He met somebody new. Vicki was still hopeful, but then today he gave the newspapers the announcement of his engagement. It was more than

Vicki could stand. I'm—I'm sorry to have to tell you all this but—"

Rebecca said, "I'll come at once. Now please go immediately to wherever Vicki is. Don't leave her alone with strangers. Call Dr. Gaver and—"

"Flower has gone to the hospital. She called Dr. Gaver."

"Good. Tell Vicki I'm on my way. Tell her—"

She heard Juanita sob. Rebecca's hand slid from the bedpost and she yielded to weakness. She sat down. "Have you told me everything? Is Vicki really still alive?"

"Yes. Yes, when they took her. But she is unconscious and they don't know—"

"All right, Juanita. You go now. I'll be there as soon as I can."

Rebecca covered her face with her hands. Her teeth were chattering, and ice was circulating through her legs and down her spine.

I'll get moving, but I need a minute first. I need it. It's so ridiculous what she's done. You don't throw your life away for a Fallon McKee. You just don't. It's too silly and terrible. How do I find out what plane goes when? Do I have to call every airline and ask them? There must be another way, but I can't think of it. I'm all in pieces and I can't afford to be in pieces. I have to think. Should I just go on out to Orly? There's bound to be a plane. . . .

Slowly she raised her head from her hands and stood up. Her legs felt stiff and very odd, but she forced them to take her back to her room. She began at once to empty the closets and bureau drawers. She needed hot coffee and she needed someone to bring her luggage from wherever it was hidden and she needed—

The phone in Vicki's room rang again, and she flew to it, the sound of her heart thudding in her ears.

Not that, God, please not that. Don't give up on her so

soon. Work with her a little, God. She was alive and she can make it if only You'll—

"Rebecca?"

Strange, she had not even thought of him.

"Rebecca, I know what you're feeling and you know what I'm feeling, so we won't waste time sympathizing with each other. We're in hell together right now and we must face it somehow. I understand Juanita was speaking to you while Barrett was calling me."

"I didn't know he was calling you."

"Yes. Are you in any condition at all to talk and listen?"

"I'm all right. I've made a start at packing. I'm going home immediately."

"I think you should. If there isn't a brighter word on Vicki before the day is out, I'll fly over, too. Barrett is going to keep me informed. Now, here's what we have to recognize. Aside from tragedy and heartbreak, we're going to have some pretty ugly things to deal with. Think of it for a moment. Fallon McKee's apartment on the night of his New York opening. And Vicki's not exactly a nobody herself. She's my daughter. This is going to be a ruddy field day for sensational reporting."

"Somehow that doesn't seem very important right now, Torrey."

"Well, if it doesn't, that's because you haven't considered the consequences. Steel yourself. I'm going to speak bluntly. Edouard was very decent to Vicki at the time of the divorce, but he expected her to be discreet. Now he's going to ask himself if she's the person to have custody and he's also going to ask that question of the French courts. What do you think the answer might be?"

"Torrey, at this point I just want Vicki to live."

"You can't afford to think only of that. If Vicki does live, she won't thank you for sitting down to weep when

237

you were in a position to make sure that she keeps her children."

"There's nothing I can do about the children."

"There is. You can take them with you when you leave."

Rebecca gasped. "You can't be serious. They're French nationals. There isn't a way in the world that—"

"Stop arguing and pay attention. Get in touch with our ambassador. Tell him the family doctor thinks that if Vicki can be promised her children are coming for a little visit it could save her life. By giving her the will to live—"

"What has our ambassador got to do with French children?"

"Take my word for it, he can help."

"I suppose you mean he can approach French dignitaries and make things move like a whirlwind and get the children on the plane with me. Well, now suppose you stop and think for a moment. Why wouldn't one of those French dignitaries inquire of Edouard if he wants the children to go to America?"

"Because Edouard doesn't have custody. Vicki does."

"But even she wouldn't have been permitted to take them out of the country."

"This is an emergency. Anyone would admit that. Are you going to lose Vicki her children for want of effort? The thing is worth a try, Rebecca. I'm inclined to come over there and do it myself. Believe me, if they were here in London I'd have them on a plane quickly enough."

"You couldn't do it."

"Don't tell me I couldn't do it. I know everybody of importance in England. Rules are made for the ignorant and the poor. We don't have to submit. Don't forget that at this minute you're the only one in Paris who knows the truth about what's happened. You have everything in your favor. Sympathy and sentiment will be on our side if you move fast. Say that Vicki had a heart attack and that you have to get her children to her at once. Say anything, but get on the plane with Ursule and Etienne."

"It won't work."

"It will if you handle it properly."

"I've never been able to do the impossible, Torrey."

"I wish I could send Jill Columbus in your place. She could cry herself out of a tank of piranhas. Once the children are in America Vicki'll have no trouble keeping them there. Possession is nine points of the law. If it became a real fight, she could even swear that Edouard's not their father and how could he absolutely prove—"

"Stop it, Torrey, stop it. Vicki may be dead, and all you can think of is perjury and kidnaping and—"

"And all you can think of is the pleasure of having a sorrow to wallow in. You can do something more practical for Vicki than cry your heart out. If she's alive, you can bring her the children. If she isn't, then you'll have them and I'll move heaven and earth to see that you keep them. It's what our girl would want. I'll even settle down in New York and help you raise them."

He would enjoy that, Rebecca thought. Charming, rakish Grandfather with a string of young mistresses and an armful of extravagant gifts for his motherless grandchildren. Adored Grandfather, who could create a holiday by simply arriving unexpectedly. Grandfather, wonderful and amusing, tender and affectionate. Ah, yes, he would be marvelous in the role, till he tired of it.

"Did you hear me, Rebecca? I said I'd help you raise the children."

"You mean we did such a fine job of raising our own?"

"That's a strange remark, isn't it? You're the one who's gone around all these years talking about your wonderful children."

"But I'm talking to *you* now. Torrey, wasn't there something we could have said to Vicki other than 'You must do what makes you happy, darling'? All her life that's what she heard from us."

"It's what she needed to hear. Vicki is a unique and complex character. We never did anything that contributed to the present misery. I've tried as hard as you have to—"

"Yes, and you've tried as hard as I have not to notice that Juanita hates all men including you and Barrett. Do you ever relate that to the summer she spent with you? Doctors do, you know."

"Oh, for God's sake, Rebecca, you need a doctor yourself. You're on the verge of—"

"And then there's Barrett. You won't mind hearing about him. I was the one who wouldn't let Frederick Benson advise him to prepare for something other than acting. Frederick wanted to let the boy know the truth. 'Now is the time to tell him,' Frederick said, 'while he's young and resilient.' Do you know what I said? I said, 'No, Frederick, I don't want him hurt.' It's to laugh. I didn't want him hurt. Now he's drunk every night of his life, Torrey, but his hurt never goes away. Oh, I guess you do get in on the crime against Barrett a little. Why didn't you tell him he would never be in your league? Why did you let him learn it the hard way?"

"What in hell has any of this to do with Vicki retaining custody? Are you going over to the embassy as I asked you to do?"

"No. It's an insane idea."

"That's still to be proven. I'll be in Paris within the next two hours, and I assure you that I'll make things happen."

She sat on the edge of Vicki's bed with the silent telephone in her hand and she thought of the things she had said to Torrey. He had angered her, and she had lost control. He was right. She needed a doctor. Only there was no time for a doctor.

She realized that she had not replaced the phone. She did so and waited in terror for it to ring again. It did not ring, and she walked back along the corridor. The sounds of morning came to her from the lower hall. The servants had begun their day. She rang for breakfast, then turned once more to the emptying of the closet. She must ask for her luggage. She must arrange for someone to take her to Orly.

But one could not leave here as though one were leaving a hotel. How much should Mademoiselle be told? How was this sudden departure to be explained to Ursule and Etienne? Ought she to call Edouard? No, Edouard was the enemy. How had Edouard become the enemy?

I'm in shock. I was never more disorganized. But Torrey is coming. He will think for me. Only I will be at Orly, maybe even on a plane, when he reaches here. Why shouldn't I wait for him? Perhaps he would fly to New York with me. It would all be a little easier if I were not alone.

Breakfast arrived, and the coffee was welcome. She would consider the eggs in a moment. Right now the coffee was what she needed. How had Edouard become the enemy? It was absurd. There was no finer man than Edouard. And Edouard was the children's father. But of course. That's how he had become the enemy. Torrey was hurrying here in an attempt to outwit Edouard, and everything depended on secrecy. She laughed a little wildly at the idea that she had contemplated telephoning Edouard. No doubt in her distracted state she would have warned him against letting the French courts know that Vicki was really not much of a mother. He already knew that she was not much of a wife. What a tremendous person he was, to have refrained from punishing her as a mother for what she had done as a wife. Ought she to have been punished?

241

Only the very worldly man made very worldly errors. The simple, unsophisticated father would stolidly maintain that a bad wife was a bad mother, and often enough he would be right.

But do I believe that Vicki is a bad mother? And can I ask such a question of myself when I am not even certain that she is still alive? Certainly, she is the exception. True, she was never a good wife, but she loves her children tenderly and would do nothing to injure them. She is thoughtless and willful but—

She heard the voices of Ursule and Etienne in the corridor and she walked out of the room to greet them. They ran to her and kissed her, and she held them tightly and smiled at them.

Mademoiselle said, "Madame is awake very early."

"Yes. When you have had your breakfast will you arrange please for a private talk with me?"

"I am in no great hurry for breakfast, Madame. The children could go downstairs without me now."

Rebecca shook her head. "Later," she said, and watched them go, the children's small faces morning-bright, their sheltered world still intact. Poor little ones, they did not know that perhaps at this moment they were motherless. And because women from the beginning of time had wept for motherless children, Rebecca wept.

This is foolish, she thought. Only if I am crying for Vicki do tears make sense. The children have almost forgotten her. She went away at a point in time which by a child's calendar is very long ago. I doubt if they ever think of her.

And that, too, was very sad, but she dried her eyes and thought what she would say to Mademoiselle. Obviously, something must be said. She could not pack and leave in mysterious silence. She decided to borrow Torrey's idea that Vicki had had a heart attack. Even when Mademoiselle learned that it had been a lie, she would think it a very respectable and proper sort of deception. Actually, a lie was all that could be offered Mademoiselle. Torrey's futile little game, which he considered worth the effort, relied on no one knowing that Vicki had wanted to die for an affair as cheap as the lyrics of a rock 'n' roll love song.

Of course, Torrey couldn't possible manage to fly the children to New York, but . . . But suppose his persuasiveness, his authoritative manner, his habit of success prevailed? Suppose the children were taken to Vicki? Wasn't that the best thing that could possibly happen to Ursule and Etienne? Vicki was their mother. Didn't most of the earth's people, civilized or not, acknowledge that no love was stronger than mother love, no need greater than a child's for the woman who had borne him?

Who am I to deny these age-old beliefs? Who am I to say that Torrey may not be clever enough to bring Vicki her children? If she survives, she will keep them, for possession is nine points of the law. If Vicki does not survive, then I will have them, and Torrey will drop by to talk theater to Etienne and to shower Ursule with pretty compliments. If we do not live through their childhood, then perhaps Barrett and Flower will raise the children while the custody fight rages on for years. And because possession is still nine points of the law, this plan of Torrey's is breathtaking. Who am I to oppose it? Who am I to say that a living Vicki does not deserve her children and that a dead Vicki would not rest easier for having them with her own family? Who am I? Well, I am Rebecca, Mrs. Winton, Mother and Grandmère.

She put down her coffee cup and went to the phone in Vicki's room.

"Madame Winton calling. Is Monsieur Dover there?"

He was not. She called the atelier. Monsieur Dover, please. Sorry, Madame. Nor was he at the factory.

"Of course it is very early. Is he perhaps on his way to his office?"

"Madame, he has gone to the south for the New Year celebration."

He had mentioned his plans, but she had forgotten. She returned to her room and dressed while awaiting Mademoiselle.

The young woman looked in surprise upon the preparations for departure. "You are leaving, Madame?"

"Yes. Please sit down."

Mademoiselle seated herself, her face expressionless.

"You told me once that because I am the mother of Madame Dover you would never disregard my wishes. The time has come to test that statement."

Mademoiselle's eyes moved worriedly from the empty closets to the confusion of heaped objects upon the bed.

"I am not subject to fits of insanity, Mademoiselle. You can believe that I do not suffer from delusions of any kind. It is all too real that something terrible has happened to Madame Dover."

Mademoiselle showed no sign of emotion, only a careful, almost clinical regard of Rebecca.

"My daughter may die. I see no reason to inform the children, but there are things you must know. Their grandfather is on his way here from London. He intends to seek a way to take or send Ursule and Etienne to their mother. This would not be in the best interests of the children."

Mademoiselle's mouth sagged in stunned amazement.

"There is no time to ponder my lack of loyalty. I am asking you to pack a few things for yourself and the little ones and to leave here."

Mademoiselle spoke at last. She said, "Why must they leave? This is their home."

"It is Madame Dover's home. By the generosity of Edouard Dover, this house and all that it contains is hers. The children's presence here is an affirmation of her custody. I want to change the complexion of the court's decision."

Mademoiselle's back stiffened. "You intend to create and fortify a position from which you may fight your former husband for the right to keep the children? Oh, no, Madame, I cannot be a party to so harmful and wicked a scheme. It is not even defensible. Neither you nor Mr. Winton has the smallest claim to the children. In the event of Madame Dover's death then Monsieur Dover is the only—"

"Of course. I telephoned him, but he is not in the city. I wanted him to come and pick up his children now, this minute, before Mr. Winton—" She paused, aware of the suspicion and doubt in Mademoiselle's eyes. "Will you go pack if I tell you that I want you to take the children to Mrs. Dover?"

"To Mrs. Dover?"

"Yes. They will be safe there, and no doubt Mrs. Dover will know how to contact her son."

Mademoiselle sat staring at her for a long moment. "It is not my wish to pry, Madame, but the situation is not at all clear. That would not matter, except that I am left with almost nothing to say to Mrs. Dover. It seems most peculiar that the regrettable illness of Madame Dover should necessitate the children's being transferred to—"

"You may say to Mrs. Dover that if my daughter dies it is understood by all that Monsieur Dover automatically receives his children." Rebecca took a deep breath and continued. "And you may say to her that if my daughter lives, no French court will refuse Monsieur Dover a new ruling on custody if he but requests it."

Mademoiselle lowered her eyes. "Will you not telephone Mrs. Dover and discuss this painful matter with her?"

"No. I don't want to do that. She will understand it all very soon. For now, I want you to tell her that she has my promise that Monsieur will never again be parted from his children if it is his wish to keep them."

"Oh, I am so certain it is his wish, Madame."

"Then go pack and please have my luggage brought up. And one thing more, Mademoiselle. You must warn Mrs. Dover against Mr. Winton. I don't know what other plans he may have or what influence he may possess. I only know that he can be forceful and logical and very convincing. You must not melt. Neither must Mrs. Dover. Do not permit him to take the children from the house, not even for a walk in the garden."

"We will respect your warning."

Rebecca nodded, and Mademoiselle left her. Rebecca stood alone in the room that had been hers through the autumn days. She thought of Mrs. Dover, the vital, clear-minded woman who would never have told her children that the most important thing was for them to be happy.

Ursule and Etienne came excitedly up the stairs. She went to them, closing her door against their view of the empty closets.

"We are going to visit our other grandmother. It is a surprise for everybody . Will you come with us?"

"Not this time, Etienne."

Ursule pouted. "We want you to come. We will miss you."

"I cannot come, but I love you both very much."

When it came time to kiss them good-bye Rebecca laughed a great deal and she gave them a gift to carry to their other grandmother. It was something that had caught her fancy in a jeweler's showcase at the Ritz. A small gold pin with a spray of turquoise forget-me-nots upon it.

"We are taking the station wagon," Ursule said, "so that Fifi also may have a holiday."

"Very good," Rebecca said, and she watched them drive away. When the car was out of sight she attended to a small detail that had come to mind while speaking with the children. She telephoned the language school and left word that she thought she now had all the French she was ever going to need and that the director could feel free to give her appointments to others. She went upstairs then and finished her packing.

After that she sat for a time in Vicki's room and she imagined how Vicki had looked on the day she had left it. The sweetly smiling mouth. The eyes joyously expectant.

Oh, Vicki, Vicki, my silly darling, you must know I did what is the right thing to do. If you had not known right from wrong you would never have engaged Mademoiselle to look after your children. If you had not recognized and admired right you would not have allowed her firm hand to guide them. I am convinced that you wanted for your children what you were unable to give, but if you live you will not speak to me. I have sent your children to better people than you or I have ever been, and because Fallon McKee's love was more necessary to you than the love of Ursule and Etienne, possession is now ten points of the law. And, Vicki, my youngest, if you are dead, then at last you are at peace and I will try not to cry for you.

She walked out of the room thinking of the children on the road to Fontainebleau Forest and she knew that that picture must sustain her in the days ahead.

When the telephone rang her heart shook, but it was the phone in the corridor. She picked it up, and Barker Kane's cheery voice was there.

"Ready, Becky?"

"Ready? Ready for what?"

"Well, we were going to get an early start. Remember? We're going to explore Bougival and have lunch at Coq Hardi."

"Oh, yes," Rebecca said. "I remember."

"So we're all set and we have the car."

"Have you? Bring it over."

"You sound funny, Becky. Are you all right?"

"I need friends to take me to Orly, Barks."

He did not ask a question. "We'll be right there," he said.

Rebecca picked up her coat and purse and went downstairs. The luggage was in the foyer. She said her thanks and farewells and she distributed francs generously.

"It is possible that the father of Madame Dover . . ." She hesitated. What a language. The father of Madame Dover. The inkwell of my sister, to say nothing of the famous pen of my aunt. She began again. "Monsieur Winton, who is the grandfather of the children, perhaps he comes here today."

The servants were looking at her, smiling politely though a trifle anxiously. So the father of Madame Dover, the grandfather of the children, might pay a call. Splendid. But there must be something else she wished to say. Was there a message? An order? They waited.

Rebecca thought how satisfying it would be if, at this moment, she could say, "I would appreciate your serving whatever manner of refreshment he prefers." But that was far too ambitious a dream when even her modest vocabulary had suddenly deserted her. No miracle occurred. She stood silent and uncomfortable before the servants. Then, with the humiliating resignation of those who can never quite vault the language barrier, she surrendered.

She walked to the butler's liquor cabinet and, with the puzzled eyes of the servants upon her, she took out a bottle of gin and set it on the table. She shrugged elaborately to indicate that this possibly could be Monsieur Winton's choice. She opened the refrigerator and a cupboard, making wide gestures toward the well-stocked shelves.

The servants were nodding now and laughing, relieved that at last they understood.

"Oh, yes, Madame," the cook said, speaking very slowly and clearly. "Monsieur Winton shall have whatever he desires."

Up to a point, Rebecca thought. Up to a point. Then she walked to the front door to watch for the Kanes.

She could think of nothing she had forgotten to do.